PRAISE FOR ANTTI TUOMAINEN

'Tersely written, full of twists and sudden violence, this is nothing less than the birth of a new genre: dystopian detection' *Sunday Telegraph*

'Tuomainen's spare style suits the depressing subject and raises a serious question: how do you find hope when law and order break down?' *Financial Times*

'This chilling novel compels … Clever, atmospheric and wonderfully imaginative' *Sunday Mirror*

'Antti Tuomainen is a wonderful writer, whose characters, plots and atmosphere are masterfully drawn' Yrsa Sigurðardóttir

'Tuomainen reaffirms your faith in the crime novel … In the genre of crime, Tuomainen has created his own style, both linguistically and story-wise. There is the social aspect, the protagonist … who acts according to his own high sense of morals, and the language: descriptive and evocative, it is at times a pure joy to read' *Etelä-Saimaa,* Finland

'Exquisite suspense without any unnecessary frills' *Helsingin Sanomat,* Finland

'You can practically taste the Nordic class – the intensity of Stieg Larsson and the deliberately faded tones of the TV series *The Bridge* … The style is close to perfect' *Kainuun Sanomat,* Finland

'The ability to use all the tricks of crime fiction and all the tools of poetry makes Tuomainen's work unique, and that combination makes the reader fall in love with his style. You cannot but value things around you more after reading *The Healer*' Sofi Oksanen

D1353125

'*Dark As My Heart* contains passages of lyrical intensity, along with bloody scenes that would not be out of place in a Jacobean revenge drama' *Sunday Times*

'*Dark As My Heart*, the most lauded Finnish crime novel of recent years, lives up to its acclaim' *The Times*

'Its sparse prose style suits the dark, treacherous, rain-soaked environment of this dystopian vision of Helsinki' *Glasgow Sunday Herald*

'In Tuomainen's first appearance in English translation, a long-unpublished poet takes to the streets of a grimly dystopian Helsinki in search of his vanished wife ... Tapani's search, which will lead him through an appalling series of cityscapes to some shattering discoveries about the wife he though he knew so well, is the stuff of authentic nightmares' *Kirkus Reviews*

'Good news, fans of Nordic thrillers! Tuomainen has won the Clue Award for Best Finnish Crime Novel and has been translated into 23 languages, so he's bound to be good' *Library Journal*

'Tuomanien's third book evocatively explores a near-future Helsinki ... Tuomainen writes beautifully ... Tapani's progression from a dreamy poet content with staying at home to a man of action elevates this bleak tale and brings a glimmer of hope to rain-soaked Helsinki' *Publishers Weekly*

'This dystopian tale snagged the Clue Award for best Finnish crime novel of 2011, and U.S. audiences should prepare to be every bit as enthralled as the Finns ... Tapani's amateur sleuthing is all the more fascinating in light of the unimaginable barriers posed by the changing city, with inhabitants focused on their own survival. Readers attracted either to dystopian fiction or to Scandinavian crime will find gold here: Tuomainen's spare, nostalgic style emphasizes the definitive nature of climate catastrophe' *Booklist*

THE MINE

ABOUT THE AUTHOR

Finnish Antti Tuomainen (b. 1971) was an award-winning copywriter when he made his literary debut in 2007. The critically acclaimed *My Brother's Keeper* was published two years later. In 2011, Tuomainen's third novel, *The Healer*, won 'Best Finnish Crime Novel of 2011' and was shortlisted for the Glass Key Award. The Finnish press labelled *The Healer* – the story of a writer desperately searching for his missing wife in a post-apocalyptic Helsinki – 'unputdownable'. Two years later in 2013 they crowned Tuomainen 'The King of Helsinki Noir' when *Dark as My Heart* was published. With his piercing and evocative style, Tuomainen is one of the first to challenge the Scandinavian crime genre formula, and he is currently working on his seventh thriller. Follow him on Twitter @antti_tuomainen, on Facebook at facebook.com/AnttiTuomainenOFFICIAL or visit his website at www.anttituomainen.com.

ABOUT THE TRANSLATOR

David Hackston is a British translator of Finnish and Swedish literature and drama. Notable publications include *The Dedalus Book of Finnish Fantasy*, Maria Peura's coming-of-age novel *At the Edge of Light*, Johanna Sinisalo's eco-thriller *Birdbrain*, two crime novels by Matti Joensuu, and Kati Hiekkapelto's Anna Fekete series (which currently includes *The Hummingbird*, *The Defenceless* and *The Exiled*). In 2007 he was awarded the Finnish State Prize for Translation. David is also a professional countertenor and a founding member of the English Vocal Consort of Helsinki. David has translated all three titles in the Anna Fekete series. Follow David on Twitter @Countertenorist.

The Mine

ANTTI TUOMAINEN
translated by David Hackston

ORENDA
BOOKS

Orenda Books
16 Carson Road
West Dulwich
London SE21 8HU
www.orendabooks.co.uk

First published in the United Kingdom by Orenda Books 2016
Originally published in Finland Like Kustannus Oy, as *Kaivos* 2015
Copyright © Antti Tuomainen 2015
English language translation copyright © David Hackston 2015

Antti Tuomainen has asserted his moral right to be indentified as the author of
this work in accordance with the Copyright, Designs and Patents Act, 1988.

All Rights Reserved. No part of this publication may be reproduced in any
form or by any means without the written permission of the publishers.

A catalogue record for this book is available from the British Library.

ISBN 978-1-910633-53-3

Typeset in Garamond by MacGuru Ltd
Printed and bound by CPI Group (UK) Ltd, Croydon CRO 4YY

Orenda Books is grateful for the financial support of FILI,
who provided a translation grant for this project.

FINNISH LITERATURE EXCHANGE

This is a work of fiction. Names, characters, places and incidents are either
products of the authors' imagination or are used fictitiously. Any resemblance to
actual events, locales or persons, living or dead, is entirely coincidental.

SALES & DISTRIBUTION

In the UK and elsewhere in Europe:
Turnaround Publisher Services
Unit 3, Olympia Trading Estate
Coburg Road, Wood Green
London N22 6TZ
www.turnaround-uk.com

In USA/Canada:
Trafalgar Square Publishing
Independent Publishers Group
814 North Franklin Street
Chicago, IL 60610
USA
www.ipgbook.com

In Australia and New Zealand:
Affirm Press
28 Thistlethwaite Street
South Melbourne VIC 3205
Australia
www.affirmpress.com.au

To my father

*'We run carelessly over the precipice,
after having put something before us
to prevent us seeing it.'*
Blaise Pascal

PART ONE
NICKEL

Finally the blood started flowing.

It rushed and flowed as the hot water caressed his body, as it pressed evenly against every inch of his skin. It was as though he'd found someone bigger than himself, someone who knew his body well, knew how to hold it, how to take it in its embrace and warm it. He stretched his short, stocky legs. The bathtub was the perfect length. He tensed his chubby thighs, his round calves, and relaxed them again. The water buoyed him up, slowed his movements. On an evening like this, after spending all day in the freezing cold, he had earned a soak in the steaming bath.

Outside the wind was whipping up a flurry of snow, the January cold and the darkness swallowing all living things. A moment earlier Pirjo had packed the boys and their ice-hockey equipment into the car and left. For the first time in what seemed like an eternity, he had the house to himself.

He moved his right arm, scratched his chest.

He leaned the back of his head against the edge of the bathtub and closed his eyes.

It is an unfortunate truth that with your eyes closed you often see much more than usual. The day's people and events all flickered behind his eyelids like a confused news bulletin. A clear indication of stress.

He opened his eyes. The pressure! All the decisions that had to be made quickly and implemented regardless of whether someone disapproved. Someone always disapproved.

He wiped the sweat from his brow. The bath water was almost scalding. He glanced at the windows. They were covered in a thin layer of steam. The lights on the veranda were switched on, and through the steam he watched the whirl of the snow. There was something hypnotic about it, something relaxing.

Maybe one day some people would realise they didn't have a monopoly on being in the right; weren't the only ones possessed of ultimate truths. Maybe…

An exceptionally dense swirl of snowflakes flurried past the window and the thick ice on the window ledge crackled as though a packet of boiled sweets had been scattered on the floor.

That's a lot of snow, he thought. He turned his head and gazed at something even more relaxing than the snow: the white tiling and dark-grey grout, the purity and cleanness of the pattern, its exactitude, its repeating logic. How beautiful, how practical. One of mankind's greatest achievements.

What was it he'd been thinking about? Ah yes, decisions. Making tough decisions. People who didn't like his decisions. That's what it had come to. Whenever you wanted something and tried to get something done…

The bedroom.

As though someone had pushed a plug into a socket.

Was there someone in the house? Surely not.

Only the moan of the wind in the chimney flue and the waves of snow washing past the window.

He lay still, and a moment later the water followed suit. This was the best thing about taking a bath: stopping, as though you had succeeded in stepping outside time itself, into its centre, a place where everything condensed. Again he closed his eyes. His breath was light and shallow. Old air out, fresh air in.

Almost as though someone was approaching.

Not quite footsteps, but something, somewhere.

He saw the bathroom's white tiled wall and through the door a strip of the bedroom. Again he heard the wind whistling through the flues. A sudden thought entered his head: something bursting into flames.

An 'electric shock' is a misleading term. The word 'shock' gives the impression that the electricity only hits you and leaves the body. That's not what happens. Electricity flows, that's what electricity does. As it courses through the body, electricity causes massive burns, interferes with the functioning of the heart, fills the lungs with water, suffocates you.

Electricity clotted his heart, burned his organs, snapped his arteries, pummelled his muscles.

He writhed and trembled. Water sputtered and splashed.

Then, a moment later, an immense calm. It was hard to establish where his body ended, where the water's surface began. Both lay utterly still, as though fused together.

A column of snow blew past the window. Snowflakes whipped against the window frame.

To: Janne Vuori <<janne.vuori@helsinkitoday.fi>>
From: Pain Increases Knowledge <<pain.increases.knowledge@gmail.com>>
Subject: Suomalahti

Hello Janne,
We have been reading your articles on tax avoidance and the grey economy.
You might just be the journalist we've been looking for. Perhaps you're not.
We'll soon find out.

You will probably be familiar with the nickel mine at Suomalahti in northern
Finland. We recommend you look more closely at both the mining complex
itself and the company administering the site. According to information we
have received, the mine is engaged in hazardous activities and, what's more,
the company is fully aware of the matter. We are convinced that we will soon
be looking at a full-blown environmental catastrophe.

A little background. The mine at Suomalahti was opened seven years ago.
Its owner, a company called Finn Mining Ltd, owns three other mines. The
Suomalahti complex differs significantly from the other three. This mine
was opened with the blessing of government authorities and the business
world. One of the mine's primary goals is to promote an innovative new
technology, using the precious metals that can be extracted from Finland's
ore-depleted ground in an efficient and environmentally friendly fashion.
This method has been extolled as the future of the mining industry, and it is
hoped that this will propel Finland towards a new economic boom, the like
of which has not been seen since the advent of Nokia in the 1990s.

This is all a pack of lies. The truth is we're digging our own grave.

If we see evidence that you are serious about our case, we will be in touch.
We guarantee it will be worth your while.

1

The mining complex must have been several kilometres in diameter; we were at the western edge of the site. I steered the car to the right-hand side of the car park and switched off the engine. The wind beat snow against the windows. Snowflakes as wide as mittens flew horizontally and vertically, occasionally gathering into fans whirling on an invisible axis, until they spun off their orbit and attacked us like a swarm of mosquitoes.

'What are we doing here?'

I took the keys from the ignition.

'Looking for the truth,' I said.

Rantanen folded his arms across his chest. 'In this weather that's probably easier than taking photos.'

I tightened my scarf, pulled on my woolly hat and checked my pockets: phone, notepad, pen, gloves. I opened the door. Snow slapped me in the face like an enormous, cold hand.

'Keys,' I heard Rantanen shouting.

'Camera,' I replied.

Jari Rantanen: fifty-four years old; just old enough to have become used to a nice, easy job in the media.

The command tower, complete with mirror-glass windows, looked like a checkpoint on the border of a closed-off country. The words PERMITS REQUIRED were displayed in large letters on the wall. Behind the building blew flags belonging to the mining company. I didn't understand why there had to be three of them on three separate flagpoles.

Snowflakes caught on my face, melted. The wind tore through my jeans and long underwear. My thick down jacket offered marginally more protection; after only a few steps it felt as though I'd been walking through a snowfield in nothing but my coat. Behind the command tower rose the silhouettes of the mine's factory buildings: the crushing plants, refineries and drainage silos. I walked up the steps to the closed door and pressed the buzzer.

The door opened, and warmth engulfed me in an instant. The man who'd opened the door was wearing a jacket bearing the company logo, and for some reason he had a hard hat on his head.

'I've come to get a permit,' I said.

The man was short and dark-haired, and the area around his mouth was, for want of a better word, untidy.

'Permit?'

I nodded towards the sign, a metre and a half tall, hanging on the wall. 'That says I can get an authorisation pass here.'

'You can't.'

'How do I get into the complex, then?'

'You don't.'

'I'm a reporter. I'm writing an article about the mine.'

'You'll have to contact head office in Helsinki. The PR people are all down south.'

'What about the people who take care of the day-to-day mining operations? Surely they must be here?'

The man seemed to think about this.

'Wait out in the car park,' he said, and pulled the door shut.

I walked down the steps and stopped by a van, which offered a little shelter – brief respite from the flurrying snow and whirling wind.

Ten hours' driving. A glacial car park.

I'd wanted this. Only a day had passed since I'd received the anonymous email.

'Hello.'

I hadn't noticed the man's arrival. It was strange, especially when I considered what size of man we were talking about. Perhaps the snow had muffled his footsteps and the wind had swept their weight away.

'Janne Vuori, *Helsinki Today*.'

The man's hand was like the fork of a truck.

'Antero Kosola, head of security. So, you're writing an article?'

The man's voice was so calm and warm, it seemed to melt the snow around us. Kosola was over one hundred and ninety centimetres tall and must have weighed about one hundred kilogrammes. Everything about him was wide: his shoulders; his jaw, mouth and nose. Only his cheeks were slender. Brown eyes, soft voice. Despite his size there was something small about him, like a bull that knows how to behave in a china shop after all. His black woollen hat was pulled down firmly over his large, round head. He smiled.

'Are we talking unofficially?' I asked.

'Off the record, you mean?'

'Yes.'

'I'm old enough to know one thing about reporters: you're never off the record.'

That was that. We looked at one another.

'May I ask, who is your superior?'

A sunny smile. No answer.

'How long have you been working with Finn Mining?' I asked instead.

'From the time the actual digging started. Two and a half years.'

'And has everything been going smoothly? Does the snow and the cold complicate things? Can, say, prolonged heavy snowfall affect the mining?'

'This stuff?' asked Kosola, and looked to the sky as though he'd only just noticed it was snowing. 'Down in Helsinki this kind of weather might make the headlines. No weather for brogues.'

Kosola looked at my feet. My leather ankle boots looked like ballet shoes.

'You can get yourselves kitted out in the village,' he said, like a tourist guide. 'If you're planning on staying around.'

I didn't say anything.

'Well, are you?' Kosola asked again.

I was about to say something when Rantanen appeared beside me. I introduced the men to one another and asked if we could take a photograph of Kosola.

'I'd rather not. I'm not at my best in photos.'

'It's to go alongside the article about the mine.'

'Well, it would hardly go on the fashion pages. One question: why are you here? The main office is in Helsinki. Everyone that can answer your questions is down there.'

'That's precisely why we're here,' I said.

Kosola looked at me. 'Thank you, gentlemen. I have to go.'

He turned and walked off towards the command tower.

'One more question,' I called after him.

Kosola stopped and turned.

'Just in case we do stick around, is there a number where we can contact you?'

'My mobile,' he said and gave me the number, which I typed into my phone's memory.

I slipped my phone into my pocket and stood looking in the direction Kosola had left. I couldn't see him; couldn't even see footprints in the snow. For some reason I thought of a phrase from the email I'd received: ...*we're digging our own grave.*

2

He was standing at the corner of Museokatu and Runeberginkatu. It was a cold, windy January day; a blizzard was blowing, and he drew the air into his lungs.

New York smelled of hot dogs and exhaust fumes, London smelled of the Underground, Paris of fresh bread, Berlin of heating oil.

As for Helsinki…

Its innocent smell was like an old cardigan left out in the freezing cold, spattered with salty seawater, fresh pine needles caught in its threads.

He realised he had missed his hometown more than he'd ever realised – or at least admitted to himself. He'd been away for thirty years.

When he had left, Helsinki had been a small city in the truest sense – grey both on the inside and the outside. What he saw now, however, was not the same city.

He walked along Runeberginkatu, leaving the city centre behind him. Here were unchanging streets, unchanging brick houses; so familiar. He arrived at Hesperia Park and spotted the restaurant where he was planning to enjoy a late lunch. The restaurant looked exactly the same as it did all those years ago: the large windows, above them the name of the restaurant in small neon letters, and in the windows the same name in almost a child's handwriting – an E that looked like a set of buttocks and a tiny circle about the I.

The restaurant itself was half full, depending on how you looked at it. (How would he have answered the old water-in-the-glass test? He might have said that when he was younger the glass was always half empty, that he always thirsted for more. Today it was nice to think there was still something in that imaginary glass, and if it was half anything, it was undoubtedly half full. This was one of the good aspects of growing old: there was more than enough of everything. Everything, that is, except time.)

He left his coat in the cloakroom at the entrance. At this time of day there was nobody working the door. He didn't imagine anyone would want to pinch his run-of-the-mill black, size forty-eight coat. He chose a table beneath the row of windows and knew instantly why he had come here: white tablecloths, artwork hanging on the walls, furniture with a certain gravitas, the small park on the other side of the windows. Now that everything was about to change again, it was important to find things that reminded him of how things used to be.

They had eaten dinner either at this table or at the next one along – nearer to the short bar by the other entrance. He remembered the roundness of Leena's face, the fortified glow of red wine in her glass and on her cheeks, how unaccustomed they were to eating out. He remembered Leena's dark, almost black hair, her beautiful, nervous hands, and how young they were.

He ordered a steak with onion gravy, a dish named after acting legend Tauno Palo, and a bottle of good old sparkling water.

A man and woman were eating at the northern end of the room. They clearly were not a couple, married or otherwise. Probably colleagues, office workers, low-level operatives in a large corporation, the foot soldiers of a sales and marketing department. Again he thought how differently life could have played out.

His dish arrived. He stuck his fork into the steak, piled onions and light-brown gravy on top of the meat and tasted it. Even better than he'd remembered.

Someone once said that our youth is a different country. For him, it was this country, this city. He had last seen Leena when they were both thirty years old.

After finishing his steak, he asked to see the dessert menu and made his decision in all of five seconds.

The waiter took away his plate and poured the remains of the sparkling water into his glass. Something about the last few drops

trickling from the bottle reminded him of his last assignment. This
happened more and more often: the most insignificant observation,
the tiniest detail, and immediately his mind began to darken in a
manner that he wasn't used to.

The trickle of water, the portly man – burned white with electricity in his bathtub, crimson blood in his eyes.

Wherever he looked, his past came to life. He tried it again now
as he waited for coffee and dessert. He raised his eyes, saw a bunch of
white tulips displayed on the counter in an Alvar Aalto vase. He could
sense their scent in his nostrils. The smell carried him back to Malaga.

*A dazzling white house with a swimming pool set into a steep hillside.
He is waiting in the garden, hidden in the shade of the trees. The smells
of a still night: roses, cypresses, rosemary, pine. A pump-action shotgun,
a Remington Express, propped against a tree, a Smith & Wesson M500 in
his belt. Gangster guns, both of them, and he doesn't like them one bit;
but the nature of his work defines the tools of his trade. He has decided
to make this look like a drugs-related killing. He hears the BMW jeep
approaching, the sound of the motor rising and falling. The driver accel-
erates up the winding village road; the sound of the vehicle breaks the
pristine night. He picks up the shotgun, shrugs it into position, positions
himself on the steps between the house and the garage and knows he's in
a spot where the car's headlights won't wash over him. The jeep turns into
the yard. It slows and comes to a stop. The driver switches off the motor;
the lights go out. In a single movement he steps towards the car, raises the
shotgun and fires. The windscreen shatters and the driver's upper body is
blown apart. He fires a second time, a third, throws the weapon to the
ground, walks once round the car, removes the workman's boots, which
are far too big for his feet, and changes them for the trainers dangling
from his belt, then stamps them into the mud, walks round to the passenger seat, takes the revolver and shoots the driver another five times in
what is left of his torso. Two shooters. He picks up the shotgun, walks into
the woods and disappears. That night the thousands of flowers around
him smell more pungent than ever.*

The waiter brings his crème brûlée.

3

Our arrival in the village of Suomalahti was at once gradual and sudden. At first it was impossible to think of the houses at the edge of the road as being linked to one another, but when we finally reached the heart of the village we realised we'd arrived some time ago, that the houses slowly getting closer together formed a chain leading us directly to the centre of 'The Hidden Gem of Northern Finland'. The dots were missing from the 'i's. Perhaps the wind had mistaken them for snowflakes and had whipped them away with the same force as it battered the landscape around us.

I told Rantanen we'd take a short tour of the village, conduct a few interviews and take some photographs to lend the article a bit of local colour. Rantanen replied with a sigh. I drove slowly. A branch of the Cooperative Bank, a supermarket, Kaisa's Hair and Massage Parlour. Petrol station, church, Hyvönen's Motors & Snowmobiles. Funeral services, the optician, a hotel, and Happy Pizza, where today's special appeared to be a faded ham-and-pineapple. Sports Retail Ltd, the local high school, and Maija's Munchies.

The village came to an end.

I glanced in the mirror. The road was empty in both directions. I spun the car with a handbrake turn and pulled up in front of the snowmobile rental firm.

The shop floor smelled of new motors. A moment later a folding door opened in the wall and a man of about my own age stepped towards us. Close-cropped hair, thick arms, and a stocky chest beneath his hoodie; the crest of the Finnish lion round his neck, a round face and blue eyes. He introduced himself as Hyvönen. I explained we were researching an article about the mine.

'It's brought the village nothing but good,' Hyvönen said without hesitation.

I continued with a few follow-up questions. Hyvönen agreed to be photographed, as long as his snowmobiles appeared in the background.

We heard a largely similar story at the salon. The mine was a good thing.

We returned to the car. Rantanen informed me that it was time for lunch. We drove a few hundred metres and I pulled up in front of a detached house. Maija's Munchies on the ground floor, the family home upstairs.

The place was as deserted as the forty-minute drive from the mine into the village. We'd seen nothing but snow and forest, hills and straight roads. The wind had kept us company all the way. As we took the steps up to the door I looked behind: a metre of snow, and plenty more in the sky.

We stepped into the restaurant. A bell jingled above the door. All four tables were empty. We decided to sit by the window. Rantanen placed his camera on the table and pulled a collection of memory cards from his pocket. I could hear someone coming down the wooden staircase and into the kitchen. A moment later a woman walked into the restaurant; I guessed this must be Maija. We exchanged a few quick words about the wind, the snow and the game pie, and with that Maija retreated into the kitchen.

Rantanen was flicking through photographs on the camera's small screen.

'We've got a few decent ones,' he said. 'That should do.'

I tried to see whether he was telling the truth or whether he simply wanted to get back on the road. There were a few good shots. The article would probably feature a lot of graphics and only one photograph – maybe the one with the three company flags fluttering in the blizzard. Behind them the mining complex glowed like a sickly sun.

Maija – I still assumed this woman was Maija – brought us our game pies and mashed potatoes. The brown gravy was piping hot and there was plenty of it. Rantanen had unzipped his jacket. His old woollen jumper was already tight around the stomach, and flashes of his green vest showed between the loose stitches. We ate heartily and agreed that I'd give Rantanen a lift to the airport.

'You're really going to stay on?' Rantanen asked, bemused, even though we'd already discussed the matter.

'I want to look around.'

'You won't get into the mining complex.'

'But the mine is here. Believe me, if there's anything to see, it's right here in front of us.'

'What does it matter?' Rantanen asked. 'We're in the middle of nowhere.'

'There's always something to see, even in the middle of nowhere. And here in particular. This place has got something there's a shortage of everywhere else: clean, untouched nature.'

Rantanen took a mouthful of mineral water, puffed out his cheeks as though to burp.

'You've got an agenda.'

'No, I haven't. I want to write an article.'

'You're an eco-warrior.'

'I am not.'

'So what's going on?'

I explained what I'd found out with just a few quick phone calls and a little reading. The mine at Suomalahti was a nickel mine. One of the main uses of nickel is in the production of steel, which is then made into supporting girders for bridges and other, smaller components. The mine was owned by a company called Finn Mining Ltd, which also owned another three mines. Finn Mining Ltd had bought the rights to the Suomalahti site for only two euros. The public explanation for this low sale price was that, at the time of the purchase, undertaking mining operations here was only a theoretical possibility. Getting started depended on a variety of factors: the quantities of ore in the ground, the results of exploratory digging, the projected environmental effects, securing sufficient funding, among dozens of others. Still … two euros. The project quickly garnered cross-party political support: on the one hand from those who on a national level backed policies based on flagrant vested interests, policies that were incredibly detrimental to the national economy; and on the other from those for whom any project that might employ a handful of people in a remote community – no matter how many millions of euros that project would swallow up, or how great an impact it would have on the environment or the health of local residents – was a fantastic, unrivalled investment oozing innovation. Of the two hundred MPs in the Finnish Parliament, roughly one hundred and ninety-eight fitted into these two categories. The remaining two would doubtless have supported it too, had they bothered to read the final report on the project, which was brimming with misleading superlatives cooked up by a bunch of bribed lobbyists.

But that was getting off topic, I told Rantanen, and returned to the subject of Suomalahti.

Only seven or eight years ago it seemed that the only projects left in the world were building projects. The nickel mine should have been a goldmine.

Rantanen didn't laugh at my lame pun. He dipped a piece of bread in his gravy and munched on the soggy mess.

Critical voices, of which there were very few, claimed that the ore body near Suomalahti was highly depleted, with a low nickel concentration. Those in favour of the project said this didn't matter because the mine would be using a process known as bioleaching, whereby oxidising bacteria are injected into the ore body in a jet of water, where they break down the rock and enable the extraction of the metal. While this method was profitable, it was also deemed highly environmentally friendly. And that wasn't all that was going on at Suomalahti, I told Rantanen.

'I'm sure it's not,' he said, a glob of brown sauce in the corner of his mouth.

Finn Mining Ltd, which now owned the complex at Suoma-lahti, used to be called the Finnish Mining Corporation, a company

founded in 1922. It had been run by the Mali family for generations. In the interviews I'd read, Matti Mali, the current CEO, had
talked about how much the company meant to him; how important it was that the family business and the mines they owned were
governed responsibly; that their vision extended into the long term;
and how he wanted to take all the important decisions personally.
These interviews gave the impression of the septuagenarian Mali as
an old-school industrial leader, a man of principle and honour, a
man for whom the continuation of his ancestors' traditions meant
everything.

'Well?' was all Rantanen said after I'd finished my commentary.

'I don't know yet. That was just the background. It's our job to
call a spade a spade, to tell people what's really going on. If there's
anything going on at all, that is.'

'Meaning?'

'Tell people the truth.'

Rantanen wiped his mouth. 'You're after a scoop – another feather
in your cap.'

I glanced outside. Snow. I decided not to tell Rantanen that he
sounded like my wife.

'Just drop me off at the airport,' he said.

We drove for half an hour through the dark, lunar landscape and
arrived at the airport – a well-lit building the size of a local corner
shop. It had been built to serve the needs of the ski resort forty kilometres away. And it was now packed: people, ski bags, the thirst for
beer in the air. The bar was overflowing with customers. Rantanen
headed straight for the counter.

Driving by myself, the steering wheel felt colder in my hands and
the road back to the village seemed all the longer. Darkness wrapped
its fist round the car and I found myself involuntarily thinking of my
last argument with Pauliina. The car lurched to one side as I reached
under the seatbelt and rummaged in my jacket and trouser pockets
for my phone. I scrolled down the log of calls to find Pauliina's

number. She answered almost instantly. After the standard greetings, the line fell silent. Both of us were waiting for the other to take the initiative, to cross the icy chasm between us. I was already surrounded by frozen weather and decided I might as well take the leap into the unknown place our relationship had become during the last twelve months.

'How are you doing?' I asked and realised that my tone of voice sounded as though I was talking to a distant acquaintance.

'I'm at work,' said Pauliina. 'It'll soon be time to pick up Ella.'

The silences between us felt unavoidable. The beams of my headlights ate up the snow-covered road.

'I'm in Suomalahti,' I said. 'We paid a visit to the mine.'

'Have you paid Ella's nursery fees?'

I stared at the landscape ahead. 'I'll do it when I get to the hotel.'

'They were due last week.'

As if I didn't know.

'I'll take care of it.'

'Like you took care of the shopping before you left town?'

I could visualise the almost empty fridge, the forgotten shopping list on the kitchen table. There were eight hundred kilometres between me and them, yet they stood before me now, as tall as mountains. I pressed the phone to my ear and listened to the buzz of the PR office in the background.

'It's nice to know we're important to you,' said Pauliina.

'Come on.'

'It's not me. You bring this on yourself.'

'This trip came up suddenly.'

'They always do.'

'I'm working.'

'Emphasis on the word *I*.'

'At least I haven't sold out to corporate giants.'

Pauliina sighed. Then silence again. Or not quite. I could hear the disappointment humming across the universe.

'Well, I think I'll get back to selling myself then,' she said. 'So we can afford to pay the nursery fees and put food in the fridge. Your idealism doesn't seem to make that happen.'

I couldn't remember when things had become this bad. We'd met three years ago, and Ella was born a year later. Now we'd reached the point where we could barely agree on anything. I couldn't remember the last time we'd laughed together or shared a joke. Pauliina accused me of concentrating solely on my work and said I neglected everything else, particularly my family. I accused her of abandoning journalism and moving to the dark side, which was what we at the newspaper's editorial office called consultants, and communications and PR officers. We had good reason. Most of Pauliina's work involved making black look white. It wasn't out-and-out lying, but it meant using your journalistic skills to manipulate the facts and distract your audience. When we argued, I asked her when she was going to tell our daughter that her mother was up for sale. Pauliina replied by saying she'd tell her as soon as her father managed to pull his head out of his sanctimonious arse and realise that seeking out the truth didn't mean masturbating at the thought of my imagined superiority, and that everything I'd ever done I'd done for myself and not for a single noble cause. Our arguments, which at first had always ended with torrid make-up sex, were now like black mud into which we sank a little further each time.

I arrived back in the village of Suomalahti. I drove past the supermarket, the hairdresser-cum-massage-parlour and a pub called The Pit. From the windows on the upper floor of the two-storey prefabricated hotel building you could see over the stone wall running round the church and into the old cemetery. Perhaps this was to comfort the guests: if you stayed here long enough, there was always a final resting place.

I hadn't booked a room in advance. It turned out I should have done so; all eight rooms were taken.

I returned to the car and sat with the engine running. The heater beneath the seat was pretty ineffective. While my toes were tingling from the cold, my backside was burning. The dial showed I was almost out of petrol and snow spinning from the sky built up on the bonnet.

It was a quarter to five in the evening. Judging by the dark forecourt, the illuminated red-wooden church and the emptiness around me, you might have thought it was later. Hutrila, our editor-in-chief, would call me within the hour. I knew this, though we hadn't agreed anything beforehand. Hutrila had recently remarried and had become a father again, and he liked to clear his desk early in the evening. This habit annoyed people. Members of our team said he was always in a rush and called him Hurrila, which certainly didn't do anything to lighten the general mood in the editorial department of a paper that was already beset with financial woes.

Snow crunched beneath the tyres as I slowly pulled out of the hotel drive. The red light of the petrol dial was staring at me furiously. I didn't know why I bothered flashing the indicator as I accelerated and turned into the main street. Illuminated windows here and there; signs of life.

The lights of the petrol station flickered in the distance. Two pumps, a roof above them and a mechanic's workshop. Only as I pulled up to the pump did I notice what looked like a small bar or café to the right of the forecourt – two large windows from which a gentle light spilled on to the even, unploughed snow outside. I filled the tank. The pump's handle was so cold, it ate into my hand, gnawed my fingers to shreds and then spat them out, numb. I closed the fuel cap and walked up to the door.

There was a thin line between the café and the drivers' break room. Where did one end and the other begin? The distinguishing features of the break room were its general shabbiness and the belongings left lying around: a manly power drill with a set of bits on a table; two people's plates, cutlery, napkins and glasses of dried milk on another. A third table was empty, but it was wobbly. At the café end of the space was a tall counter complete with pots of coffee and a vitrine displaying pastries, and behind that you could see a section of the kitchen, flooded with fluorescent light. Directly in front of me, opposite the front door, was the door into the toilets. The blackness of the area around the handle revealed this was in heavy use.

The man sitting at the wobbly table looked up.

'You paying for petrol?' he asked, and scratched his chin.

'I could try.'

'Over there,' the man nodded.

I looked at the unmanned counter. 'Okay.'

Once I had reached the cash register the man stood up, the legs of his chair screeching across the floor, walked behind me and round to the other side of the counter.

'Pump number one. A hundred and eight euros and thirty cents. Anything else?'

I glanced at the pastries on display, then at the coffee pot. Five minutes. It might perk me up. I could phone around for a hotel room. I added a coffee and bun to my bill, carried them over to the table with the power drill and sat down to sort myself out.

My phone wouldn't work; there was no signal. The coffee stung my gums; the bun felt scratchy and dry. The drill was pointing towards my stomach and it was snowing again.

I turned to the man. 'Sorry, can I bother you for a minute?'

The man looked up as though he'd been reading a paper. Except the table was empty.

'Maybe,' he said.

'My phone won't work. I'm looking for a hotel…'

'Opposite the church.'

'It's fully booked. Is there another…?'

'No. But if you drive a bit further, you'll find something.'

'Which direction?'

'You go that way, turn right and drive about seven kilometres until you reach the sign for Koitaniemi; take the turning and drive a few kilometres and you'll find the Casino in Varpainen.'

'Casino?'

'It's a summer place. They call it the Casino. These days it's open in the winter too. Because of this mining business.'

'Talking of the mine … I'm a reporter. Janne Vuori, *Helsinki Today*.'

A new expression spread across the man's pocked face. Perhaps it was curiosity. 'Something to do with those activists, is it?'

My face must have been just inquisitive enough. The angular, fifty-year-old man leaned back in his chair.

'I mean, they were from Helsinki too. Pulled up here, filled their tank, ordered a cup of tea and sat here eating their own packed lunch even though we had hot pot out the back. I listened to them while they were talking; made me think it won't be long before things start happening round here.'

'Before what starts happening?'

'Something they were cooking up together. You know, the way they were talking about the mine.'

'What way were they talking?'

The man glanced outside and I instinctively did the same. The lights in the forecourt turned the snow yellow.

'The way these people usually talk. They say a lot but they don't know what they're talking about. And I recognised one of them – from his picture in the paper. Blue hair. What kind of man has blue hair, eh? Environmental activist or not.'

'When was this?' I asked.

'A week ago, week and a half, maybe.'

'How many of them were there?'

'One woman, three men. I'd better not tell you what I thought of them.'

'How old were they?'

'In their thirties. Seems that's why you're here, after all.'

The man might have been right. I'd be sent a tip-off and I was following it.

'I'm writing an article about the mine,' I said, trying to change the subject.

'Why?'

'Why not?'

The man tilted his head. 'Is that what you lot live off down south? Traipse round the country, talking a lot of waffle? It doesn't seem right in the head to me. You got family?'

'A wife and daughter.'

'Proud of you, are they?'

The garage owner's estimate of seven kilometres was about right. The signpost appeared just as the man had said, and I turned off towards Koitaniemi. The road narrowed, the verges of snow piled either side growing taller. Fortunately, there were no cars coming from the other direction. My phone still couldn't find a signal. I switched the thing off and booted it up again.

I thought of the words that the garage owner had used.

The blue-haired environmental activist was someone I'd seen in the media.

Like thousands of others, I'd watched a YouTube video showing the activist's now infamous stunt: Santtu Leikola, a thirty-year-old man with hair dyed a bright, electric blue, who had become disillusioned and rescinded his membership of Greenpeace, stared at the camera and told the world what he was about to do and why. The image was effective in its simplicity: Leikola's pale, pocked, badly lit face; his blue, scruffy hair jutting out here and there against the black wall.

Through a series of crude, amateurish cuts, the camera followed him as he packed his equipment: a long steel pole, which could be extended and retracted like a telescope and fitted into his rucksack; a flag four metres by eight in size; a length of rope; a number of distress flares; and other associated paraphernalia. Leikola's voice was that of a fanatic: clearly agitated and utterly humourless. I couldn't remember his exact words but the frankness with which he made his threats and the names of those he mentioned had stayed with me. Once Leikola had shrugged the bag on to his back, the picture jumped again.

Next the viewer was in the Töölö neighbourhood, behind the Parliament House.

The camera moved jerkily as the activists (for there must have been at least two of them) climbed on to the roof of the Parliament. Once they were there, the image stabilised. In the background, the winter sun hung in the cloudless sky above the city. Leikola took a power drill from his rucksack and attached the telescopic flagpole to the ventilation shaft with a set of long steel screws. The pole was attached firmly, and, from watching his movements thus far, you could tell Leikola was quick and strong, and good with his hands. The flag was hoisted up the pole, fluttering in the brisk south-eastern wind, and then Leikola began to prepare the flares.

Again the picture jumped suddenly, and the next time we saw Leikola and the flag, the angle was completely different.

Now we were standing in the sloping garden outside the Music Centre across the street from the Parliament. The bright-yellow flag billowed and the distress flares glowed blood-red in the skies above Helsinki. NUCLEAR WASTE – SHUT AWAY FOR 1,000,000 YEARS, read the flag as, at that moment, parliament voted on commissioning the country's fifth nuclear plant. The stunt garnered lots of publicity and earned Leikola a fine. But the most important element was the video itself: rough, punchy and produced with a sense of earnest. Then there were the threats it contained. Leikola's comment about 'rather two hundred dead MPs than a million dead, innocent civilians' had caught on – a macabre slogan that had been twisted into numerous memes.

It was almost exactly a year since the stunt took place.

Before I realised I'd arrived in Varpainen, the headlights hit the sign outside the Casino.

BEACH – CASINO – HOTEL

HOLIDAY FUN FOR ALL THE FAMILY

GAMES, EVENTS, THEME PARK, MASSAGE

A few minutes later I could just make out the contours of the faintly lit building through the darkness.

This wasn't exactly Las Vegas.

The Casino had been built by knocking together – from left to right – a detached house, a roadside motel and a spa complex, all from different decades. The lakeshore probably lay behind this mess. The ground floor of the detached house looked like it must be the reception; in front of it was the parking lot, where a few cars stood partially covered in snow. I took my bag from the back seat.

The woman in her sixties standing behind the reception desk looked as though she was expecting me.

'You're in luck,' she smiled when I said I needed a room. 'We've got one left.'

I'd just parked in an almost deserted car park.

'Really?'

'We've been really busy these last few months. Breakfast is from six till ten. The sauna is on until eleven. You can stay in there until twelve but the stove will be cooling down.'

'Any chance of food this evening?'

'There's game stew with mashed potatoes and lingonberry jam at the bar.'

I thanked her, took my key and went up half a flight of stairs to the motel wing. Room 16 was at the end of a long corridor.

I placed my laptop on the desk next to the old TV and started my writing routine. First, the essentials: I wrote down everyone I'd talked to, copied their comments from my notepad and got down the basic information. Then I added atmosphere and first impressions: snowfall, the village, the distances. Though my article still didn't have a focus, I knew some of this material would come in useful at a later stage.

I wrote for an hour and a half, read through what I'd written and thought for a moment.

Helsinki Today was going through tough times. We were the last daily newspaper of our type in the country – serious but also populist. We had to fight our shrinking corner. I'd told Hutrila, that there might well be the beginnings of a big article up north. What I'd written didn't yet amount to much.

We didn't have the resources of a larger news corporation. So we had to do something the other media outlets weren't doing. We had to get to stories first, look more closely, find our own angle and dig at it until we reached the heart of the matter – whether that was a story, a person or both. We had to be faster, more inventive, more persistent and determined. And I knew only too well that my own angle on this story was something right in front of my eyes. It was always like this. Something obvious that wasn't obvious at all.

I wrote for another thirty minutes, shaped the text into some kind of coherent whole and sent it to Hutrila – if nothing else, as proof I'd actually been here.

I switched off the computer and thought how much I deserved a cold beer.

The bar was an oblong room with a low roof and three booths at one end, each with a view down towards the lake, presumably. Though not in the dark. Or in the winter. The pallid light from the outdoor lamps was enough to show it had stopped snowing. Along the left-hand wall was a long bar, and to the right was a low stage. I was one of three customers: the couple sitting on tall bar stools by the door and leaning the full weight of their upper bodies against the bar sounded exceedingly drunk and very tired. I sat down at the other end of the bar, ordered a beer and was about to raise it to my lips when I heard a man's voice.

'Hey, you.'

I turned just enough to see the couple. The woman leaned back then forwards again. The man stopped her leaning any further. He tried to focus his eyes on me. In his forties, thick arms, a weary face.

'Hi,' I replied.

'Aren't you on night-shift tonight?'

'I am on night-shift,' I said and raised my pint.

'You're full of it. That shit won't disappear by itself.'

The man appeared to be deadly serious.

'What shit?' I asked as neutrally as I could. 'Where?'

The man craned his head forward, apparently to try once again to focus properly.

'Is that Nieminen?' he asked.

I got up and walked towards him. Up close he seemed even more intoxicated than I'd thought. I looked him in the eye.

'What shit is supposed to disappear?'

The man returned my stare for a few long seconds before his gaze slid to the side, first to the woman and eventually to the bar.

'I thought you were someone else,' he said quietly. 'It's nothing.'

I remembered what the woman with orange hair at the reception had said. The place was full and I'd got the last room. And yet the car park had been all but empty.

'You going to finish that drink, Tomi?' the woman asked. 'I can help you if you can't manage it.'

I looked at her and saw decades of thirst in her eyes. I fetched my own pint and placed it in front of her.

'All yours.'

The woman gripped the glass. The man cast her an angry look. Soon he would doubtless blame her for talking to strangers. The dynamics between alcoholic couples were the same the world over. I didn't hang around to witness the argument that was already brewing in the air, but strode briskly back to my room.

Jacket, gloves, hat.

Snow crackled beneath my shoes as I walked out to the car.

4

He followed people. Not right now, and not all the time, but it was an essential part of his work and, therefore, of his life. The matter sprang to mind again as he walked along the gravelled pavement on Töölöntorinkatu, arrived at Töölöntori and saw windows lit on all four sides of the square.

How many lives had he stepped into? How many apartments, homes, summer cottages, villas and hotel rooms, to watch the way people lived and behaved? He had come across tidy homes that looked as if nobody lived in them, where it seemed not a single object belonged to someone, where nothing gave him a clue about how the people living there survived the changing of the seasons or the course of a day. The other extreme was every bit as mysterious: people who lived surrounded by ingrained filth and piles of rubbish, their floors disappearing beneath layers of trash.

The more he saw, the quicker he became.

The hallway generally told him everything he needed to know: shoes and jackets – their brands and condition, their quality and quantity; the state of the rug, any stains or marks; or no rug at all; the scent or, in some cases, smells or stenches; how in a matter of seconds all of the above came together to give him an overall image of what and what not to expect.

People thought their homes were private, that they were safe and secure.

He knew they were neither. Sometimes he hurried through the door of an apartment block behind someone with a key, took the lift to the upper floors, listened and watched as people chatted to one another, fiddled with their phones, cleared their throats, muttered something about the weather or simply stood quietly, allowing him to identify the nuances of their breathing, the weight of fatigue, a shimmer of impatience. What he always noticed was people's need to claim a space for themselves, no matter how small or fleeting it might be.

The square's cobbles, slippery beneath a light covering of snow. The illuminated windows around him, people in their homes. People in the street, on their way home. Today he walked past them, and it reminded him of what he did: his job, his life.

He followed people. Then he killed them.

5

Half an hour of dark road, the glare growing stronger by the minute, until finally, as the thick forest receded in front of me, the mining complex opened up like a landscape on the moon. I turned on to the road leading towards it. The car park was nearly full. I drove along a line of vehicles and found a place at one end. If I turned off the motor the cold would work its way inside in minutes. If I kept the motor running someone was bound to notice. Getting a permit at the command tower wouldn't be any easier than it had been earlier that day, I imagined. If anything, it would only be more difficult. I was in the wrong place.

I pulled out of the car park and returned to the road leading to the mine. Just before the intersection with the highway there was a crossroads: narrow lanes covered in fresh snow lead off in both directions. The lane to the right appeared to follow the outer limits of the mining complex. I turned on to it. The snow felt soft beneath my tyres. I drove slowly. The lane curved gently to the right. Trees, snow-covered verges. Eventually I came to a clearing. I switched off the lights.

The clearing grew wider until I found myself staring at an endless, open expanse divided into square sections. In a section at one end, near the forest edge, I saw movement. It was so far away, the two enormous diggers, illuminated by arc lights, and the men working around them – around eight in total – looked like busy ants. A moment later I realised that the sheer, square sections in front of me were in fact tanks full of industrial sewage. Their surfaces had frozen and the snow hid them from view, camouflaging them in the landscape.

What were these men doing? What kind of work had to be

undertaken at night and in this specific place? Tanks of raw sewage were no place to dig for iron ore.

That shit won't disappear by itself.

The diggers were rumbling around, mulching the ground. The arc lights pointed towards the woods. The men bustled around the machinery.

I only had my telephone, but it had a camera. I switched off the motor and stepped out of the car. The wind almost ripped the clothes from round me. There were a few hundred metres between me and the men and the diggers. The wire fence around the mine's property was tall and stretched away in both directions. To the left it ran through an area of forest.

The snow was deep, and walking through it was hard work. By the time I reached the cover of the trees, the snow had pushed its way inside my shoes, trousers and jacket. I was shivering with cold. When I finally arrived at the fence my feet were numb and so were my fingers. After wondering how I was going to get over the fence, I spotted a large boulder sitting just close enough to provide a launch pad. I climbed on top of it and jumped. It was only when I was on the other side that it occurred to me that the fence might be electrified. If it was, however, I would now be lying unconscious in snow a metre deep.

I trudged forward through the snow towards the arc lights and the diggers. The frozen wind numbed my face. I was careful not to wander off across the frozen tanks, sticking instead to the strips of land separating them from one another. I would be hidden in darkness for a while yet, I thought. My legs ached with cold and adrenaline; the frigid air clutched at my throat and lungs. I was sweating yet at the same time was worried I would freeze.

Over the boom of the diggers I eventually heard the sound of the men's voices. Behind the digging site, at the forest edge, the ground began to slope downwards. The men were excavating some form of canal, a wide ditch leading towards the woods. I took a few steps closer and came to a halt. Pulling off my gloves I dug my phone from my jacket pocket. It wouldn't switch on. I tried to warm it by blowing on it. I knelt down in the snow, held the phone between my hands and puffed. But it remained black and silent. After a few minutes of watching the men at work and listened as the diggers scraped against the frozen earth, I decided to go back to the car.

The trek was long and cold. I could hear Pauliina's voice, the way she'd described me to her friends after a drunken night out: *Janne would sell his left testicle for a good story and the right one to have his photo published alongside it. After all, what else does he need them for? He's never at home.*

The fence seemed taller than when I'd come over it before. Using a thick spruce tree for support, I struggled up, rolled over the top and landed on the other side with a thump. Again I was lucky. There were no stones or protruding branches hidden beneath the snow. I couldn't feel my feet, and it took all the willpower I could muster to get the car started and on the move again.

The motel owner's wife watched me as I limped through the foyer. I made it to my room, stripped off my clothes and, leaving them on the bathroom floor, gulped down a few glasses of water and stood under the hot shower.

Gradually the shivers and trembling subsided. When I returned to the bedroom, I tried the phone again. It felt cold in my hands and still wouldn't switch on. No goodnight text message for Ella this evening.

I stepped up to the window to close the curtains and looked out into the car park.

Snow.

A long shadow.

A man.

Everything about him was stocky. A man whose strength you could sense, whose outstretched hand was like the fork of a pick-up truck.

He was standing in the car park, looking right through my window. A moment later he was gone, vanished into the darkness.

I looked from one side of the car park to the other, from the dark edge of the woods to where the road led off into the world beyond, from the spaces between the cars to their windows. I could see nothing, nobody. The gently fluttering snowflakes heightened the sense of static, of frozen motionlessness. I was certain I'd just seen Kosola, the security officer. He had been standing only about twenty metres away and had looked me right in the eyes.

Fourteen hours later I left the car at the rental place next to Helsinki railway station and headed for the tram stop. Wind whipped across the square, making people lean forwards and walk as if they were begging. It pressed snow into their eyes and mouths. When my phone warmed up, I sent Pauliina a text message, told her I'd be home by eight at the latest. I didn't expect a reply.

A drunk was asleep at the tram stop, his shirt pulled up and his lower back bare, defying the elements. Either he would wake up tougher than before, or he'd have the mother of all sciatic nerve pains. The tram didn't disturb his sleep as it rattled up to the stop. Neither did he react when someone kicked his empty vodka bottle, sending it clinking and spinning across the asphalt. Poor man's Russian roulette.

The tram crossed Long Bridge and glided towards Hakaniemi. I got off and skipped across the pedestrian crossing, its white stripes slippery beneath my shoes. The editorial office of *Helsinki Today* was situated on Paasivuorenkatu. We constantly had to defend the decision to locate our newspaper's editorial in a building that also housed a number of trade unions and the offices of the once great Finnish labour movement. No, we weren't keeping the red flag flying. No, this wasn't a statement – moving from the hip design district around Eerikinkatu to a place where we could look out at the World Peace statue gifted us by the Soviet Union. No, we didn't yearn for the ideology of a bygone age. We were a thriving, independent newspaper.

I ran up the stairs to the third floor. Hutrila was in his office. It wasn't yet five o'clock, so he was still in his chair. After five, and well before six, he generally moved around to the front of his desk and perched on the edge, so that nobody coming into the room could sit down. Matters were kept short because reporters had to present them on their feet.

'Close the door,' said Hutrila as I entered.

The room was so quiet that I could hear the hum of his computer. Hutrila wasn't a fan of open-plan workplaces. What sensible person was? Open-plan offices only produced open-plan thoughts: messy, noisy and second-hand. I sat down opposite Hutrila. He was a short, blond man who constantly looked like he was about to launch a missile.

'I thought you were doing a story about the Suomalahti mine,' he said. 'Then I read what you sent me. This is nothing.'

'That's what I've come to talk about,' I said.

'You want to focus on this story, you want to neglect everything else, you want me to give you free rein. On what grounds?'

I looked at Hutrila, stared into his grey eyes.

'This could be a big story, if I can just work out what's going on...'

'Sure. Alongside your other work. I've read the text. Tell me what you think is so special about it.'

'Nothing yet.'

'Quite.'

'I need time.'

'Then make time. That's what everybody else in this team does. We have an editorial meeting tomorrow at twelve sharp. I'll see you then.'

A few colleagues were sitting at their desks, typing away. We greeted one another with curt waves. I sat down at my desk, put my laptop on the table and booted it up. I looked up and saw the lights of the hotel opposite. Then I read through the notes I'd made while up north and searched for anything else on the subject published in other newspapers.

Again and again I read that Finn Mining Ltd had bought the

rights to the plant for only two euros. It had been said and repeated so many times that nobody even registered it any more. Hutrila didn't register it, and I barely did either.

A business is only as good as its employees. This was, of course, a cliché, but, like all clichés, it was often witheringly accurate.

I looked up Finn Mining's website, found a telephone number and dialled it. Mali, the CEO, was not available. Of course he wasn't, I thought. What's more, his secretary was unable to give me an indication of exactly when he might be free. 'During this presidential cycle?' I asked and hung up.

I scrolled up and down the company's gallery of employees.

Marjo Harjukangas, environmental officer, member of the board of executives. About forty years old, long, dark hair with a middle parting; the sinewy face of a long-distance runner; brown, serious eyes. I dialled her number.

She answered.

It all happened so suddenly that I really did almost fall off my chair: I'd been sitting on the edge, leaning my elbow against the table. I introduced myself with a splutter, standing up and explaining why I was calling. Harjukangas didn't try to say anything. Even once I had finished my monologue, she remained silent for a considerable time.

'Would you like me to answer your questions now, or do you want to talk face to face?' she asked.

I glanced at the screen, clicked open every document I'd found about the mining company and let my eyes flit from one name in bold type to the next. Harjukangas's name didn't seem to be among them. Everybody else had been interviewed: the CEO, the chairman of the board, members of the committee, the head of production, even one of the truck drivers at the quarry.

'Face to face is always better,' I said.

'How about tomorrow?'

We agreed on a time. I hung up, went back to my chair and sat staring blankly in front of me for a moment. Lights lit up one of the windows in the hotel opposite. A traveller had arrived from somewhere, ended up across the road.

I scrolled back to the top of the website.

Suomalahti. Finn Mining Ltd.

Again I picked up my phone. The other board executives were all unavailable. I left messages with their secretaries and underlings, asking them to call me back. I read up on Development Manager Hannu Valtonen, Sales Director Giorgi Sebrinski, Finance and Investment Director Kimmo Karmio, and Alan Stilson, the Head of Human Resources. Valtonen was the only one of them who appeared to have any background in the mining industry, while the others came from various corners of the international business community. All except Valtonen had LinkedIn profiles. I flicked through the employment histories the men had listed, recognising a few of the companies mentioned. Nothing leaped out at me, however. Finally I closed the browser and looked at the notes I'd made.

The mechanic at Suomalahti had told me about the environmental activists who had arrived from the south, one of whom had been particularly memorable because of his blue hair. Santtu Leikola. His number was easily found through directory enquiries. He answered almost instantly.

I told him who I was and that I was calling about a possible article; might he have time to answer a few general questions?

'No comment,' was his blunt reply.

'I haven't asked you anything yet,' I said.

'No comment,' he repeated.

'I wondered whether there was any truth in the claim that you recently paid a visit to a little town named Suomalahti, home of the nickel mine operated by Finn Mining Ltd, and whether the purpose of that visit might have something to do with the mine and its operations.'

For a long time I heard nothing.

The call ended.

I leaned back in my chair. I opened YouTube in a new browser and found the video of Leikola and his accomplices climbing on to the roof of the Parliament. After watching and listening for about a minute, I paused the video. Santtu Leikola looked as though he was charging towards me.

I returned to the Finn Mining website.

Matti Mali's face was like a box in both width and depth. He had a square, stern jaw, a high forehead, and his blue eyes were wide open. He was seventy-three years old. Either he was incapable of relinquishing his power within the company or there was nobody to whom he felt he could hand it over.

He'd acquired the Suomalahti mine seven years earlier and incorporated it into his business without even having to tender a bid.

Two euros.

I thought about this deal from the other side. Once the contracts were signed, did all the parties involved feel this had gone well, that they had succeeded? The sheet of paper on which the contract had been typed out was worth more than the right to undertake mining operations and to enter into a huge gamble. Not to mention the coffee and cakes, and the chauffeurs who had driven people to the meeting.

My return home was almost painful. Ella's smile, *daddydaddydaddy*: it stabbed me and healed me all at once. I hugged her like I didn't want to stop.

'Let go, let go,' she laughed.

I loved her voice. It had been in the world for only two years and already it filled my own world. It was a voice that I would recognise among all other voices in the world, a voice that, as far as I was concerned, belonged to the gods.

She ran into the living room; I hung my coat on the rack and smelled the perfume on Pauliina's scarf. Her scent.

Pauliina was in the kitchen, loading the dishwasher. Ella had already eaten, her place at the table had just been wiped clean. Moist streaks from the Wettex cloth were still visible, long, even and curved, on the glass surface of the table.

'I can load the machine,' I offered.

'It's almost done,' Pauliina replied without turning round. 'Keep an eye on Ella.'

In the living room Ella was putting books on the shelf. Rarely was a book ever put back the right way up or anywhere near the place it had originally been taken from. I chatted with her for about an hour. Pauliina remained in the kitchen. A typical evening at our home in Roihuvuori.

I got Ella ready for bed, read her a story. Eventually she fell asleep. I switched off the lights and returned to the kitchen.

'Is she down?' asked Pauliina.

'No,' I said under my breath. 'I sent her to the shop to get some fags.'

Pauliina's eyes were fixed on her computer screen. I dropped two pieces of rye bread into the toaster, took the liver pâté from the fridge and placed it on the table. What else? A bit of yoghurt. I'd had lunch at a service station three hours ago, but my stomach still felt full and bloated.

'Who's taking her to nursery in the morning?' asked Pauliina. Still she wouldn't look at me.

'I can take her. I don't have to be in town until nine-thirty.'

The woman sitting at the table looked the same as the woman I'd fallen head-over-heels in love with three years earlier. Among other things it was Pauliina's stability that had made an impression on me: she seemed able to keep her feet on the ground no matter what was going on around her. There was something so potent about her sensible, bright personality that had attracted me and wouldn't let me go. Later I'd learned that these qualities also included a sense of stubbornness: if Pauliina thought something or someone was unfair, she remembered it. She wasn't being unforgiving; it was more a form of accounting.

She sat typing at her laptop. Maybe this was work from her consultancy firm, maybe something else. Pauliina never talked about her own affairs. Her glasses were reflecting the light just enough that I was unable to read her eyes.

'How are you?' I asked.

'Busy at work. But it's good, for the most part.'

I spread liver pâté on my warm bread. The pâté melted instantly, making the bread wet and shiny.

'Thanks for doing the shopping,' I said.

'Don't forget the Ruusuvuoris are coming for dinner at the weekend.'

Of course I'd forgotten. 'Sure,' I said.

'Saturday at six o'clock. It'll be a nice evening.'

'I could cook.'

Pauliina looked up. We were sitting across the table from one another. The laptop's lid was like the screen between prisoners and visitors that I'd seen in movies. Again Pauliina's eyes were hidden in the glare of the screen. From the angle of her head and general ill humour of her face I assumed her expression was serious.

'How do I know that's actually going to happen?' she asked.

'Because I've said it'll happen.'

'You've said it before.'

'That was different. The prime minister agreed to an interview.'

'You interviewed the prime minister and we ordered pizza.'

'Like I said, I could cook.'

Pauliina was silent. Then: 'How was your trip?'

'I don't know if I can talk to you about it.'

'Excuse me?'

'You used to be a reporter; you know how it is.'

Pauliina lowered her glasses and peered over the rim. She was beautiful.

'You're serious,' she said.

'And you work for a consultancy firm that has in the past represented a weapons factory and tobacco firms.'

'That was years before I even joined the company. I haven't touched those cases.'

'But your colleagues might have touched them.'

'So what?' she asked.

I ate my slice of bread. It was cold. Now the liver pâté felt like oil in my mouth, meat broth. I swallowed.

'Nothing,' I said. 'Necessarily.'

Pauliina pressed the lid of her laptop shut and stood up.

I could hear her brushing her teeth and going into the bedroom. I sat on the sofa in the living room, my computer in my lap, and flicked from one TV channel to the next. I found an American series in which the parents and children of a patchwork family were trying to get along with each other. It took a while before I realised this was supposed to be a comedy.

It really took nothing to ruin a relationship. Pauliina and I hadn't really harmed one another or done anything irreparable, but still we looked at each other as you would someone coughing on the tram.

I tried to find more information and news about the mining industry. But I couldn't concentrate any longer.

I thought of Pauliina, of how far we'd drifted away from one another. I thought of Ella, and once again I thought of how I'd grown up without a father. I remembered how I'd understood his absence, the question it had raised: there was a place this person should be right now, but he wasn't there. Why?

My father had left, disappeared from our lives when I was a year old.

I knew nothing about him.

6

He sat on the edge of his bed and leaned heavily on his thighs. It was that same dream again. It always followed real events, in a strange way almost reran them; all except the very end.

He enters the house from the garden, through the sliding doors on the veranda. The lock is easy and quick to open. He knows the lawyer is asleep upstairs. He gives himself time to grow accustomed to the sounds of the house, its climate. Soon he is breathing in sync with it. He adapts; he's a master at that. He can adjust to any conditions, any at all. He often thinks of this as the key to his professionalism – the one factor that explains why he's so good at his job. He has the ability to become whatever the situation requires. Always.

Now he is part of this two-storey, 250-year-old red-brick house, two and a half kilometres from the centre of an old, attractive city. He hears the sound of the fridge and is convinced he can hear that faint, high-pitched hum that televisions give off in standby mode. He is certain he can hear the sounds of a nearby square, the rowdy hustle and bustle of late-opening bars, and even the slow-moving water of the wide neighbouring canal. He walks up the stairs, placing both feet on each step, lowering his weight slowly, gradually. As he reaches the top he can see into the bedroom and hear the sound of heavy breathing. He takes the syringe from his jacket pocket, fits it between his fingers and removes the protective plastic cap. From the bedroom he can see the canal, its dark, glistening waters. He takes a few steps, finds a spot where the duvet has become crumpled and the T-shirt pulled up to reveal a bare midriff, and jabs the syringe in. The man wakes up. He has seen this expression dozens of times; it is a perfectly natural reaction to his arrival, to the sting of the syringe, in the middle of the night, unexpected.

Just as the man is about to shout out, he stuffs a fistful of duvet into his mouth and grabs him by the hands. Once the man stops writhing, he pulls the duvet away and listens. He cannot hear a thing. He covers the man, walks towards the bedroom door and takes one look back.

As if by chance, he glances across the bed and out of the window. There is something soothing about the canal, its black, stagnant water. And just then he sees a reflection in the window.

The movement is microscopic.

The man's toe.

A small, quivering motion.

He feels like pulling the syringe out of his pocket and inspecting it, but he knows it is futile. Something has gone wrong. He steps towards the bed. Just as the man is about to pull the covers from around him, he hears sounds from downstairs.

Someone is coming into the house from the veranda. He recognises the sound of the sliding doors.

He dives towards the bed and wraps his right arm round the man's neck. Perhaps the poison has taken effect after all; the sleeping man has defecated in the bed. He struggles and tightens his grip, and eventually shunts the man's head into the right position. With all his strength he yanks his forearm and hears the neck snap. He gets up from the bed and listens.

Downstairs everything is silent. Silence means that someone has heard what just took place.

He goes down the stairs, three at a time, trips on the threshold between the two rooms and manages to locate the new arrivals. A rapid conclusion that might be wrong but is probably right: two junkies breaking and entering – one in the kitchen in front of him, the other in the small office space behind him.

There are no options: the kitchen thief is standing in front of him bathed in moonlight, looks him in the eye, says he smells of shit and tells him he'll die if he shouts or tries to call the police. Thirty-something, his face gaunt from years of addiction, a breadknife in his hand.

He raises his hand and hears the sound of the burglar in the office coming into the living room. The kitchen thief is approaching him with the knife, tells him to show them where the money is. When the kitchen thief is close enough, he punches him right in the middle of the face, breaking his nose and probably his jawbone, then grabs the knife from the thief's hand, spins round and thrusts it into the throat of the other burglar, who has now appeared in the kitchen. This one is younger than his mate: a few weeks of straggly beard, bad teeth, metal rings in his eyebrows. He lets the thief slump to the floor and turns to face the first thief, by now lying on his back on the kitchen floor. He presses the knife into the thief's fist, stands up and crushes his skull with the heel of his boot.

He knows this doesn't look anything like the way it was supposed to, but it was the best he could do in a fleeting moment, in a situation that went bad.

He walks towards the sliding doors, looks up to the windows of the neighbouring houses to see if anyone is awake. He has already gripped the door handle when he hears soft steps behind him. Even before he turns around, he knows who is behind him. Terror and regret fill his mind. He cannot explain how he has ended up here or what has just taken place.

He turns.

His son's face is round and happy. The boy raises his hand, wants to hug him.

The dream woke him up, his heart pounding, his body awash with the adrenaline of a frantic animal. He got up, walked to the kitchen and ran the tap until the water was cold enough to numb his fingers. He filled a glass, drank and switched on his computer. Part of his skill was his ability to track people down.

Finding his son had been easy – he had either taken or been given his mother's surname and now worked in the public eye. He looked at the photograph he'd enlarged on the screen. He had downloaded it from the upper right-hand corner of a column advocating the development of the city's public transport infrastructure.

He'd read the column. He'd read it with a sense of pride.

He didn't really have an opinion when it came to the subject of public transport, but every word his son had written felt miraculous. Not because he admired the adroit choice of words or because he sighed with every sentence, but because somewhere in this city his son was committing words to paper, typing them on a screen, and through that he existed to so many people.

His son had dark hair, blue eyes and a nose he recognised as his own: rather long, slightly wide. The expression was that of a young man. Life hadn't yet etched its mark into his eyelids or the corners of his eyes; it hadn't tired him, worn him down.

The expression was one of hope.

7

In its shroud of snow, Mustikkamaa looked like an enchanted island. It was so quiet, I could hear the pine trees, the wind rustling through the boughs. Marjo Harjukangas was late. We'd agreed to meet at ten. It was six minutes past. The sun was rising, and the eastern horizon was a golden, velvety gauze, glinting like the promised land. The winter solstice had just passed, and now we already had five and a half hours of daylight.

When Harjukangas had suggested we meet on Mustikkamaa, I'd agreed straight away. I liked the place, especially during the winter. In the summer it was filled with sun-worshippers, families with little children, different groups of people, picnickers. Now it was empty. As the crow flies it was only two kilometres from the centre of the city to the island, but it felt more like twenty, particularly because, in order to get there, you had to travel several kilometres east and cross Hopeasalmi Bridge.

Harjukangas arrived. She looked like a student: a rucksack on her shoulder, a chunky scarf, a woolly hat. A slender woman used to working out. She had walked from the metro station and apologised for being late. We took off our gloves and shook hands. In person she looked the same as she had in the photograph: brown, serious eyes; a runner's furrows in her cheeks, now apple-red from the chill and the walk. She was alone.

'Shall we walk?' she said and pointed towards the beginning of the path.

We walked anticlockwise round the island. The path, covered in snow, rose and fell, at times winding close to the shore. You could sense the cold of the water just by thinking about it. We went through the background information. I learned that Finn Mining was a leader in its field, even when it came to environmental impact; that the company's mining operations were founded on the notion of sustainable development; that Marjo Harjukangas was a former top-level distance runner who, through determination and an uncompromising character, had won competitions; and that an attitude like this was important for an environmental officer. She would never be prepared to compromise on her principles. All this I learned through what was, for the most part, a monologue. What's more, it provided me with very little information that I needed or could use.

When Harjukangas started giving me inquisitive looks between sentences, I began to understand what this was about. For that reason her next question came as no surprise.

'What would you think if I asked you to stop recording now?'

We had arrived at the western extremity of the island. Across the sound, construction was under way on the new Kalasatama complex. Sompasaari would be a pile of rubble for a long time to come. I showed Harjukangas my phone and touched the red PAUSE button. She looked at the phone a moment longer, as if to make sure that the second counter really had stopped moving.

We walked on. Snowflakes disappeared into the sea.

'There's a mistake on the website,' she said. 'I'm no longer on the board of directors.'

I glanced to one side, waited for her to continue.

'I'll admit I was surprised when you called. But I recognised your name, and I thought you and I might have a shared interest in this. The more I think about it, the more opportunities I see.'

'Why didn't you tell me you were no longer a member of the board?'

'Because you might not have been as keen to meet me,' said Harjukangas and stopped. 'Am I wrong?'

'It depends,' I said. Of course, she was right.

Harjukangas's serious eyes didn't let up; her gaze didn't relent for a second.

'I wanted to meet you. As I said, I recognised your name. You've

written some good pieces. Your article about the grey economy in the
building industry was excellent.'

'Thank you.'

'You had an inside informant for that article, yes?'

There was something almost magical about the seconds that
followed: our frosted breath mingling before disappearing; the protective curtain of snow around us.

'Yes,' I replied.

'I have a proposal.'

'I'm listening.'

'I've worked for Finn Mining Ltd for eight years. Five of those
were on the board of directors. I am very proud of my work and my
achievements. You can take it from me that trying to instil a sense of
environmental responsibility into businesses in the mining industry
is not easy. There's a certain level of resistance. You learn a lot. More
particularly, you learn to see people, to know them through and
through. I might have lots of information that could be useful to
you.'

We walked onwards. The snow was wet and heavy.

'At this point I should ask the compulsory question,' I said.

'What do I want from you?'

'Right.'

'I want you to write a good article, preferably the best article
you've ever written.'

Harjukangas seemed serious. Sometimes people actually said what
they meant.

'You said you're no longer on the board of directors.'

'I was sidelined a year ago. Of course, that's not what they would
call it. According to them I was "promoted". My official title is now
*Senior Consultant on Internal Affairs and Environment–Procedural
Analysis*. It doesn't just sound vague; it is.'

'And why were you sidelined?'

'Promoted. Write that in the article. I think that answers your
question.'

'I mean, wouldn't it have been simpler to fire you and…'

'… and attract everyone's attention. Show them what the company truly thinks about environmental concerns? Publicly admit that they no longer have any significance for this company?'

Of course, Harjukangas was right. I continued my line of questioning.

'So, these sideliners or promoters – the other members of the board – did they unanimously agree that you should be moved to another brief?'

'Promoted,' she corrected me again. 'Yes. Well, I don't actually know. I never heard the CEO's opinion in person. But otherwise the answer is yes.'

'You said you learned a lot about people. Do you specifically mean the other board members?'

We crossed the bridge leading to the Korkeasaari zoo. On the other side of the narrow sound the animals prowled in their cages. The sea flowed dark between the two stretches of land.

'Apart from the CEO, there is no longer anyone on the board of directors from the time I was there. Are you familiar with these men? They are all men, of course.'

'I don't know any of them. I'm keen to hear your thoughts on them.'

'Kimmo Karmio joined immediately after me. Director of finance and investment – a passionate footballer; a former top-end player, apparently. A consummate professional, good at his job, but easily swayed by others.'

'A yes-man.'

'Not any more,' said Harjukangas, and glanced at me.

There was a flicker in her gaze, a flinch in the lines of her cheeks.

'Kimmo Karmio is no longer with us.'

'He left the company?'

'He died. Some kind of accident at home. I don't know the details.'

I said nothing. I doubted Marjo Harjukangas needed my condolences.

'Then there's Giorgi Sebrinski, our sales director,' she continued. 'Aside from his work, a mystery to everyone. A salesman in every sense of the word, both good and bad. He did a lot of work on the side, selling things we hadn't agreed on as a team.'

'Okay.'

'Hannu Valtonen is the company's development manager, a stalwart mining professional. Swears like a trooper. I'd take the word "development" out of his title. He's a manager. Very much so.'

'Power hungry?'

'That's putting it mildly,' Harjukangas nodded. 'Alan Stilson is the head of HR. Seems like a nice enough chap. His level of ambition was a bit of a surprise.'

'What do you mean?'

'Many times I've wondered whether he isn't more interested in the business side of the company than he is in the staff, which is supposed to be his area of expertise.'

'And what about the CEO?'

'Yes, Matti Mali. I don't know.'

I turned my head.

'What I mean is, I saw less and less of him over time,' said Harjukangas. 'When I first started, he was heavily involved with the day-to-day running of the company. But as time went on, I barely saw him in board meetings at all.'

The path meandered, following the contours of the shore. The sleet made me wonder whether the opposite shore existed at all.

'Can I ask your opinion on one other person?'

'I'll answer if I can.'

'Marjo Harjukangas,' I said. 'What can you tell me about her?'

Harjukangas gave a smirk; didn't say anything for a while. Then we talked about the weather, about how there was more snow than we'd had in years, how neither of us could remember the last time January in Helsinki had been so white.

When we arrived at the car park, I offered to share a taxi with her. She looked me in the eyes and said she would walk.

The editorial team's briefing began at twelve. Hutrila speedily went through the points on the agenda.

Most were the standard subjects: the government's austerity cuts ('As well as talking about the parliament, let's take a human angle on this: the average worker, how the cuts affect their lives. Nopanen, set us up with a quick online poll: what would you cut first, that sort of thing. It's boring, but readers like it when they can get involved'); Helsinki City Council's lack of money ('the capital city finances people in the rest of the country and is left scratching its arse. You don't need to say it directly, but use some graphics that make it obvious'); the usual lifestyle spread ('What's it going to be today? Detox treatments, income inequality, foster homes, rotting school buildings, junkie mothers, something else? Okay, detox therapy. Shall we say something like, "Give the little shits their Subutex so they won't have to steal our bikes from the garden?" Just joking); Russia ('Lievonen and Kuusi, come up with something, but most importantly, and like in all other papers, you can say anything except the truth').

After going through his list of bullet points, Hutrila moved on to topics that 'made us stand out from the crowd' and looked around the room. I raised my hand. Hutrila looked at me and asked Pohjanheimo, who had also raised his hand, to speak. An experienced economics correspondent, Pohjanheimo wanted to examine the government's corporate subsidies. 'Socialism for Capitalists' was the working title of his article. Hutrila encouraged him to carry on with his line of enquiry.

The others were all asked to speak before me.

The paper's culture editor, Rantapaatso, wanted to run a lengthy article about an American author currently visiting Finland. 'If he agrees to talk,' Hutrila said. 'What else is he going to do?' asked Rantapaatso. 'He's a writer. I won't get very far if he only agrees to write.' 'He must enjoy something,' said Hutrila. 'Says here he's into wrestling,' Rantapaatso read from his notes. 'Then wrestle with him,' said Hutrila.

Finally I was asked to speak. I explained the background to the mining operations in Suomalahti in a nutshell. Hutrila suggested I join Määttä, Tukiainen and Nopanen on their austerity-cuts team for the time being and continue looking into Suomalahti on the side. When I uttered the word Suomalahti, the economics editor, Pohjanheimo, turned to look at me from beneath his dark, sharp eyebrows, before continuing to read his paperwork. Hutrila repeated what he'd said earlier. First other subjects, then Suomalahti.

The meeting came to an end. Hutrila disappeared. Määttä and Tukiainen reeled off a list of names I should look into and suggested we meet to go through our material in three hours.

Back at my desk I woke up my computer with a tap and stared at the screen.

'Suomalahti? Really?'

I swivelled round.

Pohjanheimo pulled up a chair from the neighbouring desk and sat down in front of me. Behind him the day had brightened, the snowfall had paused momentarily. Pohjanheimo raised his dark eyebrows.

'That's right,' I said. 'Finn Mining Ltd. Suomalahti.'

Pohjanheimo had the body of a twenty-year-old and the voice of a septuagenarian. Cross-country cycling and heavy smoking were a unique combination.

'You probably don't remember Kari Lehtinen,' he said.

'I kind of took his place, so I've heard of him.'

'All good, I imagine?'

'Everything's relative.'

'I'm joking. Lehtinen was a good reporter; a damn good one. Stubborn, a bit of a drunk, but a good reporter. It was rewarding working with him, if you could put up with the know-all attitude, the mood swings, the quick temper and the obsessive need to be in the right.'

'I've read some of his pieces. He's an excellent writer.'

Pohjanheimo nodded.

'I was just thinking, Lehtinen had a finger in every pie, and one of those pies was the Finnish mining industry – Finn Mining Ltd and Suomalahti in particular. He and I once talked about doing a piece on their two-euro business venture, but it never came to anything. Lehtinen was the kind of journalist who didn't start writing until he thought he had enough material. That usually took time and caused problems, not least because it took him ages to prepare anything. So we never got round to Finn Mining; we spent our time on other matters.'

Pohjanheimo's blue eyes and charcoal-black eyebrows formed a hypnotic zone across his face. Many interviewees had doubtless found themselves saying things they weren't intending to say.

'People often got the wrong impression of Lehtinen, when they didn't know him well. He came and went as he pleased, smelled of old booze and didn't dress, shall we say, in the latest fashions. But I knew him and I knew his work. He was always following up on a thousand things at once; he used to sit furiously making old-school paper-and-pen notes. But more than anything, he knew people. He had contacts in surprising places, and in some mysterious way he always managed to have a little chat with them.'

'Okay,' I said. 'So he made notes about the mining industry in general and Suomalahti in particular?'

Pohjanheimo looked at me. 'I believe so.'

'Great. Where are they, and can I look at them?'

'That's just the problem.'

'Whether you can look at them?'

'No. I don't know where they've gone. Plenty of times I was working on something and thought it might be worth asking Lehtinen what he knew on the subject, read through his notes. There were mountains of them: notepads, papers, files, you name it.'

'Surely they were still in his desk somewhere…'

'That's the problem. Back then his desk was tidy, you see. The first time I looked, anyway. Everything was in order, papers sorted in neat piles. I looked through them, though of course it was kind of inappropriate. But at the end of the day I'm a reporter too.'

I didn't know whether Pohjanheimo was being ironic, sarcastic or what. And I didn't know whether it mattered.

'You say "the first time". Does that mean the next time you looked, the notes had disappeared?'

'Right. By then there was just normal stuff. Not a single one of his famous notepads, some of which even had pictures. Lehtinen drew a lot. It pisses me off that we don't make a bigger deal out of this. I'm convinced he had something. He always did. It's just that writing up an article always took him forever. That might be one reason Hutrila didn't seem all that interested in your suggestion. Any subject that whiffs of the stuff Lehtinen plagued Hutrila with all these years without ever finishing an article probably causes an allergic reaction.'

Pohjanheimo stood up, pushed the chair so that it rolled back under the desk a few metres away. The push was masterful; the arms of the chair stopped a centimetre from the edge of the desk. He walked off.

'What happened to Lehtinen?' I asked his back.

Pohjanheimo turned, glanced around him.

'Died in a traffic accident, everybody knows that.'

'I know. But what happened? Precisely?'

'He was investigating a case in Berlin. He liked going there. It's an ugly city, he used to say, but beautiful and vast. Of course, he liked to visit the bars. And so, one morning, when he rolled out of a bar and was walking home along a dark street – if you've ever been to Berlin, you'll know the streetlights aren't up to much; when it's dark, it's really dark; long, empty streets that you almost have to feel your way along – someone, apparently a drunk driver, hit him. Not hit, more like mowed down. Nasty, severed limbs and everything. They had to use DNA and dental records to identify the body. His head was crushed to a pulp.'

'What do you mean, "apparently a drunk driver"?'

'A normal driver would have stopped and phoned the police, an ambulance or both and waited at the scene. But drunk drivers, and people on drugs or in stolen cars, generally flee the scene because they know they'll get into trouble.'

'Didn't they find the driver?'

'No,' said Pohjanheimo. 'And I doubt they ever will.'

8

Again he loosened the knot, pulled the tie from round his neck and undid it. He sat by the window, holding in his hands the bespoke work of art, which he'd picked up on the Via Veneto in Rome, and stared out of the window.

The traffic along Topeliuksenkatu flowed gently towards the downtown area; the number 18 bus rumbled past the Töölö library. The bus made it round the awkward traffic bollards, just as it had done decades ago. He had exactly the view he wanted, the one he'd been waiting for. When a suitable apartment had come up for rent, he'd contacted the landlord straight away, saying his company wanted to locate their employees in the flat and that he was sure they could come to an understanding about the price.

The Töölö library stood at the north-eastern corner of a large park. Built in the early 1970s, the light-bricked, three-storey building was one of the places where he and Leena had been regular visitors. They'd read books; it was one of their shared hobbies – or passions, as people called hobbies these days. These days people said so much, about so many things.

He had continued reading over the years, sometimes voraciously, finding new books and new authors, but still the memory of the books he had read all those years ago exceeded everything that had come since. The books they'd borrowed had shown years of wear; they had been opened and closed by dozens of hands; the spines were loose, the pages stained, soft and yellowed, and they almost always had a certain smell, generally that of tobacco. Each book had always come with its own unique message, always making a bold claim: love is eternal; we will die for our freedom; the power of evil is great; fight the good fight.

When he went into the library or a bookshop these days, the books gleamed, pristine. A few years ago someone had told him that old books don't interest people any more. Now he was told that books in general don't interest people. As he looked around at airports, cafés and parks, on trains, metros and buses, he couldn't help coming to the same conclusion. People still read, that much was clear, but they read about what other people had eaten for lunch or did tests to reveal what breed of dog they were.

The tie. He couldn't get it to sit straight. This hadn't happened in years. He looked at the time. Almost six.

He stood up, turned his back to the window as the light faded across the landscape, and concentrated.

He followed the man along the pavement dusted with snow and into the supermarket. This hadn't been his original intention. He should have kept his distance and waited; waited for the right moment to present itself and come about naturally. Did he really believe in that? He had proved to himself a thousand times that you had to take the right moment, grab it the way a thirsty man drinks – greedily, concentrating on nothing else.

A few minutes in the Finnish sleet had taken its toll. His Spanish shoes were soaked through; the tweed jacket he'd bought in Edinburgh felt like it weighed a tonne. The automatic doors flew open. He stepped into the shop, took a red shopping basket from the pile next to the door and walked further in among the aisles.

He spotted the man standing at the cheese counter. He stopped nearby and picked up jars of pasta sauce, turning them in his hand, examining them. Rocket. Panchetta. Asparagus. He was about seven or eight metres from the man. The man finally made his decision and dropped a chunk of pecorino into his trolley. The man had dressed appropriately for the weather: he was wearing rubber boots, a waterproof anorak and a thick, black woolly hat, its bobble now making its way towards the bread aisle.

He wasn't properly prepared. There was nothing new about that.

He'd had to improvise a lot recently. He knew that the shop was his only option. Outside was the short stretch of pavement, filled with sleet and people, and the crush of public transport.

He glanced around him. The freezer aisle was the quietest place; nobody bought ice cream in January. Thankfully it looked as though the man was going to walk round the entire store. Many people did so; it was an alternative to writing a shopping list. Sooner or later you would spot everything you needed. He gave the man plenty of space. He only needed an instant.

The man pushed his trolley towards the far end of the store, towards the frozen-food section. He pretended to examine labels, scratched his chin, read the headlines of the evening tabloids. *Shock Divorce. Repossession. New-Found Happiness.* They meant nothing to him; he didn't know who these people were.

When the man finally turned into the furthest aisle, which ran perpendicular to the other aisles and appeared to lead to a large, confusing area stocking drinks, he lowered his empty basket to the floor and took a few brisk steps. Not fast enough to catch anyone's attention, but accelerating and rising a fraction on to the balls of his feet. The man had disappeared round the corner.

He strode to the end of another long aisle, so that he could approach the man from the opposite direction. *Improvise*, he told himself. *Just let it happen.*

They saw each other at the same moment.

Memory can be strange. It knows things before it understands them. He could see from the man's eyes that he recognised him, at least on some level, before he fully understood who he was looking at. A small delay was hardly surprising; it had been almost thirty years since they had last seen one another. He took a series of short steps, cautious and polite, towards the man.

The way the man walked, the way his feet touched the ground: light steps, his feet angled slightly outwards. And his upper body: his shoulders pulled slightly backwards, his long arms loose and relaxed at his side. The slim, dark-haired thirty-year-old man in a pair of retro glasses looked just as he had imagined he would.

Time shrunk around him, then tore itself open, forming a deep crevasse. It was all the harder to accept that, of his own volition, he'd been absent almost all the time that his son had lived on the earth and that he knew nothing at all of his son's life. There was nothing from back then that they had done together, not a single shared memory.

He had to remind himself that this had happened all too suddenly. That they had bumped into each other by accident.

'Hello, Janne,' he said.

He could see in his son's eyes that he didn't fully understand what was going on.

'I'm sorry,' he said. 'That was abrupt. I recognised you; so I assumed you would recognise me too. I've seen your picture in the paper, but you won't, of course … I'm your father.'

Emil held out his hand. Janne looked at it before gripping it.

'I saw you walking past and thought I might as well introduce myself.'

'Right.'

'It's been a while. I've been away, but I've moved back to Helsinki now.'

Janne said nothing. His left hand held the handle of his shopping trolley and in his right hand he was holding a packet of fair-trade coffee.

'Groceries?'

Janne seemed to snap back to reality.

'Yes. Guests this weekend. Just picking up some bits and pieces.'

'That's nice.'

Janne stared at him. 'So you've moved back to Helsinki?'

'Yes.'

'Why?'

'Do you have time for a glass of something?' asked Emil.

They crossed the street in the snowfall. To Emil the snowflakes seemed softer and larger than any he'd seen before. Janne carried his numerous shopping bags with a light, experienced grip. Emil saw their reflection in a shop window. A stylish, greying gentleman and a trendy young father. Again he pondered how different everything could have been.

They stepped into a pub and walked up to the bar. Emil offered to buy the drinks. Janne gave a friendly smile, first to Emil and then to the waitress; wooden discs stretched her earlobes. Janne ordered a bottle of British ale, Emil a glass of red wine. He undid his jacket, saw in the mirror that his tie was straight, the knot sturdy and neat. Though his jacket was wet, his suit had remained dry and impeccable. For some reason this all felt important.

Janne picked a table by the window. The city flowed past, people gliding through the snow. They sipped their drinks. Everything Emil had planned to say felt utterly wrong.

He smiled at his son. His son didn't quite smile back. He still hadn't answered his son's one-word question. That time would come. They could talk first…

'I have to go soon,' Janne told him. 'My turn to do the childcare.'

Emil tried to ignore the twinge in his chest.

'A daughter. She's two.'

'That's wonderful.'

'And a partner,' said Janne and sipped his beer. 'The girl's mother. She's going out tonight, so it's my turn to stay in.'

'What does she do, your daughter's mother?' asked Emil.

His son looked out of the window, then turned and looked him in the eye. 'She's in consultancy.'

Emil couldn't help but notice the almost imperceptible tightening of his son's voice. He waited for a moment.

'Is everything alright?'

Janne raised his eyebrows. 'What do you mean?'

Emil leaned back in his chair. 'If there's anything I can do…'

Janne shook his head and raised the bottle to his lips. It was already half empty.

'Unbelievable,' he muttered. 'Absolutely unbelievable.'

Emil waited. He tried to think of the right words, but saying the right words was difficult. Maybe the right words didn't exist. Janne straightened his back, filled his lungs, exhaled.

'What about you?'

'What about me?' asked Emil. The question was sincere.

'What do you do for a living?'

Emil could see that his son found it a struggle to remain friendly. It was understandable. He had made a mistake in the past, and his son had the right to think of him what he wanted.

'Human resources,' Emil replied. 'That's been my job for a while now. I'll be retiring soon. Just a few more small projects.'

Janne wasn't listening.

'Are you working on a new story?'

Janne nodded.

'Do you want to talk about it?'

Janne shook his head. 'No,' he said and again looked his father straight in the eye. 'It's at such an early stage – everything is up in the air, there's no focus. It's always like that at the beginning.'

'I understand. It must be rewarding when the story is finally ready after all that hard work.'

Janne put an elbow on the table. 'There's that. And the fact that somebody is finally telling the truth.'

'The truth…?'

Janne looked at him. 'If you think about it, what else could the purpose of journalism possibly be? If I decided my priority was something else, what would I be doing? Isn't there enough bullshit in the world without me? Is it worth going to all that trouble to tell the same lies as everybody else? However financially beneficial it might be…'

Emil realised that Janne was speaking to someone else entirely – he spoke slowly, stressing his words.

'People justify it by saying they have to make a living and feed their families. That they've got to play the game, that everybody makes compromises, that the times change. But where do you draw the line?' Janne sighed, raised his bottle, but stopped it before it reached his lips. 'You said you're moving back to Helsinki. Why now?' He took a long swig from his bottle.

'This might sound somewhat banal,' Emil began.

Janne swallowed. 'You're dying,' he said, so quickly that he seemed to take himself by surprise.

'Not as far as I know,' said Emil.

'Sorry, it's been a long day. I don't know why I said that. There's something about all this that…'

'You're thirty years old. The same age as I was when I left.'

Janne looked at him. Emil couldn't work out what was happening behind those eyes. His son's expression was impassive.

'Is that all?'

Emil nodded, tasted his wine; warm and sour.

'Welcome back,' said his son and downed the remains of his beer. 'I suppose.'

9

I had to run to the metro station and then for the connecting bus to get home by the agreed time. Pauliina was in the hallway doing her make-up.

'Ella complained of an upset stomach at nursery today,' she said. 'She still hasn't eaten anything.'

A dark-red hue spread across those lips that I had always liked so much. I put the shopping bags on the floor. Ella came into the hall, wanting to carry the bags into the kitchen. I gave her a tin of tomatoes and she set off.

'Does it smell of beer round here?' asked Pauliina.

I caught a glimpse of her blue-green eyes in the mirror.

'I bumped into someone interesting,' I said.

'Of course,' said Pauliina, pressed her lips together and looked at the shopping bags. 'You're serious.'

'Italian,' I said. 'I don't know quite what, but something like that.'

Pauliina arranged her scarf round her neck. I smelled her perfume.

'I'll be back when the parliamentarians decide it's time to go home.'

'Parliamentarians? Don't you mean MPs?'

'We already talked about this. It's a big night for us.'

'Right,' I said, though I couldn't recall a word of any such conversation.

Ella came back into the hallway. I gave her a packet of lasagne sheets and she tottered towards the kitchen. Pauliina pulled on her coat, fixed her scarf in the mirror. Ella ran back to the shopping bags. Pauliina gave her a kiss, leaving a lipstick mark on her forehead. I didn't say anything. Pauliina opened the door and wished me a nice evening.

And a nice evening of corruption and money-grabbing to you, I thought.

I thought of other things too.

Finn Mining Ltd. Suomalahti. Antero Kosola. The night-time activity at the mining site. The car park outside the Casino. Two euros. Kari Lehtinen. The missing notepads. Marjo Harjukangas. Editor-in-chief Hutrila. His reluctance regarding the mining story. Pauliina; our cold relationship and our weekend guests. My father. Him more than anything. The more I tried not to think about him, the more he consumed my mind. Father. Emil. Which one was he: Father or Emil? I didn't know.

I hadn't mentioned to Pauliina that the interesting person I'd met was my father. I wasn't quite sure why I'd decided not to tell her. Maybe there was a time I'd yearned for him to come back. Maybe the thought of meeting him had faded, worn away to nothing. It had disappeared like a passion or an obsession that you know you've had, but you don't know where it came from or why it went away.

And my father's, Emil's, explanation for his return: I was thirty, the same age as he was when he'd left us. Abandoned us, more like. As an explanation, it was about as good as any. Life rarely provides answers that satisfy everyone to the same degree.

Ella tucked in to the meatballs and mashed potatoes Pauliina had made, and so did I. When I asked if she still felt ill or whether she felt like being sick, she laughed. I sliced up an apple for dessert. I left the plates, the cutlery and the fruit knife on the table; I'd have plenty of time to clear everything up before Pauliina got home. We moved through to the living room. I turned the television to the cartoons channel.

I took my laptop with me to the sofa and tried to write. It had worked before and it would work now. You just had to start with something, anything at all, and before long the text would take over and tell you what needed to be written. Except that the living room was dominated by a two-year-old who needed constant attention.

I tried to strike a balance between the sofa, the computer and

Ella. I played with her for a minute, typed out some bullet points for another minute. A moment later, I was crouched on the floor, fishing the remote control from beneath the bookshelf where Ella had hidden it. I made a list of people I wanted to interview. I listed everything I could remember, everything I'd thought of. I ran after Ella into the kitchen and guided her back into the living room, returned to the sofa and remembered what Pohjanheimo had told me. I fetched my phone from the kitchen and scrolled down to Pohjanheimo's number. I grabbed Ella before she managed to run behind the television and rearrange the cables, and set her down in the middle of the floor where she was surrounded by her own toys and with any luck might find something to occupy herself for a few minutes.

A wave of crackling and noise issued from the phone. Pohjan-heimo was on his bike. At home. He'd once explained this to me: his eldest daughter had moved out and he'd turned her bedroom into a cycling sanctuary. He had attached a set of spools to the floor and rode his bike on them while projecting visuals of different routes on the wall in front of him. As far as he was concerned this was the best thing anyone could do during the Finnish winter.

I asked him who knew Lehtinen the best. Pohjanheimo panted that it was probably him, and even he didn't know Lehtinen particu-larly well, if at all.

'In addition to you, then,' I said. 'Somebody must have known something about him.'

Pohjanheimo said something. It was blurred by the crackling. I asked again.

I took Ella by the hand just as she was about to grab the laptop screen a little too firmly.

Pohjanheimo repeated what he'd said. 'The daughter. Maybe.' His speech came one syllable at a time. Perhaps he was cycling up a virtual hill.

'Whose daughter?' I asked.

'Lehtinen's,' Pohjanheimo gasped.

'What's her name?'

'No idea.'

I thanked him and hung up. Next I called Rantanen, who, before I could say a word, told me he was out of the office. I heard the sounds of a bar in the background. I could see him in a booth at his local pub in Töölö, leaning against the soft, velvet-cushioned chair and swirling a glass of cut brandy across the dark surface of the wooden table.

'Kari Lehtinen,' I said. 'The guy that used to write for us. Do you remember him?'

'Now he could drink,' Rantanen chuckled. 'We went out together one night…'

'Do you remember his daughter?'

For a moment all I heard was the noises of the bar.

'You're married,' Rantanen said eventually.

'That's not what I mean.'

'Sure you don't. I never met her.'

'So you don't know her,' I said, frustrated.

'I know her,' said Rantanen and continued after a short pause. 'Her name's Maarit. What's this about?'

'Kari Lehtinen,' I said.

'Thought so. In what way?'

'He was a good journalist and an interesting person.'

'That's one way of putting it.'

'Did you ever work with him?'

'Quite a lot. If you want to call it that.'

'What does that mean?'

'I took a lot of photographs for the stories he worked on, but I didn't work *with* him. We worked on the same stories at the same time. That's the way he was.'

'What was he like?'

More background noises: the Foo Fighters' 'Best of You', a fruit machine, a drunken woman's rattling voice.

'Incomprehensible.'

I ended the call and Googled Maarit Lehtinen. There were several

Facebook profiles with that name. I searched in an online directory: four numbers in Helsinki. I called the first one that came up. Maarit Lehtinen was thrilled when I told her I was from *Helsinki Today* but was taken aback when I asked for her father's name. It was Petri. I thanked her. The second Maarit Lehtinen on the list told me straight away she didn't want to take out a subscription to the newspaper. I told her she was under no obligation to do so. Her father's name was Vesa.

The third time was lucky, after all. The Maarit Lehtinen who answered the phone remained silent for a moment before asking, 'Are you a really a reporter?'

I repeated that I was Janne Vuori from *Helsinki Today* and that I really was a reporter. I told her I was doing a story about Kari Lehtinen, about exemplary journalism, and that it was an honour to speak to his daughter.

'What a load of crap,' said Maarit in as friendly a voice as she could muster. 'Nobody who knew my father wants to remember him.'

'I didn't know him,' I admitted. 'Not personally.'

'But you're writing a story?'

'For a sense of background, it would be really good to...'

'Kari – my father – always said somebody would call.'

I didn't say anything for a moment. 'What exactly did he say?'

'That somebody from the editorial would call and ask to see his papers, sooner or later. And if that person knew what they were doing, I was to hand them over.'

I stood up.

'Okay,' I said. 'So you have the papers.'

'I know where they are. Are you a reporter and do you know what you're doing?'

'Yes.'

'Then you'll know the code word.'

I took a few steps towards the window. I saw my reflection in the pane of glass, partially; just a poor hologram: half of me was dark forest and the façade of the building opposite, its illuminated windows.

'The code word?'

'You heard me.'

'Are you serious?'

'My father was very serious.'

'How old are you?' I asked.

'Are you a reporter or some kind of pervert?'

'A reporter.'

A short pause.

'Not bad looking either,' Maarit Lehtinen added in a voice somewhere between caution and open flirtation.

'Excuse me?'

'I just Googled you. You Googled me; I Googled you back. Now we're even. I'm looking at your picture, you're looking at mine.'

'I'm not looking at anything … and I don't have a code word. This is an important story.'

The line went dead. I remained standing by the window.

For some reason the meeting with my father felt all the more real with each hour that passed. I thought of our meeting, our moment in the bar. How casually I'd taken the situation. It must have had something to do with his appearance, at least in part. There was something unassuming yet firm about him. He didn't give me any reason to get upset; in a strange way he even seemed to calm me down. We sat opposite each other; it was perfectly natural. We looked one another in the eye as though we were used to doing so. I unlocked my phone to type his name into the search field, when I happened to glance in the window.

I was still looking at my hologram self, but now I saw something was missing from the picture. The very moment I began running towards the kitchen I heard the noise: first a loud crash, then a softer one – the sound of a plate smashing, the clatter of cutlery, the shattering of a glass against the stone floor.

Ella was lying on her back on the kitchen floor, still silent from the thump and the shock.

I crouched down and saw her right hand.

The fruit knife, sunk to the handle between her index and middle fingers, the curved end of the blade jutting from the back of her hand.

Then the screaming started.

The doctor on duty, who looked like she'd seen everything, stitched up Ella's hand. Stitched it and shot me suspicious glances. It was a classic Kafkaesque scenario: I tried to look like what I really was: a worried, frightened father who was nonetheless responsible and caring, and who couldn't possibly have done any more in the circumstances. Yet whose child, this once, had ended up in a state like this.

Despite the ban on mobile phones in the A&E unit, I sent Pauliina a text. I knew what would happen if I only told her once she got home. Pauliina said she'd get there as soon as she could.

Ella was brave and visibly tired. It was no wonder. In its bandage her little hand looked like a doll's limb. The doctor gave me instructions on how to clean it. I listened carefully, my gaze fixed on her overworked, bleary eyes.

The three of us took a cab home.

Pauliina kept an arm round Ella. She wouldn't look at me but held Ella as if to protect her, as though they'd both turned their backs on me. Back home I hung Ella's outdoor clothes in the wardrobe and took off my shoes in front of the mirror. I didn't look up at my reflection.

Ella was soon asleep and Pauliina came into the living room. I sat on the sofa, the laptop next to me. Pauliina nodded at it.

'I suppose that's the reason for everything that's happened tonight.'

I said nothing. Pauliina sat down at the other end of the sofa. We had made love on this sofa.

'Aren't you going to say anything?'

I looked at her. 'These things happen to everybody. Kids that age can get anywhere. You can't keep your eye on them every minute of the day.'

'What were you doing when it happened?'

'I was on the phone, but that doesn't change—'

'On the phone?'

'Yes.'

I looked at Pauliina. She was still wearing her evening attire: a black, long-sleeved blouse with three strands of shiny fabric running across her neckline from one shoulder to the other.

'I'm sure it was very important,' she said.

I sighed. 'Is there any point having this conversation?'

'That's what I've been thinking. Is there any point?'

'I took my eyes off her for a few seconds. It happens.'

'I didn't mean that.'

Pauliina's eyes focussed on the black-and-white rug in the middle of the floor.

'I want to make this as clear to you as I possibly can,' she said in a voice that was at once quiet yet charged. 'Ella is the most important thing in my life.'

'I know that.'

'If something were to happen,' she continued, without indicating that she'd registered my words at all. 'If anything were to threaten Ella or put her in danger, I don't know … no, I think I do know. Ella is more important to me than anything else. That's all I wanted to say.'

Pauliina turned her head. Her eyes were red and hard.

'I'm going to sleep,' she said and stood up.

I remained sitting on the sofa and took a series of deep breaths. I thanked God, the gods, fortune, luck, divine providence, fate, the state of things, the forces of the universe and the laws of physics: the knife hadn't fallen in Ella's eye, hadn't cut an artery.

Still I felt a sense of guilt. And as, one by one, the moments and events of the evening came into focus in my mind, I knew all the better why. What was it I'd thought only a few hours ago? Thank God I'm not like my father, who, decades after leaving, asks me for a drink and tries to connect with something that disappeared long ago and that can never return.

And what had I been thinking about in the clammy, vinyl-covered chair at the A&E unit once my immediate concern for Ella had subsided?

As I watched the doctor's hand take a needle and pierce my daughter's skin, I was thinking of Maarit Lehtinen, of the code word.

The sound of the kettle sounded like a ship leaving the dock. Emil waited. The red light finally went out and the switch flicked loudly back into the upright position. Emil poured the boiling water over his fruit teabag and felt the warm steam on his face. He swirled the teabag in the water, lifted it on to his plate, took a chocolate cookie and his cup of tea and sat down at his desk.

He opened up the instant messenger app in his anonymous Tor network programme. The profile <thingswillchange2015> had sent him a message and was still online. Emil read the message, looked at the computer screen for a minute and took a bite of his cookie before answering.

I can't take on work at such short notice, he typed.

The situation is critical, replied <thingswillchange2015>. *That's why we're taking exceptional measures. We have paid half of the sum into your account. What's more, we are prepared to pay the same again as a bonus if the job is completed by morning.*

Emil opened up another window and signed into his Swiss bank account.

The money was in his account.

Emil paused for a moment and thought. With the added bonus, it would be a significant sum of money. How much did he still need? If he wanted to retire and live in this city, he would need every pound and yen, every dollar and euro. But, more to the point, his work brought a sense of structure to his life, a purpose. Work had kept him sane, guided him in the right direction through all those lonely years. It kept his mind focussed, helped when nothing else could help him. Work had saved him; it had always saved him.

I'll get back to you in a moment, he wrote.

11

Two euros. I was brushing my teeth when it occurred to me. I almost swallowed a mouthful of Sensodyne. I rinsed my mouth, wiped my chin and thought for a moment. Text message. People can respond straight away or wait until the morning; they can answer in their own time, at their own risk. I typed the short message.

The response came instantly. *Do you want to come round now or later?*

A lot of misconceptions persist about the ease or difficulty of killing our fellow humans, especially among those who have never killed other people. One person says they'd never be able to do it; another might say it would be as easy as breathing. In, out. Many people believe that, if the person in question was a particularly unpleasant specimen of humanity – a paedophile or a brutal dictator – they wouldn't give it a second thought. On the other hand, a surprising number of people are convinced they would even respect the life and humanity of someone who had murdered their own daughter. The truth is you can't predict what will happen. Only when the critical moment arrives can we establish our own feelings about the matter.

Emil knew perfectly well what it was that had made him think back to that first time. This city, his son, leaving everything behind him almost thirty years ago. And the fact that he was about to do it all over again.

The taxi was waiting at the front door. I gave the address: Harjutori 4 in the Kallio district. The snowfall seemed to thicken the closer we came to the city centre. We crossed Kulosaari Bridge, and when I looked towards downtown, instead of the city skyline all I could see was a feverish glow.

Harjutori 4 was a colossal stone building from the 1930s. The left corner of the building was occupied by a hall belonging to the Siiloan Full Gospel Church; the door next to that led into a Thai massage parlour. From here it was only a stone's throw to Piritori, the most popular square for drug dealers in the city. The snowy night was like a soothing dream, soft and all-encompassing.

Behind me the taxi curved round the crescent-shaped park and sped off along Helsinginkatu towards Töölö. I found the wrought-iron gate that led into the stairwell, and I was startled to see a woman's face in the dusk.

'That was quick,' she said as she approached the gate.

She didn't open the gate but looked at me through the black grille.

'I can't help thinking you were just trying your luck with that code word.'

'I wasn't,' I said. 'It's been in the back of my mind for a while.'

'To your credit,' she continued, 'it was your first try and you got it right. My father must have had a reporter more like you in mind.'

'Would it be easier for us to talk on the same side of the gate?'

The woman turned the lock, pushed the gate open, took a step back. Now I could see all of her. She was slightly younger than me; shoulder-length, straight, dark-brown hair with a centre parting; she was stocky and had broad shoulders for a woman. Not at all masculine; on the contrary, a powerful young woman. Her nose was strong, long and Mediterranean, her eyes blue and self-assured. Now I had a better understanding of the voice I'd heard on the phone. Maarit Lehtinen was the same no-nonsense kind of person as her deceased father.

'Are you really writing a story about my father?'

'I'm writing about Finn Mining and the mine at Suomalahti,' I told her.

Maarit Lehtinen looked at me.

'You lied.'

'Only in part.'

'I suggest you don't make things worse by explaining any further.'

Maarit guided us into the centre of the stairwell. The lift was an original feature and so small that I stood face to face with her. We were almost the same height.

'I read a few of your articles,' she said.

I waited a moment for her to say something else, but she did not. Not another word. The old lift creaked as it hauled us up.

'So I passed the test,' I said.

A quick glance. Sharp eyes, a wide mouth, thin lips. 'We'll see about that.'

The lift juddered to a halt. I pulled the steel grille in front of us, held it open for Maarit. Her hair smelled of flowers and shampoo.

The attic was typical for a building this age: cold, damp and crammed with decades of useless clutter. Rough-cut two-by-fours and wire mesh divided the space into dozens of sections. The thrown-together feel of the place was heightened by the sections' wonky doors, secured with padlocks, some of which had been broken apart and left hanging dejectedly on the doors. The floor was littered with the protective packages for syringes, plastic cups, and tiny balls of cotton wool spotted with dried, blackened drops of blood.

At the end of the narrow corridor was another padlocked door. Maarit opened it. There was barely any light. Maarit stepped to one side. I saw several boxes, most of them cardboard. They were all different sizes – some shoeboxes, some fruit boxes.

'Everything in here belonged to my father,' said Maarit. 'For obvious reasons, I don't really want to store my own things up here.'

I stepped into the storage space and pulled one pile of boxes into the middle of the floor. A thin strip of light fell on it. I pulled off the tape and peered inside. Papers, notebooks, newspapers, CDs. I glanced to one side.

'Do you remember what you packed in which box?' I asked.

'I didn't pack them; my father brought them up here.'

I turned and looked at Maarit. 'He did it himself?'

'Yes, all by himself,' she said. 'He wasn't that bad a drunk.'

'Sorry. I didn't mean that, at all.'

I thought about what Pohjanheimo had said. Lehtinen's desk had been tidy, everything in perfect order. But if Lehtinen had packed up his papers by himself before his death, he must have known he was in danger and that these notes contained valuable information. Maybe.

I pulled another box from the pile, placed it next to the first and opened it up. The contents were largely the same. And yet they weren't. I went through the notebooks in the first box, looked at the documents Lehtinen had printed off, the newspapers left open at a particular place. I found a common factor almost immediately: vaccinations and vaccination sceptics. The other box was more difficult: maybe something to do with urban and town planning. The third box was obvious: prison conditions, sentences given for different crimes, particularly serious ones. Pohjanheimo was right. Lehtinen was thorough. Obsessive. I continued rummaging through the boxes. Halfway through I found the right one. Mining operations. Finn Mining Ltd. Suomalahti. Several notebooks, a few kilos of printed pages, CDs and a memory stick.

I stood up. My feet were numb. I'd been crouched down for a long time.

'Can I take all this with me?'

'You knew the code word.'

I packed my rucksack. It was soon full and heavy. I closed the boxes, piled them up again and Maarit slipped the lock back on the door.

In the lift we found ourselves once again face to face. This time
Maarit's blue eyes didn't look into mine. Her denim jacket was
emblazoned with badges, some of them real retro stuff: NUCLEAR
POWER? NO THANKS; MEAT IS MURDER; ACTIVISM NOW; VEGETABLE
JUNKIE. One of the badges was simply a black, shiny circle.

'Do you know anything about this mining issue?' I asked.

The blue eyes closed and opened, this time looking right at me.

'What do you mean?'

'Just thinking out loud.'

Maarit didn't say anything.

'While we're on the subject … and this might sound a bit weird…'
I stammered. 'Don't tell anyone I was here.'

'I'm my father's daughter,' said Maarit. 'I'm used to weird requests.'

I recalled what Maarit had said downstairs.

'When we met … What did you mean by a reporter *more* like me?'

'You're not the only reporter that's called me. But you're the only
one who knew what to say. My father said someone like you would
probably know to look in the right places.'

I thought it best not to tell her it was a pure fluke that I'd guessed
the code word.

'Another reporter, eh?' I said once the lift reached the ground
floor. 'From *Helsinki Today*?'

'Didn't say.'

'They must have introduced themselves?'

Maarit shook her head. Her hair moved just enough for her scent
to reach my nostrils again. We walked out of the stairwell and arrived
at the gate.

'Man or woman?' I asked.

'A man.'

'How old, approximately?'

'Hard to say. Not young but not old.'

'What did he say?'

'He said he was a friend of my father's and wanted to know whether
there might be anything belonging to him among my father's affairs.'

'What kind of friend doesn't introduce himself to the deceased's daughter?' I said. 'And how could anything belong to him if you don't know who he is or what he's looking for?'

Maarit stopped, resting her hand on the gate's lock.

'Exactly,' she said; then, looking me in the eye, she turned the lock.

The gate slammed shut. I listened to Maarit's steps until I could no longer hear them. How could Kallio at night be so quiet, so still? The taxi rank was at the other side of the crescent-shaped park, in front of a pawnshop and a bar selling cheap beer and days of blurred time.

That way.

I didn't take a step.

Through the park, its trees naked in the January night, I saw there were no taxis at the rank. But I saw something else too. To the left, at the corner of Helsinginkatu and Harjutori, a man slipped behind the building. I recalled what I'd seen seven hundred kilometres away: first in the heavy snowfall at the gates to the mine, then in the motel car park.

The corner of the building was a retail space, currently empty. As there were no lights on inside, the large windows allowed me to see through to the next street. There were no broad shoulders continuing along Helsinginkatu and I didn't see them returning to Harjutori.

On the side of the corner facing the street was a strip of brick wall two metres wide, providing just enough room to hide. The rucksack on my back was heavy.

I took out my phone and was about to call for a taxi but stopped short. I walked briskly towards the corner of the building. When I was about twenty metres from the windows, I saw the man creep-ing out from behind the strip of wall. I quickened my pace, slipped both straps of my heavy rucksack over my shoulders and turned on to Helsinginkatu.

The man had increased the distance between us. He must have run a short way. Now he walked with long, supple steps. The back covered in a black coat, the body language – both so familiar. I accelerated into a run. The rucksack bounced around on my back. The man had reached the middle of the block, where a set of concrete stairs interrupted the row of redbrick houses.

The man disappeared. He had turned and taken the stairs, which led to a large landing above, a popular spot during the daytime with the local drunks and junkies. I loped up the stairs, craning to see more with each step. I arrived at the platform. Another set of stairs rose to Aadolfinkatu. In front of me was an old university building, the gates at its entrance shut.

A brick wall stretched out on both sides. I stopped to listen. To the left the wall ended at Franzén Park. I walked towards it.

The park was set on an incline, two paths crossing each other in the middle. Even when they were black and leafless, the trees provided effective shadows, but I saw the man. He was walking uphill towards Franzeninkatu. The Kotiharju sauna's vertical sign gleamed through the snow, the letters S-A-U-N-A looking as though they were alight.

The man had reached Franzeninkatu and soon disappeared again. I ran. The bag thumped against my back. I gasped for breath.

I didn't notice the figure step out of the shadows of the wall. Perhaps he jumped out, perhaps he shoved me. I was on the ground. A shoe pressed down on my neck. The rucksack was being torn from my back. I tried to turn over. With a boot at my throat it was difficult. The man twisted my right arm and managed to slip off the strap. He twisted my left arm. I managed to free my right hand and struck out with all the strength I could muster.

I hit nothing.

The man gripped my throat. The hand was covered in a glove. He throttled me, leaning in closer. I caught the smell of garlic and fast food. I hit out again, this time with my elbow. It hit the target. The man let go.

I heard someone shouting. The voice was close by. The man let go of me and yanked again at the rucksack. It felt like my left shoulder almost dislocated, but I managed to keep hold of the bag.

I rolled over. A foot struck me in the face. Then I heard boots running away.

I sat up; slipped the bag from my shoulder and held it in my lap, hugging it close.

Emil didn't need to read any further. He looked at the man's picture, his address, checked the time on his computer. The night was young. What were his options? Tomorrow during the day or the early evening?

In Emil's experience, daytime was the most complicated. It required thorough preparation, the careful selection of time and place, and the utmost control.

A few years ago he had drowned a London banker in the Thames as he was leaving a lunch meeting. It all happened at the bottom of a set of stone steps leading down to the riverside. It was a sunny summer's day – exceptionally bright for an English afternoon. The whole operation had been so touch-and-go that Emil shivered just thinking about it. Of course someone had seen him. The location he had chosen with great care and consideration at night, was in broad daylight the route of somebody's daily walk. Emil remembered the sirens blaring as he walked to the underground station, his face stony and impassive, the legs of his pin-striped trousers wet, the squelching in his leather shoes, his muscles still aching from the exertion. Never again, he thought, as he finally took his seat on the District Line train and hid behind his copy of the *Financial Times*.

And so he only had the hours of night at his disposal.

Wait a minute...

Emil typed in a few combinations of search terms. The process of finding and gathering information had completely changed since he'd started out in this line of work. Nowadays people provided all the information he needed by themselves, quite freely. All he needed to do was put it all together. The man published the runs he'd completed on Run Keeper on his Facebook page. He ran every morning.

Judging by the map, he ran round Helsinki Central Park, usually following the same three-kilometre route. This was understandable: it was the only path for running in the local area that was maintained throughout the winter. Almost without exception his run took place between six and seven in the morning.

Emil waited three and a half hours. He didn't even try to sleep.

When the clock struck five he began to get dressed. Black running leggings, new, blue-green Asics trainers, a black skin-tight running top and a black Goretex fleece. In the fleece pocket he stuffed a pair of black gloves and a black running hat. He looked at himself in the mirror. Only his pale, wrinkled face would distinguish him from the surrounding night.

The quiet side streets around the Taka-Töölö district were deserted. Emil walked towards the sea. Once on Valhallankatu he found what he was looking for.

The Hyundai van belonging to a local plumbing firm had been left in an unofficial parking space in the shelter of the hedgerow and an elm tree. It had probably seemed the perfect parking space when it had been left here. It was perfect for Emil too. As was the age of the car – none of the newest anti-theft technology. Emil opened the door, sprung the ignition, and in only four minutes he was driving along Mannerheimintie.

He drove north and passed the former Teboil garage at Rusk-easuo. He looked left: the Pikku-Huopalahti district had sprung up in an area where there had once been nothing but wasteland, scrap-yards, junkyards, and even longer ago a dump. Emil remembered the shacks, the wonky warehouses. The poor man's high street, they'd once called it.

For all the contradiction, the idea that he was at work, that he was on his way to a job, seemed comforting – good, even. For a long time now, work and life had been one and the same thing. Work had told him who he was, what his role was in the world. It had been the rock that had always supported him, even in the years when loneliness had hit him like a punch in the gut; forced the air out his lungs.

He thought of his son and their meeting. He felt like suggesting they meet again.

Mannerheimintie ended at the newly constructed Hakamäentie intersection. There was something about the intricate tangle of roads and tunnels that made Emil feel lost in his own city. Once he reached the northbound highway, he increased his speed to the eighty-kilometre limit, and before long he sighed with relief. The landscape on both sides of the highway was familiar now. To the right was the darkness of Helsinki Central Park, to the left, the lights of Etelä-Haaga and the towers of rented apartments in the suburb of Pohjois-Haaga. At the next junction he turned off, took the first ring road and headed east. He remained on the ring road for a few kilometres.

The district of Länsi-Pakila had become gentrified over the years. The plots of land, at first divided into two and now apparently three parts, were crowded with brash detached houses that looked more like miniature castles. He remembered this area as having been occupied by a rather sparse selection of terraces and old, detached houses, which had been prefabricated, wooden constructions, built immediately after the war. These new houses, however, looked like something between modern art galleries and diplomatic residences in a banana republic.

He drove as though he was on his way home. Perhaps not home – no plumbers lived in this area of the city – but as though he'd been called out to unblock a drain or fix a leaking pipe.

The house he was looking for was at the end of a road, at the top of a rock rising steeply from the ground. He'd checked the street view to see how the property fitted into the surrounding environment. He knew that the house was relatively new – less than ten years old – and that it towered like a fortress above its surroundings. He drove a hundred metres or so past the end of the road and pulled up to the pavement.

The bourgeois sleep sound.

Was that slogan from a socialist cabaret or a Russian play? No matter, it was an apt description of the early hours in Länsi-Pakila. It was so quiet that he could almost hear his breath steaming up the windows.

He couldn't stay in the van. In a neighbourhood like this it would attract too much attention.

He remembered the topography of Pirkkola Park on the map, recalled the route of the three-kilometre running track. He drove onwards. Pirjo's Tavern, a legendary watering hole at the Pirkkolantie intersection, had been demolished.

The car park was opposite the Maunula urn cemetery. There were no other cars around. He took the photograph from his pocket and looked at it for a few minutes. He would recognise the man anywhere, from any angle.

It was now six o'clock. He stepped out of the van. His new running shoes were soft and silent in the snow.

He walked up the hill and easily located the running route. From the runs logged on the man's Run Keeper account, he had seen that the man went round the park, which was mostly forest, anticlockwise. Emil set off jogging. He was an experienced runner who enjoyed long distances, relishing the sensation of his legs finding their own rhythm.

The path sloped downwards, turned a slight corner, and a long straight section opened out in from of him. After this flat stretch, the path twisted and turned in a gentle uphill section. Emil liked such places. They would be perfect for his purposes. Only twenty metres' visibility in any direction, forest and rocks on all sides. No people around. Dog walkers never came this deep into the woods, at least not in the early morning. The only people out and about were dedicated athletes.

Through the tangle of spruce and birch trees, Emil could just make out the figure of a lone runner. He looked at his watch. The first kilometre had taken him five minutes. When the man turned on to the same short stretch of pathway lilting into the hillside, Emil recognised him instantly. In his fifties, one hundred and eighty-five centimetres tall, stern jawline, a sharp nose, the bluest eyes that Emil had seen for a long time.

Emil glanced over his shoulder. Not a soul in sight. He lightened his step, shifted his bodyweight to the balls of his feet, relaxed his arms.

The man's progress was smooth and purposeful. He came closer. Emil heard the man's steps, the tautness of his breath.

When there were only a few metres between them, Emil focussed all his energy into a single motion. He took one step to the side, slid over to the man's side of the path and raised his arm just as the man was about to push himself into another powerful stride.

Emil grabbed him. Two opposing forces collided.

Emil's movements – his bodyweight, the power of his arms, the grip of his fingers – culminated in a single, precise twist. Both of the man's legs were in the air. There came a crack. His neck snapped. His body fell to the ground, slumping like an empty sack.

Emil continued his run.

15

He didn't want to sleep. More than that, he couldn't. The nightmares had made sleeping every bit as exhausting as lying awake. He was impatient. Meeting his son had opened a door, at least that's how he thought of it. A door that had been closed for thirty years had opened a fraction, and the brightness that waited on the other side not only brought him warmth but made him restless. How should he proceed? He had to admit to himself that he had no experience of situations like this. A long time ago he had decided not to allow himself to become attached to people or things. For years the person closest to him had been the person whose death he was planning. If that isn't loneliness, what is?

Meeting his son had pushed something into motion, something that, almost unbeknown to himself, he had dreamed of. It had given him a chance.

After he'd left his wife and son, he'd loathed himself profoundly. Then, as the years passed, he had begun to see those events in a more reasonable light: they were young people who had behaved in what they understood to be the best way. And he had done what he'd had to do, striven for that which everyone strives for: survival.

He sat down at the dining table in his furnished, one-bedroom apartment and stared at the sun slowly creeping up behind the window. How small it was to begin with, how inexorable the light and beginning of a new day always was. The trees stepped forward from the darkness, acquired new branches, grew and twisted. At first all he could see were the thickest branches, the ones that looked like arms as thick as girders, but soon he could see the thinner ones too, until even the tiniest twig came into focus against the pale fabric of the morning.

How many mornings did he have left? Did it make any difference? All that mattered was what those days contained and how he approached them.

He sat, drinking his coffee and eating some rye bread with peppered ham. The same happened to the Töölö library as to the trees around it: it was gradually dressed and undressed by the approaching morning. First, the darkness and the dusk were lifted from above it, then it took on form and shape, and it was filled with light, with new angles and dimensions, width and depth.

Perhaps something similar could happen to him. At first the thought seemed too big, too heavy. Impossible. But then it did what thoughts often do. It planted itself and began to grow. If only his life could take on a new morning's worth of light, if the darkness and dusk could, at least in part, be lifted from above him.

He had returned to Helsinki and he had met his son. Perhaps this was a sign that life could change. He had to leave his work, find something else. At first he wasn't sure what that would be. Then he realised with absolute certainty.

16

Ella and Pauliina came into the kitchen together. I put my papers in one pile so there would be room for us to have breakfast at the table. Our three-person family. Sometimes, fleetingly, our happy family. Pauliina immediately noticed the swelling on my cheek and at the corner of my eye. She clearly also noticed that I'd spent the night in the kitchen, that something had happened.

Pauliina made breakfast for Ella and herself. I offered to make some coffee. We sat at the table and ate. Pauliina leafed through the morning paper, said she would take Ella to nursery and told me to pick her up. Ella nattered away to herself. We both answered her, admiring her bandaged hand every time she proudly showed it off. I wondered whether Ella was able to pick up on the tension between her mother and father.

Once she had eaten, Ella wandered into the living room by herself for a moment. As soon as she had disappeared round the corner, Pauliina looked at me across the table.

'What on earth?'

'I had to go and fetch some papers,' I said and indicated the pile of paperwork, which seemed to have grown in the last few minutes.

Pauliina didn't so much as look at them.

'I meant that,' she said and nodded at my face.

I touched my cheek. It still hurt.

'I'm not sure what happened either.'

Pauliina looked at me. 'I assume this is something to do with whatever it is you're investigating?'

I didn't want to talk about it. For some reason it felt wrong. Perhaps not wrong, but as though I was doing something I shouldn't. Besides, there was something else I wanted to say.

'I met my father yesterday.'

The newspaper dropped from Pauliina's hand. The business section curtsied gently on to the table.

'What?'

'We bumped into each other in the supermarket. We went for a drink.'

'You and your father?'

'Yes.'

'The man that left you and your mum before you were two?'

'One. Before I was one.'

'Okay, one. Where did…?'

'We sat in a pub for a little while. He's about to retire and he's moving back to Helsinki. He's been living in Berlin. He looks just like all the photographs – only older and more rugged.'

'Did you ask him why he—'

'Why he left, why he came back? Yes. He didn't answer the first question, but he did answer the second. He said he wants to come back because I'm thirty.'

'What's that got—'

'That's the age he was when he aban— … when he left Helsinki.'

Pauliina was about to say something but instead turned in her chair and stood up. She took her coffee cup to the sink, cleared up Ella's plate and glass, and wiped the table.

It was nine o'clock. Pauliina and Ella had already left. I looked at the papers I'd once again separated into piles placed across the table. In addition to the stacks I'd created, there was still one group: miscellaneous items. I picked up a bubble-pack envelope. Inside was a CD case. On the cover it read in felt-tip pen, DIR.MEETING/ DATE? There were no other annotations. From the living room I fetched the external CD drive and connected it to the laptop. A few clicks. I fetched my headphones. The beginning of the sound file wasn't very promising: endless silence. Then I made out the sound of footsteps, talking, people in an enclosed space. Perhaps chairs were being pulled across the floor, people sitting at a table. The sounds and voices came from different directions. The microphone picking all this up was clearly placed to one side of the room. The clink of spoons and coffee cups jingled above the conversation like church bells in a landscape.

MAN 1:   … if there's no decent coffee, forget it.

MAN 2:   There's tea.

MAN 1:   I don't drink tea.

MAN 2:   Tap water, then.

MAN 1:   You taking the piss?

MAN 3:   Clean water.

MAN 1:   What the…?

MAN 3:   Let's get down to business. If things are like you said, then how serious a situation are we looking at?

MAN 1:   Pretty fucking serious. We've got a few months. At most.

MAN 4:   If that's the case, we won't have time to drum up any extra funding without it drawing the wrong kind of attention.

MAN 2:   The wrong kind of attention? You don't think it'll attract the wrong kind of attention if we announce that we've got a problem like this? What's going on up there?

MAN 1:   The system isn't working the way it should. It just won't do its job. It works in theory, but not at Suomalahti. The mine's spewing sulphates – mercury, lead, everything except nickel, which it's fucking supposed to be producing. The vats are full of heavy metals, and when you look at it, the future's anything but bright. There's rain and snow across the whole country and it doesn't look like it's going to stop any time soon. And how fucking stupid are we going to look if we admit we hadn't thought you might get snow and rain in northern Finland? The press will rip us to shreds.

MAN 2:   First, they build you up, then they tear you down. It would be like giving them a gun and telling them to aim right at our heads.

MAN 1:   Well, I'm sure we're all agreed on reporters and the way they
          work. But if we could just come back to the—
MAN 4:   We can't ask the government for more.
MAN 2:   Why not?
MAN 4:   We'd have to tell them how things are going.
MAN 2:   Never bothered them before.
MAN 1:   Things are different these days. Everybody wants good news,
          no matter whether there's any truth to it. We were supposed to
          save the whole of fucking Lapland. Now we've got ourselves
          nuclear fallout.
MAN 2:   A nuclear warhead is the only thing that could sort this mess
          out.
MAN 3:   I think it's perfectly clear the methods we're using up there are
          far too expensive.
MAN 4:   I'm not a technical expert, but I know that changing the
          refinery operations at this stage would take years and would
          require the kind of investment we just can't afford. From a
          financial point of view, I'd look at keeping on as we are and
          trying to find a way round it for the next two or three years.
MAN 2:   Two or three years?!
MAN 4:   It could be less than that. But by that point Europe will be at
          war again and the demand for nickel will mean we can sell as
          much as we can possibly produce, and we can set our own
          price. It'll be our boom era. But, as things are at the moment,
          it's unsustainable, unbearable. It's a fact and we've got to
          accept it.
MAN 2:   You think there's anyone in this room that doesn't accept it?
MAN 1:   Changing the operating model isn't an option. And going
          public is not fucking on. But…
MAN 2:   I'm listening.
MAN 3:   I'm listening.
MAN 4:   Me too.
MAN 1:   … it's not the means of extraction that's too expensive. It's
          maintaining the means of extraction. We could explore a

different tactic. How much would we have to tweak the
refinery expenses to make this thing work? I'm talking
percentages.

MAN 4:   At a rough estimate, fifteen to twenty per cent.

MAN 2:   That's a lot. That's not just tweaking. That's a cut. That would
require—

MAN 1:   Action.

            [silence]

MAN 3:   I'm for it.

MAN 1:   Thank you.

MAN 2:   If I understand you right—

MAN 1:   We simply take advantage of the mine's location. If we can
make that fifteen-to-twenty per cent disappear from our
expenses, as it were, we can be a profitable business again.
Everyone will thank us and nobody will notice a thing.

MAN 2:   We've never discussed this, we never came to any kind of
decision and we know nothing of the factors that made this
meeting necessary.

MEN 1, 3 & 4: Of course not.

The tape ended. I realised I was standing in the middle of the kitchen
floor. I sat down at the computer. It was time to kick the hornets'
nest.

PART TWO
LEAD

BLOG
Janne Vuori, *HT*
janne.vuori@helsinkitoday.fi
Twitter: @vuorijanneht

Where can we dig? What can we say?

All that glitters is not gold. The mining industry may not save Finland after all.

As regular readers of this blog will know, the articles here are by their very nature unofficial. In addition to thinking out loud, this means that, unlike in my journalistic pieces, I also present claims, counterclaims and conjecture. In other words, anything goes.

There are currently fifty mines in operation in Finland. Several new projects are in the offing, and the promises made by those lobbying for these projects – about using renewable resources and the projected increases in employment in the local areas – grow bigger by the year. This, despite the fact that the world around us and the earth beneath our feet cannot support such promises. The enthusiasm for the mining industry is partly understandable. The country's economy is stalling, there is no new Nokia in sight, and northern Finland is fast becoming an uninhabited wasteland. This is precisely the gap in the market that mining investments seek to fill. They are expected to bring prosperity and – due to the location of the mines themselves – much-needed jobs to those areas of the country where unemployment is most acute. But are the mines really the saviours they claim to be?

The facts are brutal. Finland's soil is famously ore-deficient. Most mines currently in operation are unprofitable. The majority of those mines are owned by foreign companies, which naturally has a direct impact on how much they can benefit the Finnish economy. Many of the projects currently pending may, according to some estimates, actually have a negative impact on their surroundings. This is largely to do with the sheer size of the initial capital required and any subsequent environmental effects. Mines require an infrastructure of roads, electricity cables, train tracks and numerous other structures, which will all be built with taxpayers' money. Any potential profits, however, will be siphoned off into the bank accounts of the international mining companies, most of which are run from offshore tax havens.

And if this doesn't sound bad enough, let's just say that mines put considerable strain on the local environment. Every mine. Everywhere.

How heavy the environmental strain is depends on a variety of factors. Every mine currently in operation pollutes its immediate environment to some degree, often quite significantly. This is a fact. Another fact is that cleaning up a mining complex is an expensive business, and it's generally the taxpayer and not the mining company that ends up having to foot the bill.

What's more, the effect of the mining industry on employment figures isn't all that impressive either. The fifty mines in Finland employ only a few thousand people in total. That's the same number that Stockmann's department store employs in Helsinki alone. If politicians are truly interested in creating jobs for people, they would naturally look to places where new jobs might realistically appear. But this is about politics, about what looks good and sensible, although it is neither. Of course, every newly created job in remote areas of the country is something to be celebrated, but if the cost of that job runs into the millions, it no longer looks like such an attractive investment.

The factors outlined above raise larger questions about the overall feasibility of the mining industry in our country. Why should Finland – a country with some of the cleanest countryside in the world – wilfully destroy and pollute its own environment when it gets nothing in return? Is it possible that, if there is to be a global shortage of something, it won't be gold, chrome or nickel – and it certainly won't be industrial sewage? As things currently stand, it seems that clean soil, water and air are commodities that may soon be in short supply. All the evidence points to this being the case in a matter of decades.

There are pollutants and ruined natural environments the world over. Recent environmental predictions indicate that there are areas of the planet where breathing will soon become difficult, if not impossible. In a situation like this, a country that already has plenty of clean drinking water, vast areas of land not yet made uninhabitable by sulphates, and lakes as yet undestroyed by metallic slurry, might have a lot to give. For that reason alone we must talk about the implications of continued mining in Finland.

In the next few weeks I will be digging deeper into the nickel mine at Suomalahti. Partly thanks to a contact on the inside, I predict that the mine – both the project and the mine currently operating – will embody the problems of the Finnish mining industry, which at best can offer only a brief spell of employment for a few dozen people. But which means significant profits for a very few people, at extortionate cost both to the environment and the Finnish taxpayer. Our taxes are disappearing like smoke into the air. Most of the areas affected by the mines' pollutants will be lost for generations to come.

It's time to ask why.

1

The front door of the house across the street opened and closed like the gills of a large, grey fish; people walked in and out, mostly in – they were sucked inside the building and disappeared. He stood beneath the shelter though the snow had stopped. It was almost nine o'clock.

At last he saw the woman he would have recognised anywhere, any time. He began walking.

The woman looked in his direction, but her eyes didn't settle on him. How could that be? he wondered. Time had passed, he had to admit; it had started when he did something he could never undo. He strode across the road and caught up with the woman just before she reached the door.

'Leena.'

She turned. From her eyes he saw that, after looking at him quizzically for a moment, she finally recognised him.

'Emil,' she said.

Leena didn't seem at all surprised to see him. What was she thinking? Emil couldn't say. Leena looked around.

'Where did you…?'

'I wanted to see you. I looked up your name, found this place, your work. I thought it would be better to come and talk to you in person than over the phone. Telephone calls are…'

A bus drove past, its juddering almost knocking them to the ground, they were so close to the edge of the pavement.

'I met Janne yesterday. I wanted to meet you. I wanted to…'

Yes, what exactly do I want? To start a new life? To go back and start again?

'…I had to see you.'

'And now you have.'

'How are you? How have you been?'

'I'm very well.'

'That's good to hear. There's something … I'm moving back to Helsinki.'

Leena froze, stared at him. There they stood at the western end of Bulevardi, the piled-up snow on Hietalahti Square next to them.

Most of Leena's hair was hidden beneath her woollen hat, but the strands pushing their way from under it showed that she too had aged. Her dark hair was now tinged with grey and silver. Her face was familiar, small and narrow, her skin didn't shine as it had done all those years ago, and deep furrows ran the length of her cheeks, but she was still attractive. And her eyes: that stare that was constantly reading other people; the brightness shining into the distance. The caution in her every gesture.

'Why do I need to know that?' asked Leena.

'It's been thirty years, Leena,' he said. 'Forgive me.'

The words flew from his mouth before he had a chance to think about them. Everything seemed blurred and confused.

'I was so young back then,' he said. 'I didn't appreciate that everything has a cause and an effect.'

'Of course you didn't,' said Leena.

They stood there, gazing at each other. Emil knew what he wanted.

'I don't…' Leena began; paused. 'There doesn't need to be any bad blood between us,' she added hurriedly.

'That makes me very happy.'

'I don't know what else to say,' she said and made to leave. 'I have to get going.'

'I've come to stay.'

Leena thought about this for a moment. 'I have to go…'

'Can I call you?'

Leena stopped. 'Why?'

Because you are the one I've been thinking about all these years.

'So we can talk. We have a grandchild now: Janne's daughter.'

Leena's body seemed to stiffen. It wasn't a large movement, but he noticed it.

'You want to be a grandfather, is that it?'

Her tone told Emil there was no point replying.

'Emil, you've been away for a long time, and in that time many things have changed. I'm not sure you can just turn up and announce that Grandpa has returned.' Leena paused for a moment, her breath steaming in the frozen air. 'I might be wrong, you never know.'

'Leena…' He handed her a slip of paper with his phone number on it.

A snowplough rattled past along the cobbled street. The noise hurt their ears. Emil saw the reflection of the streetlight in Leena's eyes. Then she raised a hand, took the piece of paper and walked off. Emil filled his lungs with the chilled winter air and sensed the bitter taste of metal in his palate.

2

Someone had printed off my blog post and left it on my desk. In felt-tip pen they had written the word THE TRUTH on the left-hand side of my photograph. I looked around, but nobody seemed ready to own up to playing a practical joke. Everyone was sitting at their desks, their faces glued to their screens or their cheeks pressed against their phones. I fetched some coffee and spread out more of Lehtinen's papers across my desk. I was just wondering where to begin when my laptop beeped as an email appeared in my inbox.

Mr Vuori,

I sincerely hope life in Helsinki is going swimmingly, that your caffè latte is frothy and you have the strength to carry on the struggle for loony-left laziness and long sushi lunches in your fancy landscaped offices. Here in the north life isn't that easy; for the most part the wind is cold and biting, and unemployment is doing its best to break the 30% barrier. From time to time, when we are finally offered work a hundred-kilometre drive away, we learn from amateur environmentalists in Helsinki that what we're doing is wrong. These self-same privileged tofu tossers, who whinge about a two-minute tram journey, think we in the north should live on the smell of pine trees and the bubbling of the pure springs.

It is largely thanks to the spineless herbal-tea brigade and others of your ilk that things in the country are so well and truly fucked up. You write that the mining industry is not financially viable. Is it financially viable, then, to support your lifestyle? I Googled your name and learned that you have been awarded at least three grants to fund various media projects. Until reading your article, I'd never heard of you, so it appears your writings haven't been all that successful. It's no wonder. If you wrote them with the same intellectual input as you did your recent essay on the mining industry, they were doubtless used to wipe at least two or three backsides before being carefully sorted into the recycling bins you so worship.

What irks me more than anything is the arrogance of you and people like you. You've never done a proper day's work in your life and yet you spend all your time writing about what people should and shouldn't do in Finland, what we should and shouldn't think, how much we should hug one another, understand one another. Do you ever wonder why so many people despise you? Does it even occur to you, as you sit there nodding in your woolly hats and fiddling with your iPads? Do you understand that you are the problem you're sitting there in your designer spectacles trying to solve? Of course you don't.

You claim to want to protect the environment, though you'd be lost in a hectare of woodland. You whine about climate change, then in the same breath you buy a new smartphone and book a city break abroad. You claim to love trees and demand to have them growing outside your favourite café, though the only tree you would recognise is the Christmas tree you buy from the market downtown. (What's more, when you buy a Christmas tree for eighty euros you're paying seventy-nine euros more than the real value, which serves you right, of course, but is yet another tragicomic example of your all-encompassing ignorance.) You believe the world's problems are caused by people who are greedy, racist meat-eaters.

Thankfully, justice will be done, and you will eventually drown in your own shit. And by that I don't mean the infinitesimally small amount of metallic waste produced by a few mines. Not at all. You will drown in the shit that you, sir, represent: self-righteous know-it-allism, weak morality and endless inbreeding.

To round off, I cordially invite you to the grim, hard-working north. You might enjoy yourself so much that you'll never leave.

Yours sincerely,
Raimo Minkkinen
Retired journalist, Suomalahti

I'd never heard of Minkkinen, but his message was the most civil one I received that morning. The messages that followed were far more direct and, of course, anonymous. According to these writers I was a communist, a loony leftist; I was kissing the Green Party's arses and sucking their organic cocks; I was the inbred offspring of the hard-left activists of the 1970s; I was trying to turn Finland into Somalia, probably growing cannabis in my back garden, lived on mung beans fertilised with my own faeces, and deserved to be stoned to death or 'escorted behind the sauna', as one writer euphemistically called it.

Not a single correspondent thanked me for my blog post, let alone suggested that it was timely and important.

That afternoon Hutrila asked me into his office. As usual, we remained standing.

'Where are we at?'

'The blog has received a lot of publicity,' I said and spoke quickly so as to finish my sentence before he could interrupt me. 'It lays the groundwork for further investigation. I want to write an in-depth piece. There's lots of material. I need time. There's no way I'll have it all ready for tomorrow's edition.'

'Why should we have it in tomorrow's edition?'

'I thought that's what you wanted to talk about.'

'Who is your insider?'

The question was direct and came straight from my boss. None-theless, or perhaps for that very reason, I said, 'I can't tell you.'

Hutrila raised his left arm across his chest, propped his right hand against it and placed a forefinger on his chin.

'How did Lehtinen's notes appear out of the blue?'

'His daughter gave them to me.'

'I didn't know he had a daughter.'

'It had nothing to do with his work, I suppose,' I said and shrugged my shoulders.

'How did you get your hands on them?'

We were standing opposite each other, our eyes locked.

'I knew something that everyone else knew.'

'And you won't tell me that either.'

'No.'

Hutrila continued to stare at me with his unflinching grey eyes.

'I suggest you find a bit of humility in your work.'

'I didn't mean to—'

'I'm still your boss. Have you had any feedback on the blog?'

I was surprised at the sudden change of direction. I told him about the messages I'd received, what people thought, how they viewed our paper, how they viewed me.

'Sounds good,' said Hutrila, lowering his arms and relaxing his posture. This meant our meeting had come to an end.

I walked back to my desk and read a bunch of new emails. More of the same. With one exception. I looked at the time, then made for the door.

Sleet.

3

The wet snow whipping diagonally past and the wind coming in across the sea had blown away all life in its path. Mustikkamaa was now a deserted island. There was only one car in the car park. I walked up to it, opened the door and stepped inside.

'Phone,' said Marjo Harjukangas.

I pulled my phone out of my pocket and showed it to her. It wasn't enough. Harjukangas took it, dropped it into the locker between the seats and pushed the lid shut. She wasn't in a good mood.

'Any other devices?'

I shook my head.

'Can I check…?'

Harjukangas frisked my jacket and quickly tapped the pockets of my jeans.

'Let's walk and talk,' she said.

We got out of the car. Harjukangas seemed to have chosen our route in advance. I walked alongside her, between the wintery tennis courts and football pitches, and towards the edge of the trees.

'I suppose you've read my blog,' I asked.

We were moving briskly, the sleet clamouring to breach my jacket.

'You made an amateur mistake,' said Harjukangas.

'By mentioning an insider?'

I didn't tell her why I'd thought it was necessary. The truth was, I wanted to let the people concerned sweat a little. With her anorak collar standing up and her woolly hat pulled down across her forehead all I could see of Harjukangas was a twelve-centimetre strip: eyes, nose, mouth.

'It was too soon,' she said. 'But that's not the only reason. More crucially, your boss has probably already asked about it and wants to know who your contact is.'

I said nothing.

'So I'm right,' said Harjukangas.

Her steps were a runner's, moving her forwards lightly, effectively.

'Did you tell him?'

'No.'

'I asked you once before, and I've been disappointed, so I'll ask you again. Can I trust you?'

'Of course.'

'Don't answer too quickly. It makes you seem unreliable.'

The leafless trees, the grey horizon full of heavy sleet.

'Remember,' she continued. 'If you interpret things, you have to do so correctly.'

We arrived at the southern tip of the island and followed the path along the shore. We walked along the stretch of the path that we hadn't reached last time. Harjukangas needed to let off steam. She would get to the point before long; I was sure of it.

'Remember the accident last week, in which Kimmo Karmio died?' she asked as we made our way up a small incline.

'Yes.'

'Now we've lost another member of the board: Alan Stilson.'

'What happened?'

'I don't know. But I know one thing. First, people said he'd had some kind of seizure, but now the city police are investigating both Stilson's death and Karmio's little accident. Which is still being considered an accident, at least for now.'

I took a breath. 'If the police are investigating it…'

'Precisely,' said Harjukangas.

'I'll look into it,' I said.

'I hope so.'

'Have you got any idea what might…?'

'Threats,' said Harjukangas. 'We've had them through the years. We talked about it a while ago – whether to take them seriously or not – and if so how seriously.'

'What kind of thing?'

'Death threats…'

'But why? Why would someone want to threaten you?'

'The most serious were probably from activists. I got letters: *Because you're destroying our environment, we're going to destroy you.*'

'Did you ever find out who was sending them?'

'No,' Harjukangas said quickly but corrected herself almost immediately. 'Well, one of the letters gave the name of an organisation. Black Wing. One word or two, I can't remember. The name didn't mean anything. There's no organisation registered under that name and nobody had ever heard of them.'

We walked up the hill and arrived back at the tennis courts. Behind them was the car park and the solitary Škoda Octavia.

'You'll get your phone,' Harjukangas said without looking at me. 'But not a lift. You have to earn that.'

I worked until nine-thirty that evening. I called a long list of colleagues to see if I could get a name and number at the police department that might actually yield something. I quizzed and questioned people. Everybody I spoke to instantly smelled that I might be on to something. Eventually I got a number.

Almost instantaneously Detective Inspector Halonen managed to turn the conversation back on to me. Where had I got an idea like this? When? Who had recommended I call him specifically? I ended the call before it could turn into a full-blown interrogation. I was no wiser when I put down the phone, than I had been when I picked it up.

Some of Lehtinen's papers were in a box beneath my desk. The majority of them I kept stored in one of the kitchen cupboards at home. I picked up the miscellaneous bundle and placed it on my desk. I glanced through the papers, leafed through the notebooks. I was too tired.

Pohjanheimo and Hannikainen, one of the other reporters, were both still at their desks, typing away. I said good night and walked the few hundred metres to the metro station. The freezing air embraced me as soon as I stepped outside, snow whipped up in my

face. Romani beggars in threadbare clothes were standing beneath
the shelter in front of McDonald's, eating one-euro hamburgers. A
group of strikingly young junkies, with designer trainers, jeans and
rucksacks, were hollering at one another in the ugly glass-covered
entrance to the station. I took the escalator in noble solitude, alone
in the vast metro hall. As the orange train glided into the station I
realised I hadn't heard anything from Pauliina. At Herttoniemi I got
a bus and wound my way home through the dark suburban streets.

When I opened the door, there was nothing to welcome the return
of the heroic journalist. I found Pauliina in the kitchen.

'How's Ella?'

'Fine,' said Pauliina as she tapped at her laptop.

'Did you read the blog?' I asked.

'I haven't had time. I was in a hurry to make Ella breakfast. After
I'd changed the bandage on her hand, that is.'

We looked at each other, but not warmly. I took a carton of blueberry juice out of the fridge, poured some into a glass and sat down
opposite Pauliina. She raised her head from the screen, pulled the
band from her hair and shook it loose.

'We were in a rush this morning,' she said. 'It would have been
nice if you'd said you were leaving so early. I ended up stressed about
making it to the interview in time.'

'The interview?' I asked, and realised instantly what I'd done.

Pauliina's gaze was a mixture of disappointment and contempt.

'You'd forgotten.'

Yes, I had forgotten. Now I remembered. The job interview that
Pauliina had been worrying about for a while, that she'd talked about
weeks ago.

'Sorry,' I said. 'This story of mine is—'

'That's right – of yours.'

'Things happened so quickly I—'

'To you.'

There was still blueberry juice at the bottom of the glass, like darkened blood. I don't know why it made me think of that.

'It's always me, me, me,' said Pauliina.

I was exhausted. It was late. I'd made a mistake. That gnawed at me, that and everything else. Pauliina tied up her hair again. A few flicks of the hand and the ponytail had reappeared.

'How did it go?' I ventured.

'Fuck off,' said Pauliina, very quietly but with all the more resolve.

She leaned back in her chair and folded her arms across her chest. I don't think she'd ever looked at me like this before.

'I'm not the one that stopped trying,' I said eventually.

'Trying for what? For some action? You've certainly stopped that.'

'For good reason,' I said, all too quickly. The words slapped on the table and remained there, ugly and irreversible.

'Good to know,' said Pauliina. 'You're hardly spectacular yourself.'

'Anything else?'

Pauliina shrugged her shoulders. 'You mean apart from the fact that you're at most mediocre in bed? I can think of a few things. Your breath smells of old cabbage and rotten fish. I can't have a conversation with you for more than a minute without the topic turning to you and your achievements, which, by the way, aren't nearly as impressive as you seem to think. Shall I continue?'

'Then why the hell are we together?'

'The real question is, why are you here? You're not interested in anybody but yourself. Your daughter hurts her hand; your partner has the most important interview of her career; we need to agree who takes Ella to day care and who picks her up – practical, everyday things. But you're just not interested in any of it.'

'I am interested, but it's just—'

'But this, but the next thing. Yes, but. I would do, but. If only, but. But, but, but.'

'For fuck's sake,' I said, shoving the glass back and forth across the tabletop. Blueberry juice spilled from the glass and threw bloody stains across the table. 'Enough's enough.'

'Too right,' said Pauliina. 'You're sleeping in the living room.'

*

There was no way I was sleeping in the living room. I went into the hallway, pulled on my coat, slung my bag over my shoulder and left. I walked to the bus stop, looked at the timetable, then walked on to the next stop. The snow had relented, the snowflakes were large and solitary; frost sparkled on the surface of the road. The bus arrived and I rode all the way to Hakaniemi.

Hannikainen was still sitting at his desk. He raised his head, but I couldn't tell whether he noticed me or not.

I booted up my computer, though I knew it was pointless. I couldn't be bothered to think, far less write anything. I switched the computer off again, walked outside and instinctively headed towards the city centre. Just before Long Bridge I asked myself where I was going. I couldn't answer. What was most important was to walk, to breathe. I turned towards the shore. Snow floated down to the surface of the sea and disappeared. On the deserted street running along the shore, the leafless trees looked as though they had been turned to stone. Across the black bay was the darkness of Kaisaniemi Park, the glimmer of the downtown lights hanging above it. The night air was cold and pure. I could just make out the end of the peninsula about thirty or so metres ahead.

This was one of my favourite places, a strange deserted spot right in the middle of Helsinki. If you stood with your back to the hundred-year-old stone buildings behind you and stared out across the bay to Töölö, shining in the distance, you could almost imagine being on an island. I crossed the road and walked down to the shore, where the trees leaned out across the water. The sounds of the city were far away – behind me and ahead of me. I looked up to the sky. The snowflakes felt like tiny, freezing pinpricks on my face, disappearing almost as soon as they touched me. I stood still until the cold forced me to move again.

I walked back up the verge to the road, turned at the corner and saw a broad-shouldered man approaching from the opposite direction. The movements were familiar. I turned and headed back the way I had come. There were two paths leading away from the end of the peninsula. I took the other one, and when I turned at the corner and saw the lights of Hakaniemi ahead of me, reassured that I was not alone in the world, I thought I might have been a little paranoid.

I continued towards the lights, away from the darkened bay and the loneliness of the peninsula. Then, further away, on the road curving round towards the metro station, I spied the outline of the man, the figure that looked so familiar. Still I couldn't seem to place him. I arrived at the corner of Saariniemenkatu.

The street bisected the peninsula horizontally, each end leading to the bay. At the other end of the street stood the same man. A gust of cold air struck me in the stomach, making me gasp for breath. Another man, whose frame I also recognised, began walking down the street towards me. I was in no doubt where I'd seen him before: Suomalahti, at the gates of the mining complex, opening the door of the command tower, crumbs of fast food still hanging in his beard. I adjusted my own trajectory, crossed the street, my heart thumping, and bounded up the two steps into the Juttutupa bar.

Juttutupa was swathed in a comforting, inebriated warmth. The bar was almost full. I went to the counter, downed a beer and a cut brandy and tried to explain to myself what had just happened. Either I was losing my sanity or there were people following me. And if I was being followed, where were the men now? Was I losing my mind…? The second beer tasted better than the first. It often does.

I found a seat on the other side of the bar, opposite the stage. Two men with guitars were performing a mournful, unplugged ballad. One of them was singing a story in English about a woman who had cheated on him, left him and taken his favourite frying pan. All this in country-and-western style. I finished off my drink and fetched another, plus a chaser. The beer tasted better the more – and the more quickly – I drank it. I knew that thirst like this had its repercussions, but what of it? I was being followed and I was on the brink of separating from my partner. To hell with everything. I took another swig of beer and heard a voice behind me.

'Come here for the music, did you?'

4

The book's name was *Human Monsters*. It was supposed to calm his anxiety. Emil had found it in a charity shop opposite the old sports hall in Töölö. Flicking through the book he found some instructive stories:

Apparently, the Roman empress, Livia poisoned anyone who might rival her sons, then eventually poisoned her husband, Emperor Augustus, too. Livia's sons did not attend her funeral.

Basil II's soldiers put out the eyes of fifteen thousand Bulgarian prisoners. The prisoners were sent home in groups of one hundred, each group led by a man with one eye.

Andronikos I Komnenos had the ruling king strangled with a bowstring and then married the king's eleven-year-old widow. He was sixty-five years old. When Andronikos himself was deposed, a raging mob tied him to a pole; his beard and hair were pulled out, his hands chopped off, his teeth yanked from his gums, and one of his eyes dug out.

Gilles de Rais tortured, raped and murdered two hundred young boys and girls. He hung his victims from the ceiling of his torture chamber and tied them to the floor. He raped them and tore out their innards. The most beautiful of their severed heads he preserved so that he could admire them later.

Tomás de Torquemada, the first grand inquisitor, declared that all heretics – and Jews in particular – posed an imminent threat to the soul of Spain. He ordered over two thousand people to be burned at the stake and confiscated the homes and possessions of all those he deemed to be a heretic. Confessions were brought about through torture. The *heretic's fork*, which had prongs that dug into the skin, caused sleep deprivation that brought victims to the brink of insanity. The *choke pear* crushed the teeth and jaws as it opened up, and the *rack* pulled the bones from their joints with a crack. As the procedure continued and the winch tightened, the limbs were torn from the body, starting with the arms.

Vladimir Lenin's hanging order of 1918: '1. Hang (and make sure that the hanging takes place in full view of the people) no fewer than one hundred known landlords, rich men, bloodsuckers; 2. Publish their names; 3. Seize all their grain from them. Do it in such a fashion that, for hundreds of kilometres around, the people might see, tremble, know, shout: "They are strangling, and will strangle to death, the bloodsucking *kulaks*". Yours, Lenin.'

The troops of the Croatian fascist dictator, Ante Pavelić, gave two options to those who had survived the mass executions and extermination camps: death or Catholicism. Some were allowed to experience both. In 1941, in the village of Glina, hundreds of Serbs were crammed into a small church to be converted to Roman Catholicism. The doors were bolted and the church burned to the ground.

Mao Zedong: 'We must kill. We believe it is good to kill.' While the Chinese were facing the worst famine in their history, Mao was selling grain abroad in order to buy weapons. Thirty-eight million people died. Mao never washed. Legend has it that larvae hatched on his body.

Lavrentiy Beria loved torture. Stalin loved Beria. Beria said: 'Give him to me for one night and he will admit to being the king of England.' Beria enjoyed rape. He skinned people, stuffed snakes into their mouths, tore off their tongues, their eyes, their ears. What he first did to his victims, he then did to their families.

Heinrich Himmler was a slender child, who played chess and collected stamps. He was a chinless man, whose attic was filled with books and furniture made from the skin and bones of Jewish prisoners. Heinrich Himmler was a fastidious and effective bureaucrat: in only a few years he organised the massacre of six million people.

Pol Pot created a communist utopia in Cambodia, a place where even the counting of the years was started again from zero. Everything non-communist had to be erased. Newspapers were closed down, the intelligentsia was executed. The definition of this was broad; people with spectacles were killed as 'bourgeois intellectuals'. Eventually a third of the population was killed, most of them with iron rods, axes and hammers. Soldiers were ordered to use bullets sparingly.

Idi Amin had a taste for human flesh. He visited morgues and asked to be left alone with the bodies. He hanged his victims from trees. Amin had his servants carry him around in a chair.

Saddam Hussein wanted to personally oversee the execution of his enemies. He used Sarin gas on Kurdish children. His sons were psychopaths. They all enjoyed torture.

Türkmenbaşy erected a forty-metre-tall golden statue of himself opposite his palace in the middle of the capital of Turkmenistan. He renamed the days of the week and invented some highly imaginative methods of torture. For instance, he would put a gas mask on his victim's face, close off the air vents, then put a set of headphones on the victim's ears so that the victim could hear family members being tortured. The statue rotated on an axis once a day.

Emil stood up and looked out of the window. The knowledge that, at some point in history, someone somewhere had maimed and enslaved people, pulled teeth from another's mouth, flogged people, eaten human flesh and continued to do so didn't diminish his own sins. It didn't place him in a better light, didn't offer the chance of favourable comparison with others, didn't give him permission to forget, to downplay things. It placed him on a bloody continuum of evil beings who tore limbs from innocent people, making history repeat itself in such a mindless, idiotic way that thinking about it for even a moment was enough to drive anyone crazy and lose all hope.

Something had changed. Even the night felt different. It no longer protected him. It was as though he was standing next to a great curtain and couldn't find a chink through which to slip back into the darkness.

5

A full glass of gin-and-grapefruit in her right hand, a grey packet of Belmonts in the other: Maarit Lehtinen.

'What?' I asked, genuinely confused.

'The music,' said Maarit and waved her left hand towards the performers.

I'd forgotten all about the country-and-western duo. I hadn't even been listening to them.

'No. Yes. Sit down. Sorry, you don't have to, if you've got company somewhere. But anyway. Please.'

The words came out of my mouth every bit as angular and disjointed as they sounded in my mind. Maarit seemed to hesitate before taking a seat. She sat near me on the sofa but looked slightly past me. Perhaps she wanted to maintain eye contact with the duo, which had now changed tempo for a more upbeat drinking song.

The self-confidence in Maarit's posture; the piercing brightness of her blue eyes; the exotic curve of her cheeks and nose; her bare shoulders.

'Drinking here all by yourself?' she asked.

'With any luck,' I said.

Maarit looked at me quizzically.

'It's nothing, forget it. What are you up to?'

'I came to listen to the music. The guys are friends of mine. Is everything all right?'

I took a thirsty gulp of beer. 'Everything's fine and dandy.'

'I read your blog. It was very short.'

'A longer piece needs … It'll be longer.'

'Did you find what you were looking for in my father's papers?'

I looked at her. 'There's lots of interesting material.'

'That's it?'

The tone of her question communicated more than the words themselves. It made me sit up straight.

'Can I get you a drink?' I asked.

Maarit nodded towards her glass. It was still full. 'I'll drink one at a time, thanks.'

Quite. I knocked back my glass of brandy.

'And when are you going to be writing a follow-up piece?' Maarit enquired.

'Just a minute,' I said. I went to the counter and ordered another beer and another chaser.

When I came back, the level of Maarit's drink had remained stubbornly high.

'Can I ask you something?'

'Of course,' said Maarit. 'I can always refuse to answer.'

'Were you and your father close?'

I realised I was pissed, realised I was talking to Maarit as though we were old acquaintances, as though we'd crossed the all-important boundary of friendship. As I picked up my glass, Maarit glanced past me and almost imperceptibly shook her head. It must have been because of my question. I was about to take it back when she spoke.

'To be honest, I don't really know. I can't compare our relationship to anyone else's. All I have is my own experience. We were civil to one another, told each other how things were going – with certain reservations, of course. There are things a father doesn't want to hear about his daughter, and things a daughter doesn't want to hear about her father, though they were things that at least to some degree we were both well aware of.'

'Right.'

'We were interested in some of the same things. We spoke about them quite regularly. Does that make us close?'

I took a slurp of brandy. It no longer burned my throat but tasted soft and pleasant. I looked at Maarit.

'Maybe it does,' I said at first, then added: 'Yes, it does.'

'Why do you ask?'

The sofa was soft, the alcohol warmed me, Maarit's features seemed heightened in the mellow light of the bar.

'I just met my father for the first time in thirty years. You could say we're not exactly close.'

Maarit sipped her drink. I noticed she was looking at me closely; very closely.

'I recognised him instantly,' I said. 'I recognised him, but I didn't know him. We chatted for a while, talked about what we do for a living, where we live, my family. I'm not sure what I think about it all.'

'My father didn't stay away for that long, though he was away a lot. It's a common trait for fathers. Being absent.'

A cold wind gusted through me.

Ella. Forgive me.

'I suppose so,' I said.

'Well, nobody is perfect.'

'I can't think of anyone who is.'

Maarit smiled. For the first time, the smile contained something directed at me, only me, something emanating from those blue eyes. I also noticed she'd almost finished her drink.

'What would you say if I fetched us something to drink?' I asked.

As the evening progressed I fetched more drinks many times. We clicked. Better and better all the time.

We talked about everything, we opened our hearts. When the lights were flicked for final orders, we stepped out into the frost hand in hand. I said I'd walk her home. My mind was light, and my legs too. My inebriation was fresh and strong, not numbing or fatigued. I felt that everything would work out after all. Big things were happening. I was closing in on the crux of the case. I could build a relationship with my father. Pauliina would eventually relent, given time and space to understand. If I was being followed, it must have been because I was on to something. Everything was for sale and everything had a price. Maarit. Maarit, round whose shoulders

I wrapped a warming arm to protect her from the cold. Maarit was becoming a good friend. A very good friend. A very close friend.

We stood for a moment opposite each other, our breath steaming into the renewed snowfall. It was so quiet that I thought I could hear Maarit's heartbeat. We followed the curls of our breath, our lips moved towards one another. A hot, sweet-tasting kiss so at odds with the surrounding cold and the snowflakes melting on our cheeks that we couldn't pull apart for fear of having to catch our breath. When our lips finally did part, for some reason I could taste blood in my mouth.

We unzipped our trousers in the lift. The dark wooden walls and black floor clacked and cracked, and the mechanism gave a faint shriek with every passing floor.

The sixth floor. As I yanked the old folding door to one side, it almost crushed my hand.

We collapsed on to the hallway floor.

6

The text message contained twenty-four words. Not even one word for all the years that had passed. Still, he felt time becoming so light and meaningless that, for a moment, a day and a year felt almost interchangeable. Dull thuds beat against his chest, his body was pierced with a joy and strength that felt like youth itself.

Hello Emil. I've thought about what you said. Perhaps we should meet. Morning or evening is fine, I'm at work during the day. Leena.

Emil went through his morning exercise routine, stretched carefully and tried to cleanse his mind of the chaos of dreams and reality.

For the first time in a long while he made himself a decent breakfast: fried eggs – sunny side up; rashers of juicy bacon; thick slabs of rye bread; liver pâté; frozen blueberries and fat-free yoghurt. And coffee, coffee, coffee.

He sat down by the window and watched the new morning growing brighter.

7

This was going to be a hellish day. I was lying on my back. Naked. Without a duvet. Disjointed fragments heaved through my body in waves, vague memories of what I'd said and done the night before. Particularly what I'd done. Maarit was asleep next to me. She too was naked. Our skin was pallid and white, uncovered. The wall clock, with its large, grey face and the black hands, showed me it was five minutes to nine. Pauliina had taken Ella to nursery half an hour ago. I was breathing through my mouth, trying to think of something other than running to the window and hurling myself down to the merciful embrace of the asphalt below.

This wasn't the first time I'd been in this position, but it was the first time since I'd met Pauliina. I didn't want to take the thought any further. I hauled myself into a sitting position and stretched out a hand to find my trousers on the floor. I managed to slip my feet inside and stood up. The clock stubbornly showed that another minute had passed.

'There's coffee in the cupboard above the machine.'

I turned round. Maarit didn't look as though she'd had too much to drink.

'If you want to make some,' she continued.

Again I looked at the clock. I'd already missed the one thing I should never miss under any circumstances. I didn't especially want to stay but didn't see how it could make the situation any worse than it already was.

As I measured water and coffee into the machine I began to feel even queasier. It wasn't physical; it was mental. I sat down at a small, square table. Under different circumstances I would probably have thought the studio flat beautiful and spacious: just over thirty square metres; an old spruce floor, nicely varnished; two tall windows on this wall and a smaller, square window on the opposite wall. We were high up. Glittering in the morning sunshine, the rooftops looked like a series of frozen waves.

The coffee machine puffed and sighed right by my ear. Maarit got out of bed, pulled on a light-blue T-shirt and walked into the bathroom. I flicked open my phone and checked the morning headlines.

Nobody else seemed to be writing about Suomalahti.

The thought didn't cause me the kind of joy that it should have, and, anyway, reading was painful. The hangover slowed everything down. The text seemed lumpy; the beginning of a sentence was forgotten as I tried to make sense of the final clause.

'Anything new?' asked Maarit.

She was standing next to me, looking down at my phone.

'Don't think so,' I said and darkened the screen with a click of the thumb.

When Maarit didn't move, I raised my eyes. She looked at me as though she was about to say something, but turned instead, took two mugs from the cupboard, poured coffee into both and sat down across the table. I couldn't be entirely sure of everything I'd said the previous evening and night. Maarit nodded towards my phone.

'When will we have something to read?'

At first her gaze was direct and inquisitive, then suddenly hesitant.

'Just a thought,' she added quickly. 'What with my father's papers and all…'

I pushed my phone back into my pocket and glanced again at the clock. Ten minutes had passed since I'd woken up. I stared at the black hands, as if I could reverse them. As if I could reverse everything that had happened over the last twelve hours. At the same time I realised something.

I was my father, trying to return to something that no longer existed. For him the passage of time was thirty years, for me it was a matter of hours. We were both trying to undo what had been done.

Neither of us would succeed. You didn't need to look far for a good metaphor: we'd both dug our own graves.

'If I said anything about Suomalahti last night,' I began, 'just forget all about it.'

'You didn't.'

Again Maarit looked past me. We sat in silence. I glanced into the hallway. I saw her denim jacket with all the badges and remembered what the owner of the petrol station had said while I was up north.

Three men, one woman. Environmental activists.

'Did you want me to talk about it?' I asked.

Maarit turned her head just enough so that I could look into her eyes. She raised her shoulders.

'It's an important matter.'

'How important?'

Maarit adjusted her position in the chair. There was something impatient in her posture, something that had been brewing for a long time.

'The things that are going on up there. Anyone with a brain will get it right away.'

'Get what?'

'There's no such thing as sustainable mining. It's always unsustainable. That's its nature – always has been. When you dig for nickel, you produce manganese, phosphorus – you name it. You have to do something with all the slag. Hundreds of square kilometres of land and surface water, and millions of cubic metres of groundwater, are being polluted. When the mine is closed down, the local area will never return to its natural state. It's the truth. And…'

'And what?'

Maarit looked at me. Her earlier impatient look had been replaced with one almost of regret – at her own outburst, perhaps.

'Somebody has to do something. A good start might be if a certain journalist got his act together and wrote a certain article.'

The hand of the wall clock jolted forward, the fridge whirred. Far below us came the hum of traffic.

'May I ask you something?'

'I already told you yesterday: you can ask, but I might not answer.'

'Have you been up there? To Suomalahti?'

'I know what it looks like.'

'What does that mean?'

'Exactly what I said. I've looked into the matter. Otherwise I wouldn't spend time talking about it. Remember whose daughter I am. I study things, very carefully.'

'One more question: did you turn up in Juttutupa last night by chance?'

Maarit drank the remains of her coffee. 'I'm going to have a shower. I need to be at work by ten.'

A moment later I heard the sounds of running water. I had the distinct impression that I was in the wrong place. I rinsed out my cup, got dressed and left.

He'd kept the photograph all these years. It was dog-eared, faded and soft round the edges.

In the photograph a young family was eating ice cream next to the bridge at Seurasaari. A hot summer's day; the bridge's white railings freshly painted; colourful summer clothes – shorts and T-shirts (the 1980s were a crime against fashion); a one-year-old boy in a pram between his mother and father: a family that looked young and happy.

The day that photograph was taken was one of the best days of his life.

The day he'd been forced to turn his back on the people in that photograph was one of the worst.

Emil looked at both his telephones. One was the number he'd given his son and his mother. This phone had received a single text message, and nobody had called him. From time to time Emil looked at himself from the outside, from above, and he could see exactly how lonely he was. That eye looking down on him could see that there was a ring around Emil, a circle into which nobody had crossed for a very long time. Pulling down that invisible protective wall wasn't easy.

He picked up the phone – the one whose number he'd given to the most important people in his life – and selected one of the two numbers in the memory. The phone rang, and a moment later someone picked up.

I found it just as hard to think about eating anything as I did to consider the man who'd spoken on the phone as my father. The fact was, I needed some fresh air. What I also needed – as crazy as it sounded – was a reliable, outside opinion. If the father who had been absent almost my entire life wasn't an outsider, who was?

Again it had started to snow. I took the route via the square. Passing the door of Juttutupa would have been too much to cope with at this point. I took my phone from my pocket and, at the risk of freezing my fingers, decided to call Pauliina. The call went straight to the answering machine. I didn't leave a message.

I passed the Ympyrätalo, the 'Circle House', a concrete edifice that had replaced a number of beautiful, early-twentieth-century *art nouveau* buildings on the same site, including the so-called Wendt House. Anyone who thinks the 1960s was the decade of love should acquaint themselves with the history of Helsinki architecture. Comparing what was demolished and what was built in its place, one thing is certain: the 1960s was a time of the utmost spiritual decline and immeasurable material destruction.

In keeping with the aesthetic spirit of the present occupant of the site, behind the building was a strange cluster of long-since closed-down fast-food kiosks and a mechanic's workshop of some description. With its recesses and walls and plinths ideal for sitting on, the area was the perfect junkie magnet. It was only thirty metres to the pharmacist and the liquor store inside the building; a distance manageable even in the more advanced stages of oblivion. From early morning until late at night the small hideaway was full of noise and despair. That was the case now, too. A shirtless man with a cut at the side of his eye was howling at the snow falling from the sky and a woman beside him had pulled down her pants and was urinating into a pile of ploughed snow.

I walked up Siltasaarenkatu and turned left. In the house on the corner there was a Thai restaurant, now relatively busy given the lunchtime rush. My father said he'd booked a table.

Why now? Why now when everything was coming crashing down around me?

I remember how I'd hoped my father would return home and how I'd come up with various different explanations as to why he never did. I remember my mother's awkward expression, her forced smile. When my insistent whinging carried on, her expression turned to one of impatience and eventually a look of sadness.

I'd continued explaining things to myself until my explanations came to have the same effect on me as they had on my mother. At some point in my adult life I noticed I hadn't given the matter any thought for years. I didn't know where it had gone, how it had worn away.

When I became a father myself, however, the matter took on a new significance. I had promised myself I would never leave Ella. Remembering that promise and the fact that I'd screwed up that morning brought more gloom to the already cold, grey day. I shook the snow from my shoulders and stepped into the restaurant.

My father was sitting against the back wall, facing the room and the door. He raised his hand, and in a few steps he was standing beside me. His handshake wasn't exaggeratedly strong, but I could feel the power of his grip. At our first meeting I'd noted his movements, his body language. His hair was grey in a manner generally considered stylish. His eyes were expectant; his gaze the kind that seemed to read everything twice – first registering what he saw, then looking for what might possibly hide behind that which was immediately apparent. His body was slim; his sitting position light. I found it hard to believe he was sixty.

'You look tired,' he said once we'd ordered our lunch of coriander chicken and pork with chilli and peppers. 'Too much work?'

'Yes. Well, not exactly. I've got enough work. Too much of every-thing else though. I mean, not too much. A lot.'

He didn't respond immediately. Then he continued in a soft voice. 'I read your article about the mining company. That'll keep you busy.'

'You could say that.'

'Has anything new come to light? Are we to expect any fresh revelations?'

Everybody is interested in this case. Everybody except Pauliina.

'I hope so. I'm doing my best.'

'I'll be interested to see how it all pans out. It's nice to see you take your work seriously. Work has always been important to me.'

More important than your own family.

'How long are you planning on staying in Helsinki?'

The question took on a different tone from the one I'd meant. Now it sounded like an attack. My father's eyes (would it be more natural to say Emil's eyes?) remained impassive; his body didn't flinch.

'I've been thinking of moving back here. I notice how much I like it. The people who are important to me live here.'

'Can you find work here?' I asked and was relieved to hear that my tone was friendly, neutral.

'I very much think I will.'

'The same work you've been doing before?'

My father took a sip of water.

'Can I show you something?' he asked.

Before I could say anything his right hand was in his jacket pocket and he carefully placed the something on the table.

'You, your mother and me.'

I looked at the photograph. I stared at it for a good few seconds. I had never seen this photo of the three of us. The small image said a lot. My chest winced; a cold knife sliced through my stomach. A family of three. What had I done? What had we both done? My mother had often taken me to Seurasaari; we used to take a picnic and spend entire summer days there. I don't remember ever seeing the family in that photograph on our picnics. And the next thought to flash through my hungover mind: Is this how Ella would look at photographs of her mother and father; the family of her childhood? Would she think so-and-so is missing from this one, someone else from that one?

The waiter brought our meals. A bowl of steaming rice raised a curtain between us.

'That was a wonderful day,' said my father. It sounded to me as though he was saying out loud a thought that had run through his mind thousands of times. 'One of the best days I can remember.'

I forced myself to eat. It became easier with each mouthful.

'Is there anything you'd like to talk about?' he said, out of the blue. 'You look as though something's bothering you.'

I looked at my father. We were essentially two complete strangers. But there was something about the man sitting opposite me that … I swallowed a forkful of rice, soft with coconut milk, felt the burn of chilli on my tongue. The thought appeared of its own accord. It was powerful, independent, unshakeable. For ultimately, who can a son trust if not his own father?

'I think I might be being followed,' I said. 'Because of my work.'

'Really?' he replied, his expression unruffled.

'Late last night, when I left the office. I wanted to go for a walk, needed some air, you know how it is. It had been a tough day, and things at home were a bit tense when I left. I walked down to the shore at Siltasaari…'

'Lovely place,' my father smiled. 'One of my favourite spots in the city.'

'Likewise,' I agreed. The small interruption confused me, though at the same time I felt oddly safer. 'I went there to get some fresh air, and I was about to walk back when I thought I saw a man who had followed me once before. He started walking behind me. Then another man—'

'Do you know why he was following you?'

'I can guess. If it was the same man, it must have something to do with Kari Lehtinen—'

'Who is he?'

'A reporter who left behind a lot of papers. Lots of material regarding Suomalahti. Why do you ask? Do you know him from somewhere?'

At first my father said nothing. 'No,' he replied eventually.

'Lehtinen is dead,' I said.

My father looked at me. 'You said you were walking away from the shore and the man started following you. What happened then?'

'I was scared. I'd already been kicked in the face once. I ran into a bar for cover.'

'Is that why you're so hungover?'

His smile was brief but warm.

'What happened next?' he went on.

'I ran into an old friend.'

'What about the men following you? What became of them?'

'I don't know.'

'But you're certain they *were* following you.'

'What else could it be? They were the same men I'd seen up north.'

My father's gaze focussed now; he lowered his chin, raised his shoulders a few millimetres. Nothing dramatic, but noticeable all the same.

'So you know who they are,' he said. His voice had dropped half an octave and he almost growled.

'I think they're the same men I met in Suomalahti,' I said, 'at the mine. I was writing a story and interviewed one of the guys – the head of security at the mining complex.'

My father didn't immediately reply. The lunchtime rush seemed to be dying down.

'I'm glad you told me,' he said quietly. 'You can always talk to me, about anything you wish.'

Perhaps it was the hangover, perhaps the argument with Pauliina, perhaps Maarit, or the fright I'd got yesterday; perhaps it was

something to do with my long-lost father who was now sitting opposite me. Probably it was a combination of all these factors.

'Do you mind if I take a picture of you?' I asked.

For the first time I saw a flash of bewilderment and uncertainty on his face. It disappeared instantly, replaced by a cautious
smile.

'Of course not.'

I took my phone from my pocket and raised it. The man who had
been missing for thirty years appeared in the viewfinder. I pressed the
button. Twice.

We looked at each other. Something had happened, something
more than the taking of a photograph.

If my father was suddenly so important to me, someone who had
never had a father … I thought of Ella. I looked down at my plate.
I lifted a forkful with a good combination of meat, vegetables, rice
and sauce. To my relief my father had taken the photograph from the
table and replaced it in his pocket.

Once I've written up the story, I'll fetch Ella from nursery, I
decided. I'll have plenty of time.

The snow fell in flakes that were light, bright, melting pleasantly on his face. He was walking along the southern shore of Töölö Bay. He wasn't in a hurry but still couldn't control the bounce in his step. Leena finished work at five o'clock – rather, she'd said she would leave at five, which was a different matter. They had agreed to meet in a café on Museokatu. According to Leena it was quiet and suitable for conversation, even in the evenings. Emil hadn't told her he now lived in Töölö. Saying this out loud was suddenly difficult.

What's more, he didn't know what to think of Janne's story. His son might be in danger.

His senses weren't working the way they usually did. He was too near to the people he had always loved. Up close we cannot see clearly, he remembered someone saying. That's right, the phrase was from a book Leena had once read him. He remembered the feel of the thick grass in Sibelius Park beneath his back, a summer's day long ago, Leena's smooth, young hands holding a book, the boughs of the trees disappearing into the depths of the sky.

It was true.

We don't think rationally about the things we love.

The nursery teacher's face betrayed first fright then annoyance. Of course, I realised I was the one that had made a mistake. She had simply explained the situation.

'Everything's fine,' I said, and, after trying hard, managed to force a smile to my face. 'That's what we agreed. Pauliina was going to pick up Ella. That's it.'

Needless to say, Pauliina and I hadn't agreed anything. I hadn't been able to get hold of her. The phone had rung, but she hadn't answered. I'd sent her a couple of messages, too, with the same result.

'They left an hour ago,' the teacher explained.

She was visibly exhausted. Thirty-five years old, long, thick brown hair in a ponytail, two scarves against the cold; a monthly salary only just above the minimum wage, yet having to shoulder responsibility for the safety of the children and deal with the increasingly paranoid demands and special requirements of the children's parents. A few more winters in jumpsuits, an eventual burnout, and then she would look for a new career. She would remember me as one of the hundreds of fathers for whom everything else was more important than their own children.

'Thanks,' I said. 'Too much work.'

'That's often the case.'

'This time ... Forget it. See you in the morning.'

The woman said nothing. She walked away.

I strode home, trying to swallow my disappointment. I'd wanted to pick up Ella. I'd thought it might make amends for my absence that morning. I looked at my phone. One minute to five.

In the hallway I wiped the snow from my shoulders; the large flakes had caught on my coat like spiders, and shaking them off was difficult. Ella's voice pealed from the kitchen. She didn't run into the hallway to see me, though the door clicked shut, clothes hangers clattered on the railing and my bag thumped to the floor.

I could tell from Pauliina's expression that something had happened, something other than the fact that I'd been away all night without saying anything. I concentrated on Ella. The kitchen smelled of Pauliina's risotto. At least in theory all the elements were present: father, mother, daughter, a warm stove, a fragrant meal. I sat at the table next to Ella, opposite Pauliina and took some food.

'How was your day?' I asked.

Pauliina said nothing. I scooped up some salad, placed it next to the risotto and poured some water into a glass. Just as I gripped my fork and was about to take my first mouthful of food, Pauliina lifted something from the chair next to her and slid it across the table to me. An envelope. Addressed to both of us. Pauliina's name was above mine. I glanced at Ella, who was concentrating on her food. Pauliina asked Ella if she wanted some more. Ella said something I couldn't quite make out. I placed my fork on the plate, picked up the envelope and opened it.

Two sheets of A4: a letter and a colour photograph. The photograph showed an image of a family, hanged – a man, a woman and a child, all stripped to their underwear and brutally maimed. My face had been Photoshopped on to the man's body. The letter was brief and the message clear: if I carried on with the story, the kind of damage displayed in the photograph would happen to me and my family. Above all, to my family.

I returned the pages to the envelope and placed it on the empty chair next to me. We ate our meal. Ella babbled to herself.

12

He arrived early, again. The street-level café comprised two rooms. At the back of the first room was a glass vitrine, displaying cakes and sandwiches, and the cash register. The back room, which lay behind a low, wide opening, was like a romantic salon, with table lamps and armchairs. He chose one of the two window tables, sat with his back to the wall and looked out at the continuing snowfall. The old snow was already covered in a fresh layer, several centimetres thick. It made the view seem unreal, smoothed the roughness, evened out the chaos of metal and asphalt.

He told the waiter he would order when his ... when the person he was waiting for arrived. His fumbling for words brought a friendly smile to the young waiter's lips. He turned and looked outside again. His heart was racing. He was clearly nervous; he wasn't himself. Uncertainty, faltering. Small things, of course, but he knew that every crack, every fissure begins as thin as a strand of hair.

'Hello Emil.'

He stood up, now even this gesture tainted with uncertainty. He didn't know whether to greet her with a kiss on the cheek, a short hug or a polite handshake. It was clear neither of them knew what to do. The result was a mixture of everything: dry kisses sent into the warm air of the café, a single hand placed warily on the other's shoulder and a handshake that was so short they only noticed the touch once they released their grip.

They ordered. Leena took a cup of tea, Emil some coffee, and cinnamon buns for both.

'Earlier today I was thinking of that summer's day we spent in Sibelius Park,' said Emil. 'You read something to me.'

And he saw that she too remembered it: a quick smile; and her eyes, which always said more than her mouth. But exactly what they said, Emil had never fully understood. Neither then nor now.

'I was reminded of it today when I met Janne. We had lunch together.'

'That's nice.'

Emil tried to identify the emotion in her voice – resentment, anger, indifference – but couldn't put his finger on anything.

'To be honest I wasn't surprised when I saw you,' Leena said almost immediately.

'I was just passing…'

'I didn't mean when we met right there at that specific moment. I mean that a lot of time has passed, and there is a time for everything.'

'Quite.'

'I was reminded a while back, when I received one of those pension statements. You know, the ones that document your work history, all the salary you've been paid and how much pension you are due.'

'Yes, I know,' said Emil sincerely. He knew that such statements existed, but he'd never seen one.

'I had to sit down when I received it. It felt suddenly so heavy – figuratively speaking, that is.'

'Of course.'

'I don't know if you've ever experienced something like that,' said Leena, and it occurred to Emil that he could look at that small, slender face for the rest of his life. 'Your whole life seems to flood into your arms. Everything you've ever done, everything you've ever been is right there in front of you – like a doll's house where you can see into every room at once and there's nowhere to hide.'

Emil considered the memories he had; memories that even the smallest incident could trigger. The bewildered man he had shot in the forehead; his knife slicing through a neck stiff with fear; the bellowing as he hurled a man from a balcony.

'Something like that,' he said. 'In fact that's really why I've moved back to Helsinki.'

'I knew it the moment I saw you.'

Emil looked at Leena. They ate their cinnamon buns. Emil felt the urge to wet his forefinger and pick up the grains of sugar that had fallen on the plate and lick them with a smack of his lips.

They spoke for some time about surprisingly mundane things, such as how Helsinki had outgrown itself, how it had become an international city, and reminisced about what the city had looked like when they'd first met. If Leena is experiencing even a tenth of the nostalgia that I am, thought Emil, her heart must surely be taking extra, wistful beats too.

They sat quietly for a while. Both had turned to look out of the window, into the street where snow was falling, heavy and silent. Emil looked at the woman he had lost so long ago.

'We're not young any longer, Leena.'

'Perhaps that's a good thing,' she said, her voice almost hushed.

13

The envelope lay on the coffee table in front of us. An American drama about a group of crime-scene investigators was on the television. The woman running the forensic laboratory looked like a supermodel. The characters all called her a pathologist. Her fulsome lips gleaming and her cleavage showing just enough, the pathologist-cum-supermodel explained that the killer had made a mistake after all. I switched off the television and looked at Pauliina. She pulled her legs to one side, took off her glasses, placed them on the sofa and rubbed her eyes.

'Pauliina,' I said and nodded towards the envelope, 'It's harmless. It's just … you know. A bit of mischief.'

'How do you know that? One side of your head is still swollen. Ella's hand is in a bandage.'

'Those are two different things. And you don't need to worry about me.'

'It's not you I'm worried about.'

We sat in silence.

'I'm not interested where you were last night,' said Pauliina. 'Truth or lies, I don't want to hear it. Neither makes any difference; neither would solve anything. You have brought something so unpleasant into our home that I simply can't accept it. And I don't just mean that envelope.'

'It's important to bring things out into the open.'

'Maybe, but those people don't need you to do that. If you'd been a genuine environmental activist, you would have passed your information to someone looking for a big break and you'd be satisfied that the matter had been made public. You did this for your own reputation, your own glory. You wanted your name and photograph in the paper.'

I said nothing.

'That letter is a wake-up call,' Pauliina continued. 'It's woken me up, makes me wonder what we're doing here. Everything was so quick three years ago. I got pregnant straight away; we bought an apartment without getting to know each other. Ella was born, and since then there hasn't been time to think about anything else.'

I looked at the blank television. It seemed to stare back at me. A black hole ready to suck me into its depths.

'I don't know what you mean. We live together, we know each other.'

'What's my shoe size?'

'Thirty-eight.'

'Thirty-nine. Where do I work?'

'At the … consultancy firm … the communications office.'

'Called?'

'Korhonen &…'

'That was my last job. When did I land my current job?'

'Your new…? You didn't say anything. I have asked though. Congratulations on your new job.'

'What music do I like?'

'Well, we went to at least three gigs before Ella was born…'

'Right, listening to your favourite bands. What do I like?'

'In general or something specific?'

'What do I like?'

'Ella.'

Pauliina's eyes were cold. 'You and I have nothing in common.'

I sighed. It didn't matter what I said.

'It feels as though all this was a mistake … a misunderstanding,' she said.

I looked at her. 'A mistake?'

'Yes.'

'A misunderstanding?'

'Yes. I should have seen that work is what's most important to you. At first there was something almost alluring about it – that someone could be so dedicated, so determined, that you knew what you wanted. But when work started coming first time after time, I should have realised. Everything else just disappears. Even a passing interest in the person you live with.'

'You can't say I'm not interested in Ella.'

'You still haven't paid the nursery bill.'

'I forgot about it when I was at the motel up north and … I just forgot about it.'

'I've already paid it.'

'I'll transfer the money into your account.'

'It's not about the money.'

'It's just a nursery bill.'

'It's not just one nursery bill. It's everything. Your whole life.'

My phone beeped on the table. I leaned over to see who the message had come from.

'This is exactly what I mean,' said Pauliina.

'What?'

'In the middle of our conversation. You can't help yourself. Do you want to know why I haven't asked anything about your father? Because I already know. He's exactly the same as you. Back then he thought and acted just like you're doing now.'

'I don't think so. He seems…'

'Different? So did you. Now he regrets it and wants to form a relationship with you again. Am I right?'

'It seems that way,' I admitted.

Pauliina shook her head. 'I don't know what to say. Except that things can't go on like this.'

'What do you mean?'

'Exactly what I said. This can't go on.'

Pauliina leaned over to the table, snatched the envelope and threw the photograph in my lap. The image looked all the more sickening: a dead family, a hanged child.

'Pauliina, things like this don't happen. To us. It's just intimidation.'

'I don't care what it is. But it's come to this. And I'm not just talking about that photograph. I mean everything. You could easily ask to be transferred to the food-and-drink section or the film reviews, anything at all, and decide to be a father to your daughter.'

'I can't leave this story up in the air…'

Pauliina's face seemed utterly expressionless. She wasn't angry, wasn't upset, as I might have expected.

'I don't…' I began, but didn't know how to continue.

Pauliina swung her legs to the floor and was about to use her arms to propel herself up from the sofa.

'I'll look,' I said quickly. 'I'll look for alternatives.'

Pauliina thought for a moment.

'I hope so,' she said quietly, stood up and walked out of the room.

14

The tallest building in Finland rose up between a metro station and a shopping mall in the district of Vuosaari in the east of Helsinki. Emil knew the building was almost ninety metres high. In addition to the ventilation room and the helicopter landing pad at the top of the tower, there were twenty-four storeys of apartments, two floors below ground and a ground floor reserved for retail outlets and an entrance hall. The twenty-sixth storey featured a sauna and a rooftop terrace giving panoramic views across the city. That's where Emil was heading, for the sauna slot beginning at eight p.m.

If Helsinki had changed in the intervening thirty years, the changes in Vuosaari had been more rapid and more radical. Built up during the 1960s and now called Old Vuosaari, the furthest and most easterly neighbourhood in the area had been reduced to a small enclave surrounded by enormous residential buildings. New Vuosaari had been built in the 1990s and the building work was still under way.

Emil walked and listened. Immigrants. Languages he couldn't understand. Aurinkolahti: a district within a district. Apartment blocks constructed along the seashore – expensive condominiums, their balconies facing out to sea. If he disregarded the temperature, now ten degrees below freezing, it was as though he had walked a few thousand kilometres south.

The calm, chilled winter's evening. The fresh, sharp air. He walked for a long time. He knew he was walking in a circle, but he needed it. His hour and a half with Leena had turned out to be far more pleasant than he'd dared to imagine. Yes, they'd spoken about shared memories, but, more than that, they had talked about the present: what they thought about different matters, what life and the world looked like.

Sparse, lazy flakes of snow fluttered to the ground. He walked onwards. In his mind he ran through everything again, one last time. It was his way of getting into his work, it was like a mantra with which he banished from his mind everything not related to the task at hand. Eventually it was always effective. In any line of work, what was most important was focus and preparation. There were no shortcuts. If you tried to look for one or took a diversion of any sort, you made mistakes.

He looked out at the sea, the darkness of the horizon, took a deep breath and turned back. He guessed he must have walked around a kilometre and a half. It was only a guess and he couldn't check on his phone. Naturally, his phone was in Töölö. Not because someone might have known the phone belonged to him, but because you could never be too careful. Phones reveal everything about us, particularly where we have been and when.

The building was like a square column, almost a hundred metres high and with white walls, like fifteen enormous sugar cubes piled on top of one another.

Emil's first attempt to get in the door failed.

He had timed his own steps perfectly, but when he was five metres from the door a man dropped something and crouched down to look for it in the snow and gravel. Emil was forced to walk past the door, to continue on his way and cross the street. At walking pace he circled a small roundabout, watching to make sure the man had found what he was looking for and had disappeared inside the building. Emil took slow steps, as though he was waiting for someone. Eventually he spotted what he was looking for.

Opposite the main door of the apartment block was one of the entrances to the shopping mall; judging by the direction the woman was taking, by her opened jacket and the shopping bag in her hand, Emil could see that she was on her way home from the supermarket. As she approached the door of the apartment block, pulled the key out of her bag and pressed it into the lock, Emil walked up from the side and decisively gripped the door's long handle.

'Let me help you,' he said in a warm, polite voice.

The woman looked up and for no more than a second let go of the key ring. Emil opened the door and handed her a bunch of keys, a different one. The woman didn't notice the switch – who would expect a thing like that from a polite, elderly gentleman on a normal evening? She pushed the keys Emil had given her into her pocket and hurried towards the lift. Emil followed her, showed the magnetic card he'd just acquired to the reader and activated the panel of buttons, all the while making sure the keys were hidden in his fist.

'And you were going to…?' he asked the woman.

'Eight, thanks,' she replied.

'I'm going up to twelve,' he said and pressed both buttons.

They didn't speak on the way up.

The woman got out on the eighth floor. Emil continued up to the twelfth. When the lift came to a halt, Emil immediately pressed the button to close the doors and took the lift up to the top floor. He glanced at his watch. A quarter past eight. Perfect timing. The man would be having his first soak.

He stepped out of the lift and listened intently. The sauna was on his left. He walked up to the grey, metallic door and held the magnetic card up to the reader. The lock opened with a pleasantly soft click. He pushed the door ajar and listened again. The sounds of water being thrown on the stove.

He took off his shoes in the doorway. He did this quickly, but there was nothing panicked about his movements. He knew how much time he had. He knew that, right about now, the woman would realise she had the wrong keys and that she couldn't get into her apartment. If she lived with someone else, she would ring the doorbell and get in that way, after which it would take her a few minutes more to realise quite what had happened and draw conclusions. If she lived by herself or there was nobody at home, it would take her the same amount of time to call the caretaker and have somebody with the master key meet her at the door.

Emil had heard right: sauna, shower, steam room, behind the door to the right. To the left a panoramic terrace running the length of the building. By searching under the name of the housing association he'd acquired floor plans of the different storeys, long explanations of the building work, complete with structural information, wind calculations and locking systems, and – more importantly – the housing association's own website with a list of sauna slots, which residents could conveniently book online.

He opened the balcony door. A cold wind blew in from the south, perhaps all the way from Tallinn. The foyer was filled with perfect, almost enticingly cool air. Emil turned the handle of the door into the showers, and the door swung open by itself. He moved out to the balcony, hid among the shadows and waited.

He heard the sound of the steam-room door opening. The slap of wet footsteps making their way across the tiled floor in the shower. Then the footsteps stopped. Emil waited. The footsteps slapped across the entrance hall and made their way out to the balcony. Even from behind the man was easily recognisable. A towel wrapped round his waist, his skin steaming in the chill of the air, the man stepped towards the balcony railing.

Emil moved quickly. His thick, soft socks with non-slip rubber patches were silent and gave him a firm grip.

In any profession it is possible to reach a level at which any possible eventuality can be used to your advantage. Everything can be turned into energy, a forward motion. Every movement, whatever its original direction, can be put to use. It is this quality that differentiates the professional from even the most ambitious amateur. A professional sees energy everywhere, allows it to flow, makes use of it.

The man was about to lower his hands to the railing. Emil registered even the smallest movement. The man's final step was firm, its direction was right: his body already slightly hunched forward over the railing, his weight moving to the front. All Emil had to do was continue the motion, to give that shift of bodyweight added impetus and lift. Emil's right hand took a firm grip of the towel, while he pushed his left hand beneath the man's arm to lift him and, of course, prevent him turning round.

Their movements were identical and simultaneous, like a dance in which the bodies of two experienced performers become one, and in which one plus one is more than two. The movement was full of power and synchronised rhythm – Emil's lift and shove so perfectly timed that the man's feet were off the ground before his brain registered what had happened. By that point it was too late.

The man crossed the railing gracefully, his left foot striking the steel before he disappeared into the starry winter's night. Emil returned indoors, pulled on his shoes, took the lift down to the basement, found the front door almost immediately and stepped outside.

He dropped the woman's set of keys into a nearby rubbish bin.

Only once he was in the metro did he take off his gloves.

15

Emil had already been awake for several hours. He had done his exercise routine – a combination of yoga, old-school circuit training and T'ai chi – eaten breakfast and was sitting, reading a book by the time his son called.

'I hope I can help,' said Emil, realising he was injecting a note of caution in his voice. 'I don't want to give you advice, but I'm happy to talk about my views and experiences, if I have any.'

'Like I said yesterday,' his son began, 'I think you are sufficiently neutral and, on the other hand…'

Sufficiently neutral?

'Anyway,' said his son, seeming to change the subject, 'I'm in a bit of an awkward situation. I thought you might have some thoughts on the subject, given your age and the fact that you've made decisions in your life that have had certain ramifications.'

'Has something happened?' he asked.

'No,' his son replied, then in a quieter voice. 'Not yet.'

Emil waited.

'And I get the impression you're quite a work-oriented person too,' said his son.

'You could say that.'

'Work is important to you.'

'Very important indeed.'

'Looking back, have you ever regretted the amount of time you've spent working – the sacrifices you've had to make for your work?'

'There was no alternative.'

'That's what I thought.'

'Can I ask you what this is all about?'

'It's about the story I'm following.'

Just as work makes us something, it takes us away from other things.
The thought appeared by itself.

'What would you do without it?' asked Emil.

'Without what?'

'Your work.'

'I don't know. I've never even considered it. I can't imagine life without it … without this.'

His throat suddenly felt rough. Emil tried to swallow, make it go away.

'One decision leads to another,' he said. 'And options are eliminated one by one. In the end we all do what we have chosen, and we do it as well as we can for as long as we can.'

Who is he talking to?

His son was silent for a moment.

'I guess that kind of makes sense,' said his son. 'I've got to go.'

Emil didn't have a chance to respond.

16

Did I really call him to ask for advice? No, surely not. Perhaps I already knew what to do. I took the escalator from the metro platform up to ground level and walked the couple of hundred metres to the paper's editorial office. The sun was shining, the city rose victorious from the snow, ploughs rattled across the square, the cobblestones drumming frantically beneath them.

I said hello to Pohjanheimo and the others but didn't go to my desk. Hutrila was in his office. I asked if he had a moment.

'A moment is all you're going to get,' he said.

'The story needs a lot of work,' I said. 'But it's getting there.'

'Sounds good.'

'And there's something else.'

Hutrila leaned back slightly, placed his fingers on the edge of the desk.

'I thought I could transfer to the culture section or the food pages.'

Hutrila stared at me, holding the edge of the desk to keep from tipping backwards.

'Have you had threats?'

'Yes.'

'People at home getting frightened?'

'Yes.'

'Comes with the territory,' he said bluntly.

'I'm sure it does,' I said. 'It might be perfectly normal – par for the course. But right now I can't deal with it. I need to find something else.'

'You've thought this through, have you?'

'All the way through,' I said.

'You know how complicated these internal transfers are,' said

Hutrila. 'If I organise a transfer, there's no changing your mind. You'll go where I put you; you'll stay there, do your job as well as you can and never bother me about this again.'

'That's the plan.'

'Everybody wants to do film reviews,' said Hutrila. 'Everybody except the people who have to do it for a living.'

'I don't want to barge my way on to the film team.'

'There are no positions available there anyway,' said Hutrila and ran his fingers along the edge of the desk. 'I was thinking more of the celebrity pages.'

'The gossip columns,' I sighed.

'They are very newsworthy columns.'

'They're pointless.'

'They are some of our most popular pages.'

'Because people are idiots.'

'You came into my office.'

That at least was true. And people weren't idiots. I was. I had been. Not any longer.

'Very well.'

'You start tomorrow. I'll let Tanja know to expect company. Are you working on anything apart from the mining story?'

'Not really.'

'Finish it, send it to me. I'll assign a reporter and you can hand over the material.'

I was about to walk out of the office when Hutrila spoke again. 'About the mining story...'

'Yes?'

'Do you really want to give it up? You've got insider information, a source; you've visited the site; you've got Lehtinen's paperwork and God knows what else.'

This was the very question I'd feared.

At that moment I realised with the utmost clarity why I'd called my father: to hear the voice of a man who had lost everything.

'It's for the best,' I said.

Hutrila pursed his lips, shrugged his shoulders.

'I don't know about the best,' he said. 'But it's your decision.'

17

At first Pauliina wouldn't believe me. When I finally managed to convince her, her voice changed. It wasn't exactly warm or loving, but at least it was polite.

We agreed I would pick up Ella from nursery. Pauliina could work late at the office, try to catch up on outstanding work. I put the phone down and saw the box containing Lehtinen's papers. A twinge ran the length of my body. I tried to convince myself I'd made the right decision. Who would Hutrila assign to the case? As my eyes scanned the open-plan office, I realised what I was doing. The matter didn't concern me any longer. But the hope that this thought would bring me a sense of relief was futile. In only a few seconds I had lost the certainty I'd had when I'd stepped into Hutrila's office.

For want of something to do, I stood up and walked from one end of the room to the other. Tanja Korhonen was sitting at her computer with headphones in her ears. I tapped her golden-brown shoulder.

'Hutrila already mailed me,' she said once she'd spun round. 'Great to have someone else on the team. You wouldn't believe how much work there is here.'

'I could do something,' I said. 'While I'm waiting to see who Hutrila is going to put on the mining story. I'll brief the new reporter, then I'll be done with it.'

'You know what twerking is, right?'

Tanja pointed at her screen and clicked open a video. The music video showed curvaceous black women shaking their behinds, together and individually. Shaking, writhing, gyrating. Close-ups of round, oiled buttocks. Four and a half minutes of quivering, wiggling, jiggling, bottoms.

'Okay,' I said.

'For the online edition we need to come up with something inter-active, something like "Finland's best twerkers", or just, "Can you twerk".'

'Okay.'

'I'll write up the actual piece. You can do the online poll.'

'"Can you twerk"? Really?'

'Something like that. And something about how to do it properly. You know, actual instructions. You'll probably find the basics online – like dance steps, but for twerking.'

'The ABC of Twerking?'

'Excellent,' Tanja giggled. 'It's going to be great doing this together.'

I went back to my desk and sat down. My foot knocked against the box of Lehtinen's papers. It was all I could do not to look at it.

I fetched Ella at four-thirty. The snow crunched beneath our feet as we walked home. The pavement had been recently ploughed. The pure-white verge of snow to our right was twice as tall as Ella in her red woolly hat. Once we got back home I made some food and we sat down to eat. Ella ate quickly, slid down from her chair and disappeared into the living room. I didn't open the newspaper, didn't so much as glance at the news applications on my phone.

I'd made my decision quickly and in a whirl of guilt. I'd made the decision the way people do when they want to move on to life after their decision, whatever the cost. If you're feeling like that, it doesn't matter whether the choice you make is a good or a bad one. And so I tried to avoid anything that might cause me to regret what I had done and focussed only on things that made it feel right.

One of those things was playing in the living room. I escaped in there after her and understood perfectly well what I was doing: taking cover behind a two-year-old.

At some point in the evening I called my mother. We asked each other how things were going. As I did every time she asked, I told her we were all fine, that Ella was playing right here and sends Grandma a big kiss. For a moment the line was silent.

'I read your blog,' she said eventually. And then, almost without a pause: 'And it seems you've met your father.'

My mother's tone was straightforward; all it suggested was that she was interested. I was taken aback. I hadn't imagined that the matter of my father could be uncomplicated to her. Having said that, neither of us had mentioned the subject in years.

'Yes, I have,' I said. 'A few times. We went for a beer and had lunch together.'

'How did you feel about it?'

'I don't know,' I said. There was something about my mother's voice and her way of approaching the matter that took me completely by surprise. 'I suppose that's why I called, to ask whether you'd met him too.'

'Yes, of course. He contacted me and we met up.'

Of course?

'He seems quite…' I began and fumbled for the right words. 'He seems like quite an average man.'

My mother said nothing.

I went through what I knew so far: my father had lived in Berlin for a long time, where he worked as a consultant for numerous human resources companies. Now he wanted to retire and settle down in Helsinki. I didn't ask her what it felt like to see her former husband after a thirty-year gap. Some subjects were so enormous that they were nobody else's business. But there was one question I still wanted to ask.

'When he left Helsinki all those years ago, did it happen out of the blue?'

For a moment my mother remained silent.

'Ultimately I wasn't very surprised.'

Pauliina came home at eight-fifteen that evening. She got Ella ready

for bed and read her a story until she fell asleep. I heard Pauliina
shutting Ella's bedroom door and going into the kitchen. I found her
opening up her laptop at the kitchen table.

'I'll cook on Saturday evening,' I said.

Pauliina looked up. 'Great. The Ruusuvuoris are coming at seven.'

I leaned against the draining board.

'I wrote a piece about twerking today,' I said.

'But you were able to spend all evening with your daughter. It's
called being an adult. You give something up, you get something
new.'

What have you ever given up? And to get what exactly?

'I suppose you're right,' I said and thought how this encapsulated
the age in which we lived: wiggle your arse, or churn out column
inches about those who do.

The kitchen was quiet. Upstairs someone was tenderising a steak
or something else that required a heavy fist. Pauliina tossed her hair,
as though she was washing it in the air. The warmth I'd felt towards
her that afternoon was gone.

'What's more,' she began and pointed to a cupboard to my left,
'when I go looking for the mixing bowl I use for cooking, now I'll
actually find it and not a box of papers.'

Pauliina had gone to bed. At least, she'd gone into the bedroom,
which was essentially the same thing. Ella's birth had meant crossing
a line into a reality in which the bedroom was only somewhere that
we slept. Sex was a thing of the past; so too the long, night-time conversations; and we could only dream of lying in bed reading. Once
our heads touched the pillow, the game was over. The object of our
passions was no longer the other's naked body but the chance to lose
consciousness for as long as possible.

I'd moved Lehtinen's papers from the kitchen cupboard to the
hallway. I'd left them next to the door, where I would pick them up
on my way out the next morning. I was half sitting, half lying on
the living-room sofa with the laptop on my knee. I could have said

I had no interest in switching it on, but that would have been a lie. I hadn't read my emails; I'd not even checked them on my phone. I could see the contours of my figure in the large, black television screen. In the far corner of the room a floor lamp glowed yellow. It was surprisingly easy to imagine yourself drifting through an infinite galaxy, yearning for the warmth of the sun. 'The ABC of Twerking'; I sighed and switched on the computer.

There was a long list of new emails. Hutrila's message was the oldest.

I'll assign a new reporter tomorrow. We'll go through it in the morning. H.

The next message, sent only a few minutes later, was from pain. increases.knowledge@gmail.com.

Janne,

Did we make a mistake? Are you not the reporter we were looking for after all? Maybe you're not a reporter at all. We offered you the story of a lifetime, so what's the problem? Have you come up with too little or too much? Does somebody want to shut you up?

If someone wants to keep you quiet or if you're being threatened, we believe we can help. We have plenty of resources, but our help is conditional. We'll give you 24 hours, then we'll reassess the situation. In a manner of your choosing, you can demonstrate that you are worthy of our trust.

To recap: continue with your work, tell us who or what is threatening you and we'll take care of the rest. We don't want to see you fail.

The rest of the messages were routine things: group threads; notices of receipt; someone putting off a lunch meeting. I went back to the anonymous message. Either the sender knew about the threats, or it was a lucky guess. That, in turn, meant that either the senders were very close to me and knew details of the investigation, or they knew nothing. I thought for a moment whether or not to reply, but

I didn't think it would help. The fact was they had made me take on the story in the first place. I read the message once again, stood up from the sofa and walked into the hallway.

The wall clock said it was midnight. I listened for a moment. The apartment was utterly still; the entire house was silent. The neighbours were no longer tenderising anything – a steak or whatever else. People were asleep in their bedrooms.

I carried the boxes into the living room and placed them between the sofa and the coffee table. Very well. I would look through them one last time, and if I found something I would tell the reporter that Hutrila would assign in the morning. I placed the papers in piles on the table and got started.

Three hours later I got up from the sofa and went into the kitchen. I opened the fridge, took out a slab of Emmenthal, toasted some rye bread, opened a tub of fruit yoghurt and took everything back into the living room. I sat down on the sofa to eat, looked at the piles of papers, and reached out to pick up the tub of yoghurt. My hand stopped in mid-air.

Pasteurised milk, peach (4%), kiwi (2%), pineapple (1%), passion fruit (0.25%), setting agents (modified corn starch, pectin), aromas (incl. peach, kiwi, pineapple, passion fruit), sweeteners (Steviol glycoside), acidity regulator (sodium citrate), E211, E013, E141.

That was it. A thing can be fluttering in front of you like a flag and you still overlook it. Until you stumble into it, that is, or even put it in your mouth.

It didn't take long to find the notebook in which Lehtinen had written down all his contacts. Biologist Tero Manninen. I'd seen Manninen's name somewhere else too; but where? I leafed through the notebooks, then the loose papers, the printouts. I finally pulled out the newspaper clippings and found what I was looking for. An opinion piece torn from the paper a year and a half ago. Written along the margin in black biro were the words CALL HIM!

Who Will Pay the Price – and For What?

Finland is currently experiencing the second large-scale mining boom in its history. The newest international facility, which opened only a few years ago, is the nickel mine at Suomalahti operated by Finn Mining Ltd. However, the positive media attention the project has garnered and the large economic expectations placed on the mine itself obscure the other side of the mining-industry coin.

One of the problems of this flip side is the damaging impact the mine has on the local environment. The risk of such damage is always present, no matter what the representatives of the mining company or their most fervent supporters say. It is incumbent on the mining company to follow the course of this impact, preferably by allowing impartial observers access to the complex. At the time of writing, this is not the case.

The issues with the local environmental surveying system are well known to all of us who have at some time been involved with it. In many instances, it is clear that the authorities responsible for ensuring standards are upheld at the mines are either directly or indirectly dependent on the financial success of the mines themselves.

Naturally, this is partly a question of geography. Mines are located in sparsely populated areas where solutions to widespread unemployment and other socio-economic problems take priority over anything else. After all, who wants to report bad news about the largest employer in the local area, an employer upon which the job of a family member might depend? Who would dare demand the closure of the mine, if that meant a nail in the coffin of one's own village?

It is for these reasons that we need a wholly impartial body which – contrary to what common sense might dictate – has no direct links to the wellbeing of any particular area of the country. This impartial body would comprise experts

from different fields and it would   a body. I don't expect to be
have the power to recommend   contacted any time soon.
the mine be shut down if need
be.   Tero Manninen,
    I hereby declare my   Biologist
willingness to partake in such   Espoo

There was no need to wonder whether the text had been edited or
not. The numerous jumps in style and content showed that the original must have been at least twice as long. Lehtinen's notes contained
Manninen's phone number and email address. I looked at the clock:
3:19 a.m. I stood up from the sofa, walked to the window and leaned
against the sill. Along the top of the window frame was a ventilation strip; fresh, chilled air flowed on to my face. I thought of Ella,
my home, my family. I tried to fend off what had just occurred to
me, tried to keep it at a distance; tried not to think it so attractive.
I pressed my forehead against the cool glass and looked down at the
yard, now white with snow.

    Two figures in hoodies were wandering between the rows of cars
parked outside. Junkies. Looking for something, frantically, anything they could get their hands on, anything they could change into
money. They were out in the freezing cold; I was in the warm. They
were outsiders; I was very much an insider. And still I understood
something of the force that drove them, that forced them to risk
getting caught, to risk anything at all that stood in the way of what
they needed to do. The duo stopped at the side of a blue Peugeot; a
rucksack moved, a window shattered. The car alarm began to wail;
one of the hooded figures pulled something from inside the car. A
few seconds later the yard was empty.

    I wrote a short email to Manninen the biologist. I sent it at 3:42
a.m.

18

The men stepped into the stairwell at twenty past nine. The large snowflakes swaying down to the ground didn't prevent Emil identifying them. One of them was clearly Antero Kosola, the head of security at the Suomalahti mine – a broad-shouldered giant with large hands. Despite his size, Kosola moved quite nimbly; he walked along the slippery pavement with self-assured steps.

The smaller man with the black beard was of a different body type altogether. And for him it seemed as though the world was a profoundly complicated place: the zip on his bulging down coat wouldn't cooperate; he seemed about to slip over with each step; and as he spat, the saliva meant to lubricate his mouth became stuck in the corner of his lips, leaving him with no option but to wipe it on to the sleeve of his jacket.

The men were walking down Tunturikatu. At the end of the road they stopped by a Jeep Cherokee and climbed in. As the vehicle pulled away from the kerb and jolted over the verge of ploughed snow, Emil slipped his automatic into drive and followed them.

The men drove towards the city centre, followed the flow of the traffic past the Central Railway Station and the Ateneum art museum, then drove through Kaisaniemi and crossed Long Bridge. When they arrived in Hakaniemi, they passed the block where his son worked. After that they steered the car down towards the highway at Sörnäinen. The SUV indicated left. Emil followed the car to the forecourt of the petrol station.

The men parked, got out and walked across the snow-covered forecourt towards the café. Emil left his car at the other side of the lot, at the end of a line of vehicles.

Inside the café he ordered a cup of coffee and a warm bun dripping in butter, and sat down one table away from the two men. They drank their coffees and munched on the sandwiches they'd ordered for breakfast. The man with the black beard dribbled pieces of tomato down his jacket. More plastic than paper, the napkin made the mess worse.

Emil looked outside.

The snowfall had started at around seven that morning. He'd seen the first flakes as he'd sat at the window drinking coffee. There was always something magical about the first moments of snowfall: something began drifting down from the sky, then, before long, the earth was white.

For a long while the men sat in silence. Kosola was sitting with his back to Emil. From his stature, his body language and every gesture, Emil could see he was a noteworthy man. Noteworthy in the dangerous sense. Emil barely paid any attention to the man with the black beard. He would eventually choke on his sandwich or slip on an icy pavement before he had a chance to do any real damage.

The bun was fresh and the well of butter in the middle made it moist and tasty. It was due compensation for the ridiculous spectacle he was watching in front of him, thought Emil.

Kosola said something to the bearded man, who now had a piece of crust the size of a birch leaf hanging from the side of his mouth. Both men looked out into the car park as a white BWV station wagon curved into a free space and switched off its motor and lights. Out of the vehicle stepped a man in a suit and, despite the snow, a thin pair of leather shoes. He stepped inside the café, saw the two men and joined them at their table.

Emil could only make out a word here and there, words that didn't seem to mean anything. It's alright, he thought. If the head of security at the mine spends his spare time almost a thousand kilometres from his workplace, there must be a reason. As indeed there must be a reason why these men are meeting right now.

Emil drank his coffee and watched the traffic flow past along the highway. How much of his life had he spent like this, following people, observing them, getting close to them?

And yet there was nothing routine about his work. Emil thought of how one of the two men waiting here – probably the bearded clown with the slippery feet – had kicked his son in the face. How these men had followed his son, either to frighten him or to do something worse. It was hard to hold in check the emotions that these deeds awoke in him. But, as he had learned in the past, the surest way to add fuel to the fire of such thoughts was to try to rein them in. And so he let his feelings hang in the air and waited until they floated away, like a dark cloud disappearing over the horizon. Only by letting everything else go could he finally grasp the important elements, hold them tight. This he had learned.

The men had finished eating. Kosola looked at his phone, tapped a few buttons. The bearded man managed to snap a toothpick between his teeth and gave out a yell. By now Emil knew the men well enough.

Kosola stood up first. He was already at the door while the bearded man lumbered behind him. From Kosola's broad shoulders Emil could see just what Kosola thought of his mate. For some reason it seemed necessary to drag this fool along with him.

The Jeep drove off the forecourt. Emil watched it churn up the fresh snow on the road, swerve through the blizzard and head eastwards along the highway.

19

As the metro glided across the bridge to Kulosaari and the rocks disappeared from beneath us, it seemed as though we were driving into the very heart of the earth, white and squalling. To the left you could normally make out the silhouette of the downtown area, to the right the tall apartment blocks of Pihlajamäki, the row of houses along the shore at Arabia, and the green of the bay at Vanhakaupunki, and beneath the train, on both sides, the sea. Now all of this was a matter of faith. The doors rattled as the wind tested their strength, and the train hurtled blindly forwards.

My phone chimed. An email. Biologist Tero Manninen. I read the message and began to feel a little more uncomfortable. When I'd finally gone to bed at five to four that morning, I'd imagined I would wake up with a brighter, lighter mind and with a clear idea of what to do next. Of course I knew what I was going to do, I just couldn't yet admit it to myself. For all its conciseness, Manninen's message couldn't have been clearer: he was still willing to volunteer his services.

Upon reaching Hakaniemi, the snow did the same to humans as it had to the train moments before. It formed a tunnel around me, making me follow a narrow track, hoping it led where I wanted to go. I found the front door of the editorial office and bounded up the steps to the third floor. I knocked the snow from my shoulders and undid my scarf, only to realise that this wasn't the only reason I felt as though something was gripping my throat.

I could see right into Hutrila's office. He looked up, and he must have seen that I didn't have the box of Lehtinen's papers with me. His eyes darkened. He turned back to his computer. I took my coat to my work station, pulled a box containing some of Lehtinen's papers from beneath the desk and placed it beside my computer.

If anyone ever asks me what causes seismic shifts, I would have an answer immediately: they begin with tiny, insignificant shifts, like someone moving a cardboard box from one place to the next. I didn't fetch any coffee but instead headed straight for Hutrila's office. At the southern end of the open-plan office I saw the golden flicker of Tanja Korhonen's arms.

'You changed your mind,' said Hutrila.

He didn't raise his eyes from his computer screen.

I closed the door.

'I've got new information.'

'I think you'll find that coming up with new information is part of the job description,' he said.

I ignored the jibe.

'You haven't spoken to anyone else yet, have you?' I asked.

Hutrila moved his fingers from the keyboard to the edge of the desk and leaned back on his chair. He can see me for what I am, I thought.

'Did the folks back home change their mind too?'

I shook my head. Hutrila's face remained expressionless.

'I haven't spoken to anyone yet,' he said. 'I had the impression you weren't entirely convinced about what you were doing.'

I said nothing.

'You know what happens now, don't you?'

Yes. Hopefully. Unfortunately.

'You and I are going to make a deal,' he said. 'You look into this mining story, dig as deep as you have to, don't leave a single stone unturned. And this isn't just a play on words, you understand?'

'It's a deal.'

'You start straight away. When you're standing in that spot on Monday morning, you'll have a double-page spread of the story ready to go to print. If it isn't ready, it needs to be very close, and I need to think so too. If it's nowhere near, you won't have to ask for a transfer again. You'll start the week by proofreading the weddings and obituaries, and you'll stay there until you retire. You will cover all your own expenses for this story – travel costs, everything – and I'll decide later how much of it, if anything, the paper will reimburse. Everything depends on results. You will also agree not to ask me for anything at all for at least the next thousand years. Do we understand each other?'

Did I even understand myself? I decided not to answer my own question and called Manninen, the biologist. He said he would be ready to leave at two hours' notice; that being the time he needed to gather all the relevant equipment.

'In that case we'll leave in two hours,' I said.

I was about to hang up, when he asked me if I knew anyone with a thorough knowledge of the mining complex. When I told him I didn't, he had a suggestion of his own.

'Maarit Lehtinen.'

20

Emil pressed the telephone against his ear and glanced around him. The bookstore was quiet in the mornings, but you could never be too careful.

'I mentioned this work matter and the other … events when we met the other day,' said Janne. 'I thought I'd better tell you the rest. I've decided to go up north again. To Suomalahti. We're planning on taking some samples.'

'Planning?'

'Yes.'

'You're not alone?'

'There are … three of us,' said Janne. There was something else about his voice; as if he was talking about something other than his work. He was like a little boy owning up to something. And in this scenario he was – he had to search for the word – *a father.* That's what it must have been like, he thought. This is what it could have been like.

'This sample-taking expedition…' Emil began, and moved deeper between the rows of books. He found himself at the beginning of the crime and thriller section, a large white letter A at eye level. 'Presumably this is something … how should I put it … unofficial?'

'Very,' his son replied quickly, then paused. 'We'll have to break into the mining complex in order to get the samples.'

'Is that necessary?' asked Emil. 'Can't you do the same work here in Helsinki?'

Since when was he a parent handing out advice? What right did he have? What authority?

'The shit is up there in the north,' his son replied, quiet and determined, as though he had read Emil's thoughts.

'Of course. I understand,' said Emil, and he meant it.

'We're setting off in a few hours.'

'You'll be careful, won't you?'

His son remained silent.

'Yes,' he said eventually. 'You be careful too.'

For a moment Emil stood silently on the spot, motionless, his phone in his hand. He dropped it into his pocket, looked in front of him and saw the row of books arranged by author from A to D: *killer this, killer that, death this, death the other, murder here, murder there.*

He walked out of the store and looked up at the sky. It looked higher than it had in days. The snow clouds always hung low in the sky. He tried to concentrate on the facts, but it was hard – every bit as hard as admitting to himself that he knew what had frightened him so much about that phone call.

His son had sounded just like him.

The entirety of the conversation after which I lost my family for good:

ME: I'm sorry, Pauliina, but—
PAULIINA: Goodbye.

Manninen the biologist was driving, Maarit was sitting next to him, and I was behind Manninen on the back seat. The fresh, light covering of frozen snow whirled on the road, forming swirls and waves in the currents of air. Manninen had met me in Hakaniemi, and we picked up Maarit in Sörnäinen. Manninen praised Maarit's work as his research assistant.

'That was years ago,' said Maarit.

'Three and a half,' said Manninen. 'At the environmental information centre in Helsinki. Back when it still existed, before all the cuts. My only permanent job to date.'

Manninen's car wasn't the newest model on the market. It jolted and groaned as though it had been thrown together by a careless six-year-old with a pot of glue. The pocket in the back of the seat in front of me was bulging with papers. The logo of a familiar pizzeria peered from among them.

'You two already know one another, then?'

This was why I'd moved to the back seat when we arrived in Sörnäinen. I looked from one to the other. They didn't so much as share a glance.

'These circles are pretty small,' said Manninen. 'As far as I'm aware, it's the same with journalists. Everybody knows everybody else. Everybody gossips about everybody else – except to their face.'

'What circles?' I asked.

Manninen looked across at Maarit.

'The environmental crowd all know one another,' said Maarit.

'Helsinki is a small city,' said Manninen.

For some reason I'd pictured Manninen as slightly younger. And based on the voice I'd heard on the phone, I'd imagined him as a short, dry character. In reality he was fifty-six years old, and with his build and blond hair, the figure he cut was akin to that of the wrestler Hulk Hogan.

'That's how it is,' I said. 'You bump into old friends all the time.'

'Maarit knows her way round the mining complex,' said Manninen. He looked at me in the rearview mirror.

'Right,' I said.

'And I'm in charge of the measurements.'

His eyes returned to the road ahead.

Good, I thought. I'm writing a story, not playing your games. I know you have your own reasons for helping me. That suits me fine. But I'm writing a story, and in those circumstances all means are acceptable. Every reporter knows that; though in public we rave on about ethics and good journalistic standards. *Silly billy*, as I'd once said to Ella, tickling her under the chin. Pauliina's abrupt goodbye gripped my chest, crushed me like an anvil. I didn't want to think of the consequences. I was writing a story that needed to be written.

'When did you last visit Suomalahti?' I asked Manninen.

Maarit looked out of the window at the passing verge, where the forest sprinted past on nimble, snow-covered wooden legs. Manninen's eyes reappeared in the mirror.

'Why do you ask?'

'Happy Pizza.'

Manninen's right hand touched the gear stick then returned to the steering wheel.

'Right. About a month ago.'

'Why?'

'Just curious.'

'Did you visit the complex?'

'You mean inside it?'

'So you did pay a visit?'

Manninen said nothing. He really did look like Hogan, with his large head and thick blond hair. At times his blue eyes looked stern, at others mild, as though the ice melted and reformed every time we looked at each other.

'What about it?' asked Maarit, breaking the brief silence that had been filled only with the monotonous hum of the tyres. I couldn't see her face at all.

'I mean, if someone saw this car back then and noticed him wandering around the mine, they might put two and two together.'

'Nobody saw a thing,' said Maarit. 'It was dark then; now it's darker.'

I sighed. Another seven and a half hours of this road ahead.

The piles of snow at the edge of the road grew taller; daylight faded, disappeared altogether. The darkness that surrounded the car looked powerful enough to suck into its folds anything that strayed beyond the glare of the headlights.

The pair in the front hadn't said a word. That was fine by me. I tapped away at my laptop and wrote comments in my notebook while going through another pile of Lehtinen's papers. They proved not to be quite as interesting as I'd thought when deciding which ones to take with me. I turned on the torch on my phone and pulled a history of the Finnish Mining Corporation from my bag. The book had been published in 1994. Naturally, it didn't cover more recent developments, but you never knew what would open up new doors.

The journey continued, the hours passed.

At one point I raised my head and realised I'd fallen asleep. I rubbed my face. At that moment something seemed to startle Manninen and the steering wheel swerved.

The right-hand side of the car scraped along the verge of snow. My phone and the book flew from my hands. A truck full of logs. The cloud of snow it churned up behind it was like white mud, so thick that the windscreen wipers Manninen had flicked on sagged under its weight. We were travelling at a hundred kilometres an hour. It was as though we entered a dazzling abyss. Then visibility returned to normal and the darkness seemed like light.

My heart was racing. I fumbled between my feet for my phone. The screen had gone dark. I clicked to activate it again and found myself staring at an image of my father. It was the photograph I'd taken when we'd had lunch together. The longer I looked at it, the more I saw. I was no longer looking at a strange man. This man was my father. I could see the passing of the years in the deep ridges of his brow, the self-discipline in his slender face. The eyes revealed more. What at first I'd thought was cold and calculating, was in fact a shrewdness, a patience. He looked like a man who was used to waiting and who didn't let small things get to him. His eyes looked directly at the camera, at me.

My father was now a part of my life. I didn't know whether I should feel anger or resentment, or whether, when I'd met him, I should have thrown my arms round him and wept. I hadn't been able to do either, and still my heart was thumping. It wasn't only to do with the logging truck or Manninen running the car up against the verge. The moment I took that photograph things had changed – the balance shifted, rousing an old wish that I'd long forgotten. More to the point, it had revealed to me something I would much rather not have known anything about: it showed me the price of loss and the impossibility of return.

I only needed to look to the side and see my reflection in the window to realise who was looking back at me.

The same man, only younger.

It was impossible to reach the Suomalahti mine without first driving through the village. Perhaps I'd been worried about nothing. The darkness of the night and the thickening blizzard wrapped us up so tightly that we could only catch glimpses of life on earth. Manninen said he needed to fill the tank.

'Why didn't we fill the tank back in Kuusamo?' I asked.

'Who's driving this car?'

We pulled up in front of the familiar petrol station. The windows in the café were dark. Manninen stepped out of the car. A clank as he fitted the nozzle of the pump into the car. Maarit continued to stare fixedly ahead, slightly to the right, as she had done for most of the journey.

'So, here we are,' I said inanely.

'Wasn't that the point?'

'I suppose it depends who you ask.'

'Don't worry. You'll get what you want.'

'What about you?'

'What about me?'

'Will you get what you want?'

Maarit paused for a few seconds before responding. 'My father died. Because of this. Of that I'm in no doubt. This won't bring him back, but … it's got to be done. We have to do everything we can.'

'Is that all?' I asked.

Maarit didn't have a chance to answer. During our conversation the lights of a car I'd imagined would simply continue along the road suddenly slowed and began turning into the forecourt of the petrol station. The car had appeared out of the dark, the blizzard. For a long time its lights were directed right at us; so I could only see the make once it had turned and come to a halt on the other side of the pump. The yellow glare from the lights on the roof of the petrol station allowed me a view through the car's windows.

One glance was enough.

In a split second I dropped to the floor of the car and huddled on my side. The driver of the Jeep Cherokee hadn't turned to look our way. I heard the door of the SUV opening. I couldn't hear the stocky man's footsteps. I hadn't imagined I would hear them. I doubt I had ever heard them.

Manninen finally pulled the nozzle out of the tank and put it back in the pump with a clatter. We set off again. Once I sensed that the car had turned a few corners and felt Manninen accelerating, I raised my head. I looked out of the back window but couldn't see the vehicle, only the yellow glow of the station behind the snow. Kosola, the head of security, was back there somewhere.

'Did you recognise that man at the pump?' I asked Manninen once I'd sat up again. I wondered whether Maarit had even registered my dive on to the floor.

'Who?' he asked.

'Apart from us there was only one car at that petrol station, and only one man stepped out to fill up the only other car.'

'I wasn't paying attention.'

'He didn't look familiar?'

'No,' said Manninen. 'Who was he?'

I looked at Maarit. 'Doesn't matter,' I said.

The wind whipped up. Snow danced in the headlights, growing increasingly frantic, heavier, like the train of a dress growing weightier and more cumbersome by the minute. For around half an hour we drove, groping our way through the darkness. The road ran round the mining complex until we reached the main access road. Because we were going to use both torches and headlamps, we needed the forest for protection. There was plenty of that on the eastern side of the mine, so we drove as close to the eastern edge of the complex as the access road would take us.

Along the access road, there were many smaller maintenance roads leading to different sectors of the complex. It quickly became clear, however, that we'd have to leave the car by the side of the main road, otherwise we might not be able to get back.

We stopped, and started getting dressed. This time I'd come better prepared than before: I had packed my bag with lots of warm clothes and even some food. Manninen's bright-red bag, which he attached to his back with numerous clasps and knots, looked particularly heavy. In his hand he was carrying a borer. I was told to carry the folding snow shovel.

'It's about forty-five minutes from here,' said Maarit as we took our first steps in the snow that came up to our knees. 'If we're quick.'

The wind blew snow into my mouth and eyes. Our shoulders hunched, we plodded forwards, one after the other. I was bringing up the rear. The best protection against the cold and the biting wind was exactly what we were doing: moving. Standing still would soon become painful.

We'd been walking for about half an hour when I was certain I heard the sound of a motor, the howl of a machine accelerating very fast. The sound disappeared into the wind before I had the chance to say anything to the giant biologist panting in front of me.

Maarit seemed to know exactly where we were going. I saw her holding her wrist in front of her face. A GPS watch, I assumed. Maarit's steps were light and effective. Manninen and I had our work cut out just to keep up with her.

The snow melted against my face and the wind whipped my skin. Breathing turned to gasping, sweat poured down my back. My thigh muscles were exhausted with having to trudge through the snow. They began to ache, and my gait felt heavier with each step. Nobody spoke. The wind gusted around us. Apart from that, all I could hear was our steps. The world suddenly felt very small.

We arrived at the edge of a logging area and stepped out of the protection of the forest and into a clearing. The wind felt instantly more brutal. From here it was only five minutes to the end of the first stage in our illicit expedition. The cold pressed through our clothes. We were now walking along the frozen river. I knew this, though I couldn't make out where the land ended and the water, flowing beneath the ice and snow, began. It was dark and the fluttering snow formed a great curtain in the wind, which seemed to be gaining strength all the while.

Eventually we arrived at the spot we would have found even without our torches. We looked at one another. We were here.

The snow was doing its best to cover everything in sight, but it couldn't hide everything. The excavated drainage trenches were deep and particularly long. What's more, they were also fresh and ran perpendicular to the river, joining it at one end. On my last visit to the mine I'd looked at this part of the terrain from the opposite direction, about a kilometre away from this spot.

We made our way about five metres down the steep verge and

came to a halt. The snow was flat. Beneath it was a layer of ice, and beneath that the water. Manninen slung his borer into the snow, unclasped his bag and shrugged it from his shoulders. From the bag he pulled a torch on a tripod and a plastic bag with a zip, struck the tripod into the snow and switched on the light. A sudden brightness lit the bottom of the ditch. Inside the bag was a selection of jars with red lids.

Manninen continued his preparations without saying a word. I grabbed Manninen's borer and, without being asked, thrust it into the ice and began boring a hole. The smell wasn't what you'd expect from a pure mountain spring. I stepped out of the way so that Manninen could get to the water and held a torch up so he could see what he was doing. He used a small hand-held pump to fill the jars with water. Maarit glanced at the GPS watch on her wrist. Manninen filled the jars and secured them in the plastic zip bag. He then pulled another piece of equipment from his bag – it was the size of an old camera but sturdier – and said he was going to measure the speed of the current.

Again I made out the sound of a motor. It rose and fell with the wind, then disappeared again. Maarit was standing with her back to me and Manninen. She had heard something too. Manninen was busy with the water and didn't seem to have heard anything. The cold burned my feet, my toes ached. In the torchlight Manninen's fingers looked white. And there it was again, the sound of a motor. This time we all heard it.

'Just a few seconds more,' said Manninen.

Maarit and I were silent. Manninen focussed on his work. I felt the urge to hurry him along. The motor seemed to cut the air, coming closer and closer. Now I was sure it was a snowmobile.

Manninen pulled the contraption from the hole in the ice, took a few steps towards his bag and packed everything, then stood up to his full height, adjusted his headlamp and was just about to sling the bag on his back when a dull crack broke the frozen silence and Manninen's throat burst open as though it had been cut with a knife.

23

He had followed his son and his two travelling companions – the woman and the stocky blond man – first into the freezing, deserted village, then into the spruce forest, across a clearing in the woods, then down to the riverbed and finally to the bottom of the trench. He had watched them clambering down the steep verge, seen his son bore a hole in the ice by torchlight, and the large man who had driven the car fiddling with equipment by the water's edge.

His son's movements and his way of working had made him sigh: yet another quality, another skill that his son had, but of which he knew nothing, skills whose development he had been unable to follow.

The wind shook the trees and blew gusts of snow across the terrain, but Emil could still make out the sound of a motor – a vehicle somewhere. He had heard it back in the forest, almost as soon as he'd set off after the three bobbing headlamps, the only lights in the otherwise endless, impenetrable darkness.

At times the sound disappeared, perhaps caught by the wind or smothered by the incessant snow, but it quickly became clear that the vehicle was approaching the part of the terrain where his son was. Emil could see in his son's movements that he too had heard the sound. Emil was too far away to hear whether his son said anything. The woman turned to face the direction from which the snowmobile was coming. The stocky man continued what he was doing until he suddenly snapped to, bounded towards his bag, packed up his equipment and hoisted the bag on his back. In the light of the lamps the tall, stocky man was like a statue erected in the wrong place.

A shot. A rifle. Large calibre.

The man was standing there like a lighthouse. A shot to the neck. Fatal.

A snowmobile. Very nearby.

At that moment it was obvious: crystal clear what he was; what his role was, now and forever.

His lungs burned, his throat rasped. He trudged forwards through the snow. He saw the headlamps thrashing frantically as his son and the woman scaled the opposite verge, then the lights disappeared into the whirling snow. He imagined that Janne and the woman must have torn the lamps from their heads and stuffed them into the snow. He'd seen that they had hand-held torches too and guessed the two of them would find their way back to the car using them. Unless…

He dashed in the direction from which the shot and the sound of the snowmobile had come.

As if from out of nowhere, the lights of the vehicle appeared at the edge of the verge. Abandoned at the bottom of the trench, the lamp lit the side of the mobile just enough to show the contours of two men. The one sitting at the rear had a rifle slung over his shoulder, and he was noticeably shorter than the broad-shouldered long-armed man behind the wheel.

Emil knew instantly who they were. He had sat near them and watched them. Now he also knew why the shorter man was always brought along. Despite the dark and the snow, he had just hit a small target in the middle of the open countryside.

The snowmobile had come to a halt. The men had pulled their snow glasses up to their foreheads. The large blond man was lying on his side at the bottom of the ditch, his arms and legs splayed in all directions as though he'd been running sideways and frozen on the spot.

Emil needed only a few seconds. He pulled the glove from his right hand, opened his hunting knife and gripped it in his fist. In this situation it felt more familiar than anything else.

The driver's thumb was about to press the gas to start the engine. Or perhaps Emil simply imagined he could see this clearly. He came out of the snow, the darkness, from behind a collection of large boulders.

The driver turned and saw Emil. His large, powerful legs propelled him up. His right hand dropped his glove and moved to his waist. For his size the man was fast, immediately standing to his full height. In the same movement he had slipped his left leg over the seat and dropped down into the snow in front of Emil. His right hand found what it had been fumbling for at his waist.

A pistol.

Again Emil had to improvise. In the sinking snowdrifts, everything happened in slow motion. First, he did what was necessary; that is, what was possible. By now he was standing right in front of the man.

When the man's long firing arm was almost fully extended, Emil stuck the knife into the man's bare wrist, right the way through it. Then Emil yanked out the knife, pulled his arm back and straightened himself up again. He noted where the man's pistol had fallen and took another step closer. The man tried to lash out with his left hand. Emil dodged the punch, grabbed the man and struck quickly. The blow was quick and precise, aimed at the only bit of bare flesh, the only part of the body not covered in thick, weather-proof material. The blade of the knife sunk into the man's eye right up to the hilt. Emil pulled the knife free and sunk it into the other eye. The man fell to his knees in the snow and rolled on to his left side.

The smaller man with the dark beard might have had trouble eating a doughnut or buttoning up his jacket, but not with handling a rifle. In the brief moment Emil had spent neutralising the driver, the smaller man had taken the rifle from his back, cocked it and raised it. Emil thrust his hand into the snow and found what he was looking for. He raised the pistol and shot the bearded man three times in the face. There came a spluttering cry from inside his balaclava and the man fell backwards. The bearded man's trigger finger clenched shut. A bullet rocketed off towards the snow falling from the sky.

Emil switched off the snowmobile's motor but left the lights on. He listened. Nothing but the wind in the trees and the whirl of the snow. He looked down towards the stream.

24

After being called once more, I again walked from one end of the corridor to the other. I'd been held for interview for a day and a half, and I guessed I'd soon know the inside of the Kemijärvi police station better than I did the home of my former family.

I had told them what I knew many times over. At times I was left to try and rest in a bleak staffroom normally used by employees on the night shift, but I couldn't get to sleep.

It was nine in the morning. The door of the interview room was open and I stepped inside. Behind the desk sat a man in his forties, who stood up when he saw me and reached out a hand.

'Antero Halonen. We've spoken on the phone.'

I recognised the name and the voice. I had called him to ask whether the police were looking into the deaths of the board members of Finn Mining Ltd. We shook hands. Halonen smelled of expensive aftershave, a whiff of another world. He was wearing a dazzlingly white shirt beneath a black jacket, both clearly by top-end designers. His hair was short and dark, with a stylish peppering of grey at the sides. His jaw was wide and the stubble carefully trimmed.

'From the Helsinki crime unit?' I said.

Halonen smiled. The smile was charming.

'That's right. We're helping out a little here,' he replied. 'Please sit down.'

Halonen sat at the desk, opened the folder in front of him and took a small Dictaphone from his pocket.

'Alright if I record?' he asked, though it wasn't really a question. It certainly didn't sound like one. He picked up one of his papers, read it for a moment then placed it on the desk.

'You arrived in Suomalahti the day before yesterday. Who were you travelling with and what was the purpose of your journey?'

'I've told your colleagues all this—'

'Then you can tell me again,' said Halonen.

'Maarit Lehtinen. Tero Manninen. Me. We wanted to examine the mining complex and take some samples.'

'You knew, of course, that entering the complex is strictly forbidden?'

'Yes.'

Halonen looked at me for a moment before continuing. 'What happened?'

'We reached the spot we were looking for: the river. We took some samples. Somebody shot Tero Manninen. Maarit and I managed to run away. We reached our car, but Manninen had the keys. He had driven us all the way from Helsinki to Suomalahti. We started walking back towards the village and as soon as we could get a signal we called the police. We walked for another half an hour before the first police car arrived. And it was in that car that we were brought here to Kemijärvi.'

'What exactly happened at the river? Tell me everything in the order in which you remember it.'

'I bored a hole in the ice. Manninen took the samples. I heard the sound of a snowmobile again – I'd heard it earlier but didn't know what it was. We started getting ready to leave. Manninen packed his bag, gathered his equipment: the shovel, the bore. Then came the shot. Manninen fell to the ground, and we started running.'

'You didn't see anybody?'

'No.'

'Neither before nor after the shooting?'

'No.'

'So at no point while you were in the woods was there anyone other than you, Maarit, Manninen and the snowmobile you mentioned?'

'No.'

'What about the samples?'

'All in Manninen's red bag, which was left at the scene.'

Halonen looked at me with his green-blue charmer's eyes. 'Did you hear any other shots?'

'Other shots? No. Just one. Manninen died.'

'Were you shocked?'

'Of course I was shocked. I haven't slept since.'

'That's understandable.'

Halonen again turned his attention to his folder. He lifted the papers one at a time: one, two, three, four … At the tenth paper he leaned back in his chair. His body remained poised, but now he was looking at me as if from a distance, as if he were examining the entirety of me.

'Very well,' he said. 'You ran from the scene – you and Maarit. Were you together all the time – from that point until the police car arrived?'

'Yes.'

'Neither of you remained by the river for any length of time? Neither of you deviated from the route?'

'No and no.'

'Are you sure Maarit will tell us the same story?'

'Of course she will. Is she saying something different?'

Halonen looked at me. 'No.'

We sat for a moment in silence.

'How well do you know Maarit?' Halonen asked eventually.

'Not very well.'

'Do you know Santtu Leikola?'

'The same Santtu Leikola who…?'

'… who climbed on to the roof of the Parliament. Do you know him?'

'Not at all. What's he got to do with this?'

Halonen didn't reply. He waited for a moment. 'Let's go back to the night in question. Did you at any point realise you were being followed?'

'I just told you I heard the sound of the snowmobile. I told you Manninen died after someone shot him. So yes, we did realise we were being followed.'

'What about the journey from Helsinki?'

'I couldn't say.'

'And later on, while you were running from the scene?'

'I thought they would be following us all the while.'

'Who are "they"?'

I was beginning to lose my patience.

'The men on the snowmobile,' I said slowly. 'Maybe alone, maybe with someone else. I imagined they, he or she – would be following us.'

'So you didn't know that the men driving the snowmobile were also found murdered?'

I stared at him.

'Nobody told me anything about that,' I said.

'I asked them not to tell you.'

Silence filled the room. The Dictaphone's red eye stared at us, unflinching. The suave DI Halonen looked across the table at me, his expression neutral.

'Now I understand why I've been asked to stay here and why everyone has been asking me the same questions,' I said. 'You're hoping I'll slip up, mess up the story and suddenly reveal that I actually killed a bunch of men in the woods. Well let me help you out: it wasn't me.'

Halonen looked at me for a moment longer then closed his folder.

'Let me ask you a favour,' he said.

'What? A confession?'

Halonen ignored my comment. 'As far as possible, we're trying to keep this matter away from the media. We would greatly appreciate it if you didn't talk about any of this. For the time being.'

Halonen stared at me. He reached out his right hand, picked up the Dictaphone and switched it off. Its red eye closed.

'Like I said, keep what you saw to yourself for a while. One other thing – and this is just as important: let me know the minute you remember anything new or hear anything that might be linked to the events at the mine. You tell *me*. *Immediately.* As a reporter, you must appreciate the power of words – the devastating effects they can have.'

25

He watched as his son stepped out of the police station into the frozen morning, looked up towards the sky, glanced around him and walked to the edge of the pavement. His son looked in both directions, but didn't notice him. There were about two hundred metres between them. At that distance people only see what they are looking for.

His son walked off along the main street. Emil pressed a button and the Volvo XC70 came to life. He had rented the car in Rovaniemi using a Belgian passport and credit card. His son's steps were those of an exhausted man. The pharmacy, the bookstore, a clothes retailer, a kiosk. His son didn't so much as look at them. Only once he reached a small, two-storey hotel did he slow his step.

Emil knew what Janne was searching for. His look was hungry. He parked the car about fifty metres from the entrance to the hotel and took his black bag from the passenger seat. Despite the thermometer above the supermarket giving a temperature reading of minus eighteen degrees Celsius, it didn't feel particularly cold: the air was dry and motionless.

He saw his son at a table in the window of the hotel. The dining room was a typical, small, multi-purpose space: a breakfast room, lunch restaurant, dining area, and nightclub. Liquor advertisements on the wall, fitted carpet, dark furniture. There was a time when everybody had furniture like this. His son was fiddling with his phone, the way everybody younger than Emil did nowadays – moving from one place to the next like the walking dead, receiving instructions from the small screen in their hands. He only raised his eyes from the phone as Emil pulled a chair from the neighbouring table and placed his bag on the chair. Emil walked round the table and sat down opposite his son. Janne's eyes followed his movements, didn't so much as glance at the black sports bag.

'Morning,' said Emil when they were finally face to face. 'Breakfast time. Have you already ordered?'

'Morning. Yes.'

'What are you having?'

His son stared at him. 'Breakfast. There's only one. Porridge, eggs, bread, sausage and cheese. And coffee.'

Emil turned, looked at the waiter and caught his attention. The waiter arrived, took Emil's order and disappeared, probably into the kitchen to prepare their breakfast himself. The waiter was also probably the receptionist, the chef, the caretaker, the karaoke host and the doorman.

There was nobody else in the breakfast room. It's just as well, thought Emil. People react to things in different ways, but one thing they all had in common: people get upset when the truth is revealed. Some are more upset than others. You can never tell in advance how it's going to go.

Janne somehow looked tired – and yet not. They stared at one another.

'Human resources,' said his son.

Emil said nothing.

'It seems that covers quite a lot,' he continued.

'We both need a good breakfast,' Emil said. 'Low blood-sugar levels are the cause of many a bad decision.'

'Does a low blood-sugar level make you follow people?'

'How are you feeling?'

'How am I feeling?' said Janne, and stared at him. 'I honestly don't know.'

Emil sat still and waited. He was good at that, he'd had lots of practice.

'How did you know to follow me up here?' asked his son.

'I followed you from the police station.'

'How did you know I was at the police station?'

'You're my son,' said Emil. 'I want to know where you are.'

'You didn't answer my question.'

'I believe I did.'

'Fine father-and-son moment this is,' said Janne. 'It was almost worth waiting thirty years for.'

Their breakfast arrived. Bowls of steaming porridge, a litre of coffee in a metallic pot. Slices of cheese and pepperoni were piled up on the same plate; the bread was ready-sliced. Both ate the way hungry men should.

'What's in that bag?'

'Let's eat first.'

They were drinking their coffee when Janne looked first at Emil then again at the bag. Janne turned and pulled open the zip. Emil saw a strip of the red backpack and turned around. Apart from them, the room was empty. The fact that the restaurant was doing badly was a blessing in disguise. Janne pulled the zip shut and looked at him.

'I assume that was the reason for your trip?' asked Emil.

'You could say that,' Janne nodded slowly. 'Where did you get this?'

'I found it.'

'Seems you're quite good at finding things. You found me, my mother. A bag belonging to a biologist shot in the woods. You know I've just come from the police station.'

'I know that.'

'You know I could take that and walk right back there.'

'Life is often more complicated than it seems. Rash decisions tend to have longer-lasting effects than carefully considered ones.'

'So now you want to teach me about life, tell me some great universal truths?'

'I'm sharing the experience that comes with age. That's not quite the same thing.'

An elderly couple walked past the window. Their outdoor clothes were so colourful that he could almost hear them as they shuffled past. Janne leaned back in his chair, folded his hands across his chest.

'Who are you?'

'I'm your father.'

'I don't mean that. What are you? What do you do?'

Emil looked outside. A small, cold northern town on a winter's morning. Emil, sixty years old. This is where he had ended up. This is what everything had come to. It happened to all of us: the place where we ended up always came as something of a surprise. Emil met his son's eyes.

'I kill people.'

Sometimes time leaps forwards, sometimes it crawls. Sometimes time disappears and leaves us floating in space. After that, all that is left for us is a free-fall back to the earth, a return to a life that has changed irrevocably, become fragile and startlingly unfamiliar. They were two men who had once again met each other for the first time.

'You're serious,' said Janne. 'People?'

'Men,' Emil clarified. 'Men who deserve it.'

'How can anyone deserve that?'

'By crossing a line.'

Janne looked at him. 'And you decide when that happens, do you?'

'Never. They do it themselves.'

'How?'

'We all know when we've done something we shouldn't.'

'That's quite a vague definition.'

'Actually it's quite specific. To cross the line I'm talking about, you always need to make a conscious decision. I only take on assignments that meet that criterion.'

'So you're a hitman?'

Emil said nothing. Again he looked his son in the eyes. *Into your hands I place my life.*

'I don't know what to say,' said Janne. 'Either you're telling the truth or … But you have Manninen's bag and you know what's going on here. I just heard that the man who killed Manninen is dead. I don't know how he died, but I doubt it was a heart attack. So there's only one question left. Why are you telling me all this?'

Emil was surprised. This was happening differently from what he had expected. On the other hand, everything happened this way.

'You have a family…'

Emil heard his son sigh. Janne placed his elbows on the table and leaned forwards.

'I had a family.'

'*Had?*'

'My wife is bored of me. She wants to separate, wants me to move out.'

'Are you going to?'

'I don't think I have many options.'

'I'm sorry.'

'You're sorry.'

'Family is the most important thing we have,' said Emil, and understood the weight of his words, how they reflected on him. 'The people closest to us.'

Janne sat back. 'Let's not turn this into a family therapy session. Considering what you told me a minute ago.'

Janne's standoffishness – it was a mask, thought Emil. If it wasn't, then Janne was just like him. The thought was as uplifting as it might have been under different circumstances.

'I was going to say: there comes a point in your life when…' Emil fumbled for the right words, knowing he would never find them. '… When you want to see what you were – what you are; to see what is left. It's always about people. I don't know how to put it any better, any more gracefully.'

Janne looked out of the window, then back at Emil. So far everything had gone far better than he had imagined.

'Thirty years,' said Janne. 'It's too long a time.'

'Too long for what?'

'Too long for there to be anything left, anything to look back on.'

It seemed Emil had celebrated too soon. 'I'm sorry you feel like that…'

'You're sorry, again.'

'I am, I truly am. From my perspective thirty years isn't too long a time. It's not a long time at all.'

Janne shook his head. 'I don't know what's worse. Have you any idea of the situation I'm heading into?'

'I know what it feels like to lose my family.'

'Lose? You didn't lose anything. You left us. You are … I don't even want to say what you told me you are. That's if it's even true. How do I know?'

'I know what it's like to feel lonely.'

'What do you want?'

To forget. To remember.

'To be your father.'

The waiter appeared and collected their plates, leaving the coffee pot. Emil poured them both a fresh cup. Only the most significant moments in life can be this mundane. Life doesn't come crashing down around us when a champagne bottle is popped open. Life creaks at the seams and the sun and the stars shine in the sky as you sit down on a bus, unsuspecting, and stare through the sleet at the landscape beyond the window, or as you wash the dishes, your back aching. The phone rings, your heart stops. It's at moments like this that a partner, whom you've trusted for years, tells you over supper they are leaving, that they've found someone else and will be moving out the very next day.

Emil didn't want to foist himself or his thoughts on Janne. Neither did he want this moment to evaporate, to lose the chance before him.

'What exactly can you offer me as a father?' asked Janne. 'Teach me various ways of killing people?'

The question was sarcastic and meant, at least in part, as a blow below the belt.

'Of course not,' Emil answered honestly, again staring around him. The room was empty. He wouldn't have wanted to have this conversation in a packed restaurant.

'What then?' asked Janne.

'I can listen. We can talk.'

'About what?'

'About life, anything at all.'

'Okay, let's talk about life,' said Janne. He placed his elbows firmly on the table, raised his shoulders. 'Let's start with the fact that you lied to me when we met the first time.'

'I did that to protect you. Parents do things like that.'

'Hardly for children in their thirties.'

'Particularly for children in their thirties. The things you haven't talked about by then will remain unspoken forever.'

'I disagree.'

'Good. Now we're having a conversation.'

'Does my mother know about you? About what you do?'

I believe she does. On some level, in some way. Because of what happened back then…

'No.'

'Are you going to tell her?'

'No.'

'What if I tell her?'

'That's up to you.'

'What do you think she'll say when she finds out?'

'She'll say what has to be said.'

Janne looked at him. 'What does that mean?'

'It means I believe people have their own reasons for doing and not doing things. Whether or not I understand those reasons is a different matter.'

'Why did you tell me this?'

'You're my only child. You are my son. I want you to know me.'

'You're taking quite a risk.'

'I know that.'

'I'm a reporter, and, to all intents and purposes, you and I are complete strangers. I can see the story now. A lengthy article in the weekend supplement. A portrait. It will be touching and personal because we're related to one another.'

'I don't believe you'd write something like that.'

Janne picked up his glass of water and took a sip. He emptied the glass.

'Did you kill those men in the woods?' he asked.

'Yes.'

'Why?'

'One of them shot your colleague. I was afraid they might harm you too. The shooter was very skilled. In many ways they had the upper hand. A snowmobile, a rifle, two excellently trained—'

'So there were two of them?'

'Yes.'

'And you killed both of them?'

'Yes.'

Janne stared at him. The dark rim of his glasses heightened the intensity of his eyes.

'Only one of the men shot at us,' he said quietly. 'That means the other one was innocent.'

'He would have harmed you. I knew him. I don't mean personally, but I know men like that. I know what they are, what they're capable of, what they do.'

'Isn't…?' Janne began, then fell silent.

Emil turned, saw the waiter approaching. He wanted to clear the table before lunch. Emil asked for the bill. Together or separately, he asked. Together, said Emil. Separately, said Janne. The waiter was frozen to the spot. *Together*, Emil said in a tone of voice that left no room for ambiguity, and the waiter walked off.

'Couldn't you just have stopped them following us instead?'

'Everything happened very quickly. Like so many things in life. Nothing happens for a long time, then everything happens all at once.'

The waiter returned, placed the bill in front of Emil and left.

Neither of them glanced up at him. The two men sat looking at one another.

'You could say that,' said Janne.

'I have a car. If you're going back to Helsinki...'

'I'll take the bus. To Rovaniemi. I'll fly back from there or I'll get the train.'

They remained sitting opposite each other for another few seconds. Then Janne stood up, pulled on his coat, wrapped a scarf round his neck, threw the black bag over his shoulder and walked out.

26

The snow-covered landscape was full of motion: it rose and fell, twisted and turned, stretched out flat. At times the forest rushed past, then the trees disappeared and the world was again nothing but endless sheets of snow. Apart from me, the back seat of the bus was empty; the window breathed cold air on to my face. I held my phone in my hand for a long while before managing to make the first call. I explained that I wanted to run some tests on water from the well at my family's farm and that I'd taken the necessary samples. I learned that the laboratory was in Vantaa and that I would have to bring the samples and fill out a form explaining various legal formalities, such as the specific location of the farm. That would be no problem, I said.

It also took a moment before I sent my first text message. Maarit answered immediately. She said she was already back in Helsinki and that we could meet. It seemed she too preferred communicating by text message; neither of us wanted to hear the other's voice. I wondered about everything I suspected Maarit might be involved in; what she suspected of me, and what was truly going on. Many uncomfortable, inappropriate things had taken place between us. We'd witnessed a man dying, and we had played a part in making it happen. On top of that, what had happened earlier: a drunken, passionate night, which was either a mistake on both our parts or a shared, concerted attempt to use each other.

And my father, our meeting, the things we'd spoken about – everything was swirling through my mind. Words took on new weight, the space between the lines disappeared. My father's voice echoed and dissolved, at times close, at others as though it was carried away across water. What words meant, what they expressed, shifted from the incomprehensible and the utterly shocking, to the mundane and perfectly sensible. I tried to think of him as a person – a sixty-year-old man trying to form a bond with people he had left behind long ago. The emotion was a mixture of sorrow and fright. What made the feeling so difficult was that I could relate to it so completely. I understood my father. In part. But as for the rest, what he claimed he had done – and still did – felt like a nightmare.

Halonen had told me to contact him directly as soon as I remembered something or if any new information came to light.

More than anything, the thought of Ella weighed on my mind. My daughter, my child. As much as I wanted to believe that I would never repeat my father's mistakes, that was exactly what I was doing, and it was all happening too easily. It didn't take much imagination to see myself explaining my choices to Ella, trying to assure her that she could trust me, which, of course, merely demonstrated that I knew I had betrayed her trust by disappearing from her life.

There was one thing I had learned, though. Work keeps us sane. Focussing on work helped when nothing else could. I was writing a story. The key to the story was right here in the bag beside me. I knew many things that nobody else knew. At least, no other reporters.

A mining company trying to increase profit margins by destroying the environment. A company whose board members might have been murdered. The thought brought to mind the activists. Did the police suspect them? And was Maarit one of them?

I did what I often did when I found myself without a pen and paper: I wrote myself a text message. A list of the facts so far: *Nickel mine at Suomalahti probably polluting the environment (confirm samples). Action deliberate. Responsibility with mining company.*

After typing the contents of the text message, I realised that here was my first article. I made another list of historical context: *price of company purchase, history of mining company, family business for generations.* All at once I realised that everything led back to Matti Mali. I Googled his picture. If the members of the board had been dying, perhaps it wasn't a group of activists that was behind it. They were energetic and came up with stunts that garnered much publicity. That was it. I couldn't see them – not even Santtu Leikola, who'd climbed on to the roof of the Parliament – actually laying a finger on anyone. For Matti Mali, on the other hand, everything was at stake: the future of his family business, his life's work.

I had considered Mali in various ways during my research, but had always dismissed him. Marjo Harjukangas's stories about threats must have played a part in my reasoning.

The bus came to a halt at the airport. I stepped off. I checked the jars of samples, wrapping my woollen jumper round them tightly for extra padding, and lifted the bag on to the conveyor belt.

The flight to Helsinki took an hour. Two sales representatives behind me were getting in the first drinks of the evening. I listened to their conversation until I dozed off.

At the other end, every minute I waited for my luggage felt torturously long. My bag appeared, and I checked the jars. Everything was intact, nothing had leaked. I rushed out to the taxi rank.

The laboratory of Water Analytics Finland was in a redbrick office building built in the 1980s. In the fading light and freezing emptiness of the winter's afternoon, its illuminated windows and the warmth that enveloped me in the foyer felt cosy. That said, the very fact I was considering a sterile office building near the airport a welcoming place spoke volumes about my state of mind.

I explained to the receptionist why I'd come, and was asked to fill out the form. I decided to locate my fictitious farm in Suomalahti, about ten kilometres from the mining complex. Once I'd filled in the form, I asked to meet the lab technician who would be examining the samples. The receptionist, a very young woman – probably still a student – looked at me for a moment and made a brief phone call.

We waited. The young woman gave me an awkward look. Eventually the sound of footsteps echoed down the corridor, and before long the technician appeared.

Susanna Salmela must have been in her forties. Her short dark hair revealed ears with more piercings than I could count at a quick glance. She was wearing a long white coat and a pair of Birkenstock sandals. I handed over Manninen's samples, explained that the matter was very urgent and important, and said that money was no object. The final comment was an out-and-out lie. I only had a few hundred euros in my account. That would go on next month's mortgage repayment. What's more, I was sure I'd exceeded any expenses Hutrila would be prepared to pay for.

Susanna Salmela placed the jars in a tall, silent trolley with soft wheels and assured me she would get back to me as soon as possible. Then she pushed the trolley back down a corridor lined with doors looking like hatches on a Christmas calendar – some opened, some left ajar, some still closed.

Back at the editorial office I casually greeted those who were still at work. Nobody asked where I had been. Fortunately Hutrila's office was empty. I didn't want to talk to him quite yet. I had to write something first.

Writing was thinking, a way of bringing order to the world. By writing I worked out what I was actually doing, formulated my true opinion on things. When I was writing I could shut off everything around me. That was my secret; it was the truth about my work. Regardless of what else was happening in my life or in the world, when I was writing I was happy; or as happy as someone can generally expect to be. Even if I was writing about something other than what was preoccupying me, the act of ordering words and forming sentences on paper helped with those very preoccupations. For me, writing was what made each day lived, balanced. When I didn't write, it soon started to show – at least to me; and even after only a few days. Everything began to become patchy. And the longer I didn't write, the more scattered and restless my mind became. Eventually I didn't know what I thought about anything; didn't know my place; didn't remotely know what I was doing.

I booted up the computer, fetched some coffee and sat down. How banal everything seemed right here, right now. But on the periphery of my thoughts – places my concentration couldn't reach – waited Ella, Pauliina, my father, Manninen the dead biologist, Maarit, and the events of the night in the forest. I looked around. An average day in the editorial department of an average newspaper. Nothing out of the ordinary. Except…

I began.

The more I wrote, the more clearly the pattern began to emerge.

Matti Mali. Everything started with him: things I knew for certain and things that were still only theories. I left a message for Marjo Harjukangas, asking her to call me back. The story grew longer and longer. I took short breaks. At some point I noticed that everybody else had left. I stretched my legs. In the window I saw the faintly lit park; the blank tree trunks and branches; the lights of the hotel across the road; a part of myself. I turned and went back to my desk.

I wrote until I was exhausted, until I simply couldn't continue. The story was long, but it could be reworked. As soon as I had the lab results I would add them to the text. The story's protagonist: Matti Mali. Working title: LORD OF THE DUNGHEAP.

I went to the bathroom. When I returned to my desk, I saw that my phone had rung. Marjo Harjukangas. I looked at the time. Nine o'clock in the evening. I called her back. She had news.

Someone had tried to murder Matti Mali.

PART THREE
GOLD

1

Leena's eyes were warm and wise. Emil didn't imagine the warmth was intended entirely for him – let alone only for him. He enjoyed what he could of it, though. At some point in our lives we make a decision, he thought, a choice that, though we don't understand it at the time, will be final and will define how the years will treat us. It is a fork in the road that we only realise we have crossed much later. Leena had chosen a good path. It showed. She could have chosen another path, after what Emil had done. He knew that.

But there she sat, wise and attractive, here, in the same restaurant as thirty years ago, at the very same table. Emil couldn't remember what wine they had drunk back then. Today a bottle of dark, fragrant Chilean red stood open on the table. Across the table was a woman whose hands, once young and uncertain, now held a glass between her firm, relaxed fingers.

The passing years. We either disappear within them without understanding a thing, or we accept them as a gift. Something like that. Emil realised that he had been silent for a long time.

'Thank you for coming,' he began. 'I wasn't sure whether this would be appropriate. This place, so soon.'

Leena smiled; it lit up her whole face.

'I was happy to accept your invitation. I think I said at our first meeting that…' Leena interrupted herself, raised her dark eyebrows then continued. '…at our first meeting for thirty years … that it's probably for the best that we're not young any more. I know an elderly woman – she prefers to use the word old, because she thinks it better describes the true state of things – who says that the good thing about each passing year is that there are fewer things about which you need to give a damn. Excuse my language. I agree with her. When I was younger I might have thought coming here with you would be needlessly nostalgic, that I should have more self-respect, and that you should try harder. That I should decline your invitation at least once, make sure I seemed to hesitate, something like that.'

Emil could have listened to Leena all evening. He couldn't understand men who complained about their wives' endless chatter. Why didn't those men choose women whose talk they wanted to hear?

'As we get older,' Emil began. 'I think we have a better idea of what we really want.'

Leena put her glass on the table.

'And we know what we don't want.'

They looked at each other. Leena's face was at once serious and somehow at peace with everything that had happened. Emil noticed he was no longer hungry.

'I understand why you left,' said Leena. 'I understand why you didn't keep in contact. But we don't have to talk about that. You did what … you had to do.'

Again they looked at each other. The iceberg inside Emil was beginning to melt. The conversation with his son; telling the truth; Leena's words.

'And besides, it's done now and it happened a long time ago,' she said. 'What happened all those years ago…'

Risto Hukkinen phones Leena twenty times a day, calls her a whore and threatens to attack her, to rape and violate her; to cause her financial difficulties. Time and again, day after day.

Leena changes her telephone number. Risto finds out the new one in a matter of days. Risto appears outside Leena's workplace, outside the front door to the house. Risto sits down in the tram and stares at her without saying a word. Risto follows her home in the dark. Risto suddenly appears on the running track, at the cinema, the library. Risto sends her letters in which he talks as if they are still a couple.

The harassment has been going on for about a year. Seven days a week, twenty-four hours a day.

Risto and Leena had dated each other for three impossible years. Leena soon realised she'd made a mistake. In fact, from Leena's perspective, most of the three years had been spent trying to end the relationship, trying to get away.

Risto is a manipulative liar, a pig whose true character is only revealed once it is too late. She can do nothing about him. Nobody can do anything about him. The police shrug their shoulders; friends and relatives listen for a while then lose interest.

Leena meets Emil. They fall in love, and before long Leena is pregnant. Emil quickly realises that hanging above them is a dark cloud casting a constant shadow on Leena's face. Emil tries to answer the telephone, tries to walk alongside Leena as much as possible. But it's never enough. When Emil answers the phone, there is nobody at the other end. When Emil walks with Leena, they don't see anyone following them or standing across the street. And yet the phone at Leena's workplace rings incessantly, and she continues to see Risto whenever she walks anywhere by herself.

Leena and Emil get on with life as best they can. They have a son. Risto disappears. Emil can see that Leena is bursting with joy. Their life is full of love. At least it might have been, had Risto not returned, now even worse than before. In his eyes, having a child with another man is the final deceit. One dark November evening Emil answers the telephone. Risto's voice. The whore and the child deserve to die.

Emil puts down the receiver and tells Leena he is going to the shop. Leena has told him where Risto Hukkinen lives. Emil takes the bus to the Munkkivuori neighbourhood. There is no snow yet; the ground is wet and bare. The asphalt gleams, black and oily. Emil looks out into the freezing rain, which so resembles his spirit. He steps off the bus at the Munkkivuori shopping mall. He walks round the shops – the shoe repairer, the bookstore. The rain numbs his face, trickles down inside his jacket collar.

In the lightless evening the rows of tall houses along Ulvilantie look like space rockets. The front door is open. Emil looks at the list of residents in the hallway. Sixth floor. The lift is small and slow, and Emil can see his face in the mirror on the wall. It is a face he has never seen before.

On the way up, his life races through his mind. He thinks of his parents, now long since dead: his violent, alcoholic father and his mother, beaten and frightened into submission. He thinks of the jobs he has done: chauffeur, builder, butcher. He thinks of people that have given him something better: the boxing instructor who encouraged him outside the ring, too; the librarian who gave him both love and books – a combination that can save lives, as Emil knew only too well. And then, the greatest of all gifts: Leena and Janne, his family.

Emil rings the doorbell and waits. He rings again. He opens the letterbox and sees a few, dimly lit square feet of the hallway floor. Shoes. Both men's and women's. So Risto Hukkinen lives with one woman and spends his time threatening another.

Emil recalls everything Leena has told him. Risto Hukkinen is a motoring enthusiast; he has an old Ford Mustang with which he is constantly tinkering. Emil returns to the yard, finds a row of garages between the tall houses. One of the doors is open, and a warm yellow strip of light cuts across the wet asphalt. Emil walks towards the door, pulls it open further. The beautiful, sleek bonnet of the white Mustang is propped up and Risto Hukkinen is bent over, his head leaning into the motor. Emil stands in the doorway for a moment then steps inside. Hukkinen notices that someone has appeared and stands up straight. It takes him only a fraction of second to recognise who it is.

Risto Hukkinen smiles. He has nothing to be afraid of. Emil is thirteen centimetres shorter than him and twenty-two kilos lighter.

Hukkinen is a big man, tall and stocky. He is wearing a T-shirt. His arms are the same girth as Emil's thighs. Emil cannot help himself thinking of Leena taking punches from a man fifty kilos heavier than her. The air in the garage is warm.

Hukkinen is a structural engineer, an expert when it comes to strength calculations; a man of steel and concrete. Hukkinen adds, subtracts, multiplies. He looks at Emil and sees a man in his thirties – a thin, sinewy figure whose face betrays the fact that there's little fat on his body. Hukkinen sees him as nothing but a punching bag.

'Tell me,' Emil begins. 'Tell me what will make you stop?'

Hukkinen's smile narrows somewhat. His bright-blue eyes look directly at Emil.

'Stop? Stop what?'

'The harassment. The phone calls, the stalking, the threats, the scare tactics. Everything.'

'You believe all of that?'

Emil says nothing. He stares at Hukkinen.

Hukkinen laughs.

'A man under the thumb,' he says.

They size each other up.

'Leena enjoys it,' he continues. 'Besides, what the fuck has it got to do with you?'

The light from the fluorescent lamps on the ceiling is bright, but still much of the space remains unlit. Hukkinen reaches a hand down under the bonnet.

'Do you beat your new girlfriend, too?' asks Emil.

'Whores always get what's coming to them. And I could have you charged with breach of the peace, with defamation. I'll call the police.'

'Do it.'

Hukkinen stands still, all except for his right hand, hidden beneath the bonnet. That moves. The beard and moustache around his mouth glisten, making Hukkinen look like a bear that has just eaten.

'Leena is nothing but a whore,' he says. 'You can't trust her. The kid is someone else's. It's a bastard.'

'You're all the same,' Emil says, and again feels the frozen rain whirling inside him.

Hukkinen stares at him fixedly.

'Men that beat their wives are full of excuses,' Emil continues. 'I'll tell you something I've never told anybody. When I was six years old I watched as my father battered my mother's head against the wall, yanked her right arm so hard it dislocated, and kicked her in the groin while she was lying on the floor. Later on I listened as he told his relatives she'd fallen off her bike. And I listened as he explained to my mother that he'd had to do what he did because she'd betrayed his trust. There's an explanation for everything. Every time.'

The garage is so quiet that the buzz of the fluorescent lamps rings in their ears.

'Boo-hoo,' says Hukkinen eventually.

Emil shakes his head.

'You don't get it. That's not why I told you.'

'So why did you?'

'Because I don't respect you. What is a man who doesn't command respect? Nothing. You're nothing.'

'And who the fuck are you to decide?'

'I don't decide anything. It's the truth.'

'The truth,' scoffs Hukkinen.

'You're nothing,' Emil says again. 'And you've only got yourself to blame. I don't know what it feels like, but I doubt it's a very comforting thought.'

Hukkinen looks at Emil. His eyes are full of hate, of burning rage.

'Do you think I'm afraid of you?'

'I don't care one way or the other. What you think doesn't matter.'

Hukkinen's right hand has found what it was fumbling for. Emil can see it in his posture, which has begun to tighten and move in the opposite direction.

'And I thought you'd come here to tell me what to do.'

'So did I. But I've changed my mind.'

'So you're not asking me to stop doing whatever that slut says I've been doing?'

'I'm not asking you for anything,' says Emil. 'The time for that is over. I understand that now.'

'Then you'll understand you can get the hell out of here, too.'

'I can't do that.'

Hukkinen shifts his weight to his left leg, the thigh pressing against the Mustang's fender.

'Why not?'

'For Leena's sake; for my son's sake,' says Emil.

Again Hukkinen smirks at him. 'What will they say when you go back with your tail between your legs, whimpering about what a bad world it is out there?'

'I'm not…' Emil begins, '… I'm not going back.'

'You know what?' Hukkinen says, more a statement than a question. 'Before I beat the living daylights out of the snivelling cunt that sent you here, I'm going to teach you a little lesson.'

'Leena didn't send me. She knows nothing about this. Nobody knows.'

Hukkinen is thinking about this. It's in his eyes, in the angle of his head. He's weighing up his next move. Something about his calculations seems to please him.

'Well then,' he says. 'It's just you and me.'

'That's right,' says Emil.

The sound of rain can be heard on the garage roof. Emil looks Hukkinen in the eye. Hukkinen lunges at him, pulling his right hand out from beneath the bonnet of the car. His punch comes surprisingly quickly. Emil manages to raise his left arm to stop the blow, the wrench strikes his elbow, his arm goes limp. Pain swirls round his body in an intoxicating rush.

For a thickset man, Hukkinen is fast and nimble. The heavy wrench swings in all directions. They are at the side of the Mustang. The wrench shatters the passenger-seat window. From the look on Hukkinen's face, Emil knows this is the final straw. To Hukkinen's mind, the smashing of the car window is Emil's fault. Hukkinen is dripping with rage, says he is going to kill Emil. Again the wrench flies through the air. Emil tries to dodge it but doesn't get out of the way in time. The corner of the wrench scrapes across his cheek.

Emil feels his skin ripping, blood spurting from his face. He ducks, and dashes past Hukkinen to the front of the car, where there's more space.

Again Hukkinen lunges for him. Emil's left arm still won't work. Hukkinen is on top of him, and the two of them fly towards the wall of tools. The blow knocks the air from Emil's lungs. Hukkinen presses him against the wall, the metal tools digging into his back. Some of them press painfully, others seem to burst their way through his skin and flesh.

Hukkinen's face is right next to his. His left hand grips Emil by the throat and squeezes. Emil can feel his windpipe is about to snap; breathing is impossible. The pain is indescribable. With his right hand Emil manages to grip the hand holding the wrench. He squeezes the wrist with all the force he can muster, pressing it on the inside. His thumb sinks between the bones of Hukkinen's forearm. If it goes any further, it'll come out the other side, he thinks. He presses his fingers hard and twists. The wrench falls from Hukkinen's clutch. Emil releases his grip, clenches his hand into a fist and punches Hukkinen square in the face. Hukkinen's nose breaks on impact and his hand falls from round Emil's throat. Hukkinen takes two or three steps backwards. The punch, which would have knocked out any average man, only dazes Hukkinen for a second. Blood is pouring from his nose. It comes in spurts, soaking his beard and moustache.

Hukkinen lashes out with both hands. Emil only has the use of his right and he can't breathe properly. He can still feel Hukkinen's grip on his throat. Perhaps his windpipe will be permanently damaged. Emil dodges the blows. Hukkinen is unable to find his target. He suddenly sees the wall of tools behind him and snatches up a knife. Emil realises there isn't much time. He can't breathe, and Hukkinen is brandishing a sharp, glinting blade.

Emil dodges Hukkinen's blows and takes a risk by diving behind his attacker. This takes Hukkinen by surprise, and, at this, Emil wins a few crucial fractions of a second. He manages to snatch the wrench from the garage floor. Again Hukkinen lunges towards him. Emil moves to one side. The last remnants of air in his lungs are gone.

Emil leaps forward, turns the wrench in his hand so that the jaws are in his fist. Hukkinen lurches forwards, and Emil slams the handle right into his open mouth. Hukkinen's face twists towards the ceiling, and at that he falls to his knees. The force of his lunge is such that the fall is powerful. Emil stands up as Hukkinen comes crashing down. Hukkinen's knees strike the floor, and Emil stands upright above him. Emil thrusts the wrench handle all the way down Hukkinen's gullet. The sturdy handle of chromium-vanadium steel smashes everything in its path. Emil releases his grip. The jaws of the wrench are protruding from Hukkinen's mouth like a set of unnatural dentures. Hukkinen slumps to the ground, thrashes for a moment, then lies motionless on the concrete floor.

Emil is on his hands and knees. Entire minutes pass before he is able to breathe enough to stand up again. A pool of blood has formed round Hukkinen's mouth.

I'm not going back.

That's what he'd said.

'Where did you drift off to?'

Emil noticed the peppered steak on the plate in front of him, the hum of conversation in the restaurant, Leena's quizzical, friendly eyes. How long had he been daydreaming? Perhaps only thirty seconds. He smiled at Leena.

'I was remembering something,' said Emil. 'I'm sorry.'

'You have nothing to apologise for,' said Leena.

2

'Why are you calling?' she asked.

'Why do you think?' I said.

I switched off my phone, read through my text again and saw all the holes – the gaps and flaws that I hadn't noticed while I was writing them. There on the screen they laughed at me, mocked me. *Here we are, right in front of you, and you still can't see us.* I closed the file. Most of the text was beyond salvation.

Someone had tried to kill Matti Mali – at the same time as I'd been having that unforgettable breakfast with my father. According to Marjo Harjukangas's account, Matti Mali had been on his way to work when an as yet unidentified person had accosted him outside his house. There was no information as to whether the assailant had used a knife, or whether Mali had been shot at. He can't have been too badly hurt, because he was now recovering at home, as Harju-kangas put it.

I couldn't get any more information out of her. She asked me to stop mentioning my insider source in my articles, and told me not to contact her again. She was clearly in shock and couldn't explain why she was calling me in the first place. I don't know, she said and hung up.

I called Pauliina, just so I could hear Ella's voice. They had gone to Pauliina's parents' house. I imagined only too well everything Pauliina must have told them about me – about us, our plans to separate, about what had driven her over the edge.

Ella was only able to concentrate for a few seconds before the phone was passed back to Pauliina. All we said to each other was goodbye.

The dim, empty office slowly began to wake up, the silence filled with sounds and words, movement in the shadows. When I could no longer force myself to concentrate on my writing, all the things I had pushed from my mind began flooding back. People, conversations, things I had done. I threw on my coat and left.

Maarit arrived in Juttutupa half an hour after me. I saw her in the doorway the moment she stepped inside; something lurched in my stomach. My heart didn't know how to beat. Maarit kicked the loose snow from her boots, looked around and spotted me.

I was sitting at a table in the corner with a pint of beer – the second of the evening. The bar was busy as usual, but tonight there was nobody on the stage. It felt like an eternity since the last time I'd met Maarit in this same place.

Maarit went to the bar, took two steps up to our booth, placed a bottle of Czech beer on the other side of the table, quickly shrugged off her coat and sat down.

'When did you get back to Helsinki?' I asked and watched as she adjusted the scarf round her neck until she was satisfied with its position.

'Yesterday,' she said.

Maarit looked at me, and I looked back. I sipped my beer. It didn't taste of anything.

'I'm sorry about Manninen,' I said. 'You were friends. It's hard to say anything else. My condolences.'

'Thanks,' said Maarit, turning the bottle of beer between her fingers. The label spun anticlockwise, the text moving from the end to the beginning.

I kept my eyes fixed on her. The way her hair framed her face made her look so stern, it was hard to read her expression; I could only see the essentials: her eyes, her nose and mouth. Something remained hidden. So far she'd said only two words.

'So you got back yesterday,' I said.

Maarit nodded.

'What have you been up to today?'

Maarit looked as though she had only now truly arrived at our meeting, as though she had just noticed my presence, registered me.

'Sorry?'

'I said what have you—'

'Nothing much,' she said. 'Why?'

I sipped my beer. How much of this would I have to drink before it tasted like beer? Maarit shifted position. She sat up, back straight, eyes focussed, pulled her broad shoulders back slightly. None of the changes was very big, but when you put them together the difference was clear. I glanced at the coat she'd folded on the chair next to her. I couldn't see any badges. No – I could see one. It was completely black. Finally I put everything together. I was about to open my mouth when Maarit spoke.

'It had to come to this.'

I said nothing.

'I always thought I'd never go as far as my father, in anything. The world doesn't need any more fanatics. And yet … I knew the way. I took us there. Manninen trusted me.'

Maarit took a sip of beer, swallowed, pursed her lips and continued. 'I wanted to do something positive, honestly; do something for the common good. It felt important. It is important, I know that. It still is important, but it doesn't feel like it any more.'

'You're still in shock,' I said.

Maarit looked at me more acutely than at any point during our meeting.

'Maybe,' she said and didn't look as though she was in shock in the slightest. 'What about you?'

'I'm writing a story. And I will write it.'

'Still?'

'Why shouldn't I?'

Maarit glanced first to the left then the right, then turned to look at me again.

'You weren't scared off by … what happened?'

'Should I be?'

I tried to look for signs in Maarit's expression, signs of anything at all.

'I don't know,' she said again, still turning the bottle in her fingers. The bottle drew small, wet scratches across the table, which for a fleeting moment gleamed like the purest rain. 'I don't know anything any more.'

'I'm sorry,' I said. 'Well, I don't know if I'm sorry. I just don't believe you.'

Maarit looked up at me, and for the first time that evening I saw something in her face. She said nothing. I took a breath and leaned forward.

'The badge. A group of environmental activists called Black Wing. The threats received by the board members of Finn Mining Ltd and their subsequent deaths. You and your surprising, and not-so-surprising, appearances in various places. And what happened this morning. You and your friends, whoever you are and whatever you call yourselves. You're responsible for people's deaths.'

Maarit looked at me. Still she remained silent. It seemed as though there were more shadows on her face than a moment ago. Perhaps it was the light, perhaps the angle of her head, perhaps the thick hair outlining her face.

'I apologise,' she said. 'But only for one thing. I'm sorry for what happened to Tero Manninen.'

'That's probably the only thing you don't have to apologise for. Manninen knew the risks. He wanted to take those samples.'

Maarit's eyes glistened. 'Anything for a good story, is that it?'

I stared back at her. 'Anything for the cause, you mean?'

Maarit shook her head. 'I don't know what you're talking about.'

'Yes, you do. You and your friends have been murdering the Finn Mining board members. And this morning, as if to crown everything, you tried to murder Matti Mali. Your group includes, or at least it used to include, Santtu Leikola and the deceased Tero Manninen. I can't prove anything, but I'll be satisfied if you just tell me I'm right.'

'I can't tell you that,' said Maarit.

'Why not? Are you afraid someone will try and kill you, too?'

Maarit's eyes shined all the more; tears appeared in the corners of her eyes and trickled into hiding beneath her hair. Her expression remained fixed. She was sitting upright, leaning against the table.

'I've lost a friend. That happened because we all wanted to do something good. We wanted to reveal what's going on, show these wrongs for what they are. We wanted the truth to come out. We thought that you, as a reporter, might share that sentiment. We thought you were on the same side as us. I'd read your articles and … I thought it would be worth getting to know you.'

She looked down at the table.

'Of course, it wasn't by chance that we met here. Santtu texted me and said our favourite reporter was here. I was on the tram on my way home, but I thought I'd pop in and ask what was going on with my father's papers, whether they've been of any use. What happened afterwards happened all by itself.'

'Santtu Leikola? Is he behind all this?'

'Behind what?'

'The killings. The attempt on Matti Mali's life this morning.'

Maarit looked up at me as though I'd spilled her glass.

'It's hardly surprising we hit it off,' she said. 'We're similar, you and me. Doesn't matter what gets trampled on, what you lose, just as long as you get what you want. Or what you think you want. I knew it the moment we started talking. Your relationship is falling apart; your father turns up after thirty years; and you can't think of anything but your work – your own aims and objectives. You're like me. I'm like my father.'

I waited for a moment. 'You didn't answer my question.'

'In a way I did. But to put it more plainly: no, I am not a member of a damn terrorist organisation and Santtu … Santtu is only responsible for the emails you've received. Other than that, he's only been behind his own stunts. If he'd done anything else, I'd know about it within the space of a minute. Santtu tells me everything, every single thing, all the time. He's a lovely guy, but sometimes he's too open for his own good. That's why we didn't even think of inviting him when the three of us went up to Suoma-lahti. As for this badge – this black one here – it's just a black badge. That's the whole point. It draws people's attention for the simple reason that it's nothing more than a black badge. Sometimes things really are exactly what they seem.'

Maarit placed her coat back on the seat. We sat for a moment in silence. Her eyes had dried. She took a sip of beer.

'Santtu is a lovely guy,' I repeated.

Maarit didn't look up.

'Yes, he is,' she said quietly, but in a tone of voice that it was impossible to mistake.

'Jesus Christ.'

'Just look at yourself. You've got a partner and a little girl. You're a father. Hypocritical little shit. You think it's okay for a man to sleep around but not for a woman?' She looked up. 'Are we done here?' she asked.

Maarit shunted the bottle to one side. There was still a third of the beer left. She began pulling on her coat. The black badge caught the light of the lamp and glinted, as though it was sticking its tongue out, mocking me.

'Can you forgive him?' I asked.

Maarit had put on her coat but remained sitting.

'Who?'

'Your father. Can you forgive him for being the way he was?'

'Of course. But he's dead. It's too late for anything else; anything other than forgiveness. There are plenty of other things I can think of doing.'

She stood up, zipped her coat. 'Good luck with the story.'

She walked across the room, pulled her hood over her head and slipped through the door into the winter's evening. I raised my pint to my lips. Beer didn't taste like it once had.

*

I went back to the office and sat at my desk for a moment. It was only then I realised quite how exhausted I was. I stood up, walked to the window. It had started to snow again. The first snowflakes were floating in the still air, so slow-moving, it was as if they were gazing in amazement at the world around them.

3

Emil presses his thumb against the man's Adam's apple and crushes it. The man's eyes reveal surprise, fear, and eventually peace. Emil keeps his hand firm, pushes the man through the front door and lays him on the hall rug, little by little relaxing his grip. The man lies on the floor as though he is asleep. Emil pulls the door shut behind him and walks past the man into the kitchen, takes a packet of Italian liquorice ice cream from the freezer, finds a dessert spoon in the top drawer and sits down on the sofa. The man's family is sitting there; Emil sits down between them. To his left are an exhausted mother and a boy playing on his phone; to his right a girl who has dyed her hair pink. They are watching television, which seems to be repeating the same silent scene over and over. In the images on the screen Emil can be seen strangling the children's father and placing him on the hallway floor. Again and again. Emil raises the tub of ice cream and is about to sink his spoon into it, but stops. The tub is full of the eyes of dead men: surprised, frightened and peaceful, content with their fate.

Emil snapped wide awake. His shirt was glued to his chest as though he had spilled a litre of water while trying to drink. He looked at the time: 4.19 a.m. The more good things that happened to him, it seemed the worse his memories and nightmares became.

After their pleasant evening he had escorted Leena to the taxi rank, where they had exchanged a warm kiss on the cheek. Then he had walked home.

He had drunk only one glass of wine with his meal, and that had been soaked up by the food. Once he was back home, he collected the details he'd been sent the previous day in a folder in his TOR network profile. He'd pulled on clean clothes, walked to the car park

by the Olympic Stadium, stolen a car and driven to the suburb of
Mankkaa.

He had hanged the man in his garage, then returned to Helsinki,
and driven to the Cable Factory arts centre, all without feeling the
least satisfaction – without feeling that he did a job at which he
excelled and which he could concentrate on fully. This wasn't his life
any more. He'd parked the car by the sea, looked out at the thin strip
of lights across the water in Lauttasaari, and walked back along the
shore to his apartment. He'd taken a warm shower, drunk a cup of
tea and fallen asleep, only to awake in the grip of a nightmare.

He stood up and took a few steps, felt the cool of the parquet floor
beneath his feet. Darkness stared back at him through the window
with all its force. He heard the lift judder into motion, the door
opening. Out on the street a taxi sped off towards the city centre. The
world was spinning on its axis, but he had stopped still.

One more.

Then he would have done his bit.

4

'And what do we know today?'

Steps. The door. Bright light. I hurried to sit down. That's right: I'd been watching the snow for a while, then nodded off for a moment on the conference-room sofa.

Halonen stood in the doorway.

'What's the time?' I asked.

'Seven minutes past seven. Why are you sleeping at work?'

Where else can I go?

'I like this sofa.'

'Pulled an all-nighter?'

I nodded.

'What are you working on?'

I got up from the sofa. Halonen kept his eyes on me. It felt awkward having to stretch and straighten my clothes under the watchful eye of the detective inspector. I thought I knew what Halonen meant by his question.

'I haven't written a word about what happened.'

'The murders at the mine, you mean?'

'That's right.'

'Good.'

Halonen looked like he'd just stepped out of a photo shoot for a glossy lifestyle magazine. The dazzling white shirt, the top button open, no tie, the smart, fitted suit. He stepped into the room and closed the door behind him. It was unnecessary. I could see through the glass wall that the editorial office was deserted.

'That's why you've come here, isn't it – to make sure I've kept my word?' I said.

Halonen put his hands in his pockets. He was standing at the other side of the room, but still I could smell his expensive after-shave. Clementine, incense, forest.

'You've probably already heard that someone tried to murder Matti Mali.'

'Yes. It's been all over the news since yesterday, and I didn't—'

'That's not what I mean. The first time you called me, you asked whether the police were looking into a certain series of deaths.'

Kimmo Karmio. Alan Stilson. The members of the board of Finn Mining Ltd.

'I remember.'

'Not very many people know about them. They're not exactly classified information, but, again, I'd appreciate it if you didn't speculate about the deaths in public or write anything about them – or about yesterday's attempt on Matti Mali's life.'

I didn't say anything.

Halonen's expression seemed open and honest. Perhaps he'd said what he'd come to say.

'And?' I asked.

Halonen lips pursed almost imperceptibly. 'In return I'm sure I could give you something.'

'When?'

Halonen raised his hands. 'Right now, if you like.'

I waited expectantly.

'If you've received any threatening letters and wondered who sent them, I can tell you with almost one hundred per cent certainty that they were sent by one of the two security guys murdered at the mining complex. It seems these guys were working for one of the now-deceased board members at the company, and perhaps someone else too.'

'Thanks for the information.'

'My pleasure,' said Halonen.

We remained standing where we were for a few seconds. Halonen continued looking me fixedly in the eyes. Then he took his hands from his pockets, straightened his jacket and turned towards the door. The gesture was practised, stage-managed – this I understood almost at once – but it worked. He had half turned round when he stopped and turned back to face me.

'Have you met up with Maarit Lehtinen? Since coming back to Helsinki, I mean.'

Before I could say anything, Halonen answered the question himself. 'You have.'

I nodded.

'You talked about recent events,' he said, and I realised instantly that this was no longer a question.

Halonen took a step closer to me. This time he didn't put his hands in his pockets, but kept them by his sides.

'Did Maarit perhaps mention Santtu Leikola or any of the other activists?'

'Well, only to say that … he's not that kind of person.'

'Had Maarit met up with Leikola?'

'Why don't you ask her that?'

Halonen didn't answer. His eyes seemed infinitely deep.

'Violence; the death of a close friend,' he said eventually. 'You're still shocked by the events in Suomalahti.'

Again he slipped his hands into his pockets, assumed a more relaxed position, the kind of pose that someone might interpret as backing away. I thought of Maarit, our conversation.

'If you suspect Maarit—' I began.

Halonen interrupted me straight away. 'Who says I suspect her? She's made an impression on you. I'm not surprised. She makes an impression on everyone.'

'She hasn't done anything.'

'She – and you for that matter – scaled a perimeter fence, forced your way into the mining complex and witnessed a man's murder. She is part of this investigation.'

'I mean, she's innocent,' I said. I knew it was true. Maarit was as innocent as all innocent people. Ella. Pauliina. I was the guilty one.

'Innocent,' said Halonen under his breath.

'Yes.'

'Somebody once said that, once we reach a certain age, nobody is innocent. What would you say that age is?'

I looked to one side, then back at Halonen. His face was impassive.

'It's a bit early for the big philosophical questions,' I said. 'I don't know the answer.'

'Neither do I. That's why I'm asking. And you know the other reason I'm asking?'

'I can't imagine.'

'It's my job.'

'Great.'

'What's your job?'

'It's not all that different from yours,' I said.

The room was beginning to feel smaller, and yet I still couldn't help opening my mouth. 'Do you have a suspect for the murders in Suomalahti?'

'Why do you ask?'

'Because it's my job.'

Halonen smiled, quickly and almost imperceptibly. 'Got someone in mind, have you? So you do remember seeing something out there?'

'You don't have a suspect.'

'No comment.'

Silence. Again.

'Anyway, thanks for the little chat,' said Halonen. 'We understand each other. That's the main thing.'

Halonen turned, and this time he didn't turn back. He left the door open as he walked out and disappeared down the corridor. I waited a moment, then checked that he really had left, took my phone from my pocket and made a call with what was left of my battery.

Detective Inspector Halonen had mentioned three murders and one count of attempted murder. That really was true. Giorgi Sebrinski had committed suicide by jumping from the balcony outside the sauna suite at the top of his apartment block in Vuosaari. He had plummeted almost seventy metres to the ground. Although there was about a metre of snow on the ground, it didn't do much to soften his fall.

At the same time, Halonen had helped me to focus my attention. He seemed convinced of the role played by Maarit and the other activists. Of course, this was logical.

Question: Who would want to kill the entire board of directors?

Answer: Someone who knows they are complicit in something gross and unforgivable and who wants to make an example of them.

Ergo: The activists, who in the past have operated without regard for laws and regulations and who have now decided to up the ante, to take things to the next level.

I didn't know whether Halonen had any proof. Even if he did, he wouldn't have told me. It didn't matter. For, even as Halonen's gaze buried deep, straining for the obvious and the logical, he looked right past the target.

Three dead: Karmio, Stilson, Sebrinski.

One injured: Matti Mali.

One remaining: Hannu Valtonen.

5

Mankkaa was at its busiest at eight in the morning. In Mankkaa, that meant large SUVs taking children to local schools and bilingual nurseries; estates, station-wagons, in which sales directors, choked by their expensive ties, texted their mistresses at the wheel, spilling coffee on their suit trousers in the process.

The taxi pulled up behind an empty police car. The driver looked up in the mirror and asked if this was the right address. I looked at the number on the door of the house Yes, I said and paid him. I stepped out of the car and walked towards the two-storey white-washed building.

The fresh snow that had fallen overnight crunched beneath my feet. The air in the quiet suburb was crisp. The road hadn't yet been ploughed, so I walked along the furrows made by the passing cars. The windows of the surrounding houses were mostly still dark, the yards empty. People had already left to get on with their day. All except Hannu Valtonen.

An oblong garden sloped down to the road; I walked through it, up towards the house and the garage, where a white BMW and an ambulance were parked. This couldn't have been an emergency call: the ambulance was empty and none of the lights in the car were switched on. As I walked past I glanced inside the BMW. On the backseat and in the boot were suitcases; on the front seat a bulging leather satchel – hand luggage. It looked as though someone was about to head off.

I stopped at the open door of the garage. It was high-ceilinged and spacious, and was divided into two sections. To the right was a beautifully restored 1960s Triumph sportscar, and around it were a variety of workbenches and tools. On a set of tracks running the length of the ceiling hung various cables and other equipment. This was a motoring enthusiast's space. The left-hand section of the garage was empty, showing only an expanse of concrete flooring. Two police officers stood there, along with the ambulance crew, of which I assumed at least one had to be a doctor. Between them on the floor lay a grey body bag, its zip firmly shut. From the track running directly above the bag hung a metre of white rope, which seemed to have been cut in the middle.

'Who are you?' asked one of the officers upon noticing me. He was young and stout. 'Are you a family member?'

'No.'

'Then I'll have to ask you to leave.'

'What's happened here?'

By now the officer had appeared beside me and gripped me by the shoulder. Before I noticed it, we were walking in the same direction, away from the garage. Out in the garden I came to a halt.

'What's happened?' I asked once more.

'A man has died.'

The officer still had hold of my shoulder. His grip was firm.

'Please leave the property.'

'Hannu Valtonen?'

The policeman looked at me for a moment, then raised his hand. I took a few steps back.

'No need,' I said. 'I'm going.'

I returned to the road, knotted my scarf and buttoned up my jacket. From my bag I took a hat and a pair of gloves, then I walked away.

Editor-in-chief Hutrila crossed his hands behind his head, closed his eyes and calmly breathed in and out, three times. He arched his back; it looked like a yoga position. I'd told him everything I was at liberty to reveal. Then I asked. Hutrila opened his eyes.

'More time?'

'Yes.'

'You realise other journalists will get in there first and write up anything they can get their hands on?'

'They'll write up whatever they can get their hands on, yes,' I said. 'But nothing more. And I've got more, I promise, and soon there'll be even more than that. That can be our angle, it's what will make us stand out. Other papers take care of the basic story, report it on a general level. Then, once readers are familiar with the story, we jump in with all the details. We'll have a scoop that other papers can only dream about.'

'Are you sure?'

I'd come back from Mankkaa by bus. As the sun had risen, drawing out the contours of the horizon, I'd made my decision.

'One hundred per cent sure.'

'When you went up north, we agreed you would have a story ready by the time you came back.'

'Things got complicated.'

Hutrila thought for a moment. 'You've asked for extra time every step of the way. You've asked to be transferred; you've overspent your budget, then turned up here without a story. What's different now?'

'Now I have a deadline. Tomorrow morning, nine o'clock.'

Hutrila lowered his arms to his sides so slowly that I was beginning to think this really was yoga.

'That's the first sensible sentence I've heard you say in a long time.'

6

One more. This one would be the most difficult. It was the most difficult because it was the last.

By this point the risks were greater than ever; Emil knew that. He'd witnessed it countless times before; watched people letting go in the final straight, becoming careless and sloppy, lulling themselves into a false sense of security. It was understandable; it was human.

It happens to all of us.

When the finish line comes into view, it feels like you've already crossed it. You start living the life that comes afterwards. You imagine the rest of the journey will fall into place by itself, run on its own steam. You think you can concentrate on admiring the scenery, building a future. You see yourself doing different things, enjoying this, that and the other, without a care in the world. Your hand reaches for the trophy, your eyes focus on the podium.

You imagine there's no space at all between you and the finishing line.

But in that space, there's everything.

7

I hauled all the boxes containing Lehtinen's papers into the conference room and closed the door. I sorted the papers, the notebooks and newspaper clippings into separate piles. The pile of papers was the tallest. That was a good starting point. I read through every page again, as if with fresh eyes, making notes as I went. I set myself the task of finding on every page something I hadn't noticed before. As I'd said to Hutrila, other papers would start by reporting on what was happening right now, what might happen next. That would set up my story about what was really going on. I fetched my phone and called the laboratory.

I asked the switchboard to put me through to the technician, Susanna Salmela. They connected me straight away. The results hadn't yet come through. I asked whether she was able to assess the samples based on what she'd already observed and on her overall experience in the field. She paused for a moment. This isn't about a gut feeling, she said. That's the whole point of these tests. We only tell people what we have measured and what we can prove. That's just as it should be, I admitted. I asked her to call me as soon as the results had come through.

But, just as I was about to hang up, Salmela asked me something. I didn't hear her question and asked her to repeat it.

'Have you seriously been using this water for everyday consumption?' she asked.

Two hours later I fetched some food from across the street, stuffed the burger and fries into my mouth and swallowed. Next, the newspaper clippings, the articles Lehtinen had saved. I went through each and every one of them; some of them I even read from start to finish. Then the notebooks. I picked a retro-looking, A4-sized hardback notebook from the top of the pile.

The pages were full of Lehtinen's handwriting. I'd flicked through this notebook once before, but on that occasion I hadn't paid enough attention to the sheets of A4 he had stapled in, in various places. Now I realised this was because unfolding them was difficult. The staples were firm, and in some instances the pages were attached in several places. Lehtinen must have had a good reason to do this. I prised opened one of the sheets.

They were printouts of emails, but not Lehtinen's own. The recipients included Giorgi Sebrinski, Kimmo Karmio, Hannu Valtonen, Alan Stilson and Matti Mali. They were communications between the board members of Finn Mining Ltd.

I went over to Tanja's desk and asked to borrow something to remove the staples.

'I'm a bit disappointed you didn't do the twerking story,' she said and handed me an implement that looked like an angry, metallic mouth. 'Twerking is what everybody's talking about right now.'

I returned to the conference room and began removing the staples, at the same time reading through Lehtinen's notes. They weren't directly related to the content of the emails. Perhaps this was intentional, perhaps not. Eventually all the attachments were laid out loose on the desk. I sat down and began to read.

Half an hour later I fetched my laptop and searched the relevant terms, and when I found the name of the company I was looking for, I ordered all the material I could find about it – documents from the register of companies; credit histories; a financial statement; staff reports. Then I printed them off. I checked to make sure everything fitted chronologically. I picked up one of the printed emails, laid it out in front of me and checked that it truly said what I thought it did.

Finally I called Marjo Harjukangas and apologised for contacting her again.

When she had given me a two-word answer, I thanked her and hung up.

8

The sky glowed above him, bright and blue. The snow that had built up on the window ledge overnight sparkled like millions of tiny mirrors. He had been getting dressed, but stopped now and walked to the window. He leaned against the window frame, felt the cold stone under his palms and a draught against his wrists.

He looked out into the forecourt where children in jumpsuits were climbing to the top of a pile of snow, stumbling and sliding down again on their plastic toboggans. Once in a while a child succeeded in sliding all the way down to the gritted pavement. There was a crackle as the plastic toboggan met the gravel and the child came to an immediate halt. He didn't want to see it as some kind of premonition, but for some stubborn reason that's what it looked like.

He had been given a deadline. He'd always liked that word. It described what he did, what his work was really about. But more than anything, he liked the literal meaning of the term. He liked timetables, time restraints. But he also noticed that the word hid a paradox. A deadline liberated him, stripped away any sense of indecision, helped him to concentrate, to focus his energy. When everything was hanging in the air, floating in the wind, nothing could ever be completed. And a suitable time never seemed to appear. He should be content right now. Everything was going as planned. And still…

Looking for answers on the outside was pointless.

The world hadn't changed one iota.

He had changed.

He stood by the window a moment longer, then continued getting dressed. He pulled his skiing suit on over the layers of warm clothes, attached the bag round his waist and checked to make the sure it contained everything he needed: sunglasses, ski wax, an energy bar. And the key.

9

I got off the number twenty bus at its final stop – at the far end of Lauttasaari – and walked across the bridge to Kaskisaari. The island was small, extremely affluent and unknown to the majority of people in Helsinki. This was hardly a surprise. The island was exclusive, not only because of its location, but also because of the price tag on its properties. In places the detached houses looked like airports, with their extensive rooftops, long private roads leading up to their gardens, and windows several storeys high. The fences running round each of the properties were tall and were fitted with security devices in various shades from bright yellow to fire-engine red. I walked along the recently ploughed street and squinted. The snow and the sun made everything brighter. Between the houses I caught a glimpse of the sea. Across the water to the west lay Espoo. The towers at Keilaniemi rose up on the horizon like dull, grey teeth. To the east, across the sound, was Seurasaari; the outdoor museum exuded a stillness over the whole island. The protracted freezing weather and the constant snowfall had frozen the sea. The dots moving around on the ice were skiers enjoying the sturdy packed snow and the smooth, unimpeded surface of the ice.

The house I was looking for was on the western side of Kaskisaari. It was the penultimate building on the street leading to the shore. It was one of the oldest buildings on the island, built perhaps in the 1930s. Judging by the location and the era of its construction, the architect must have valued privacy and quiet. In those days the only way to reach the island was by boat. Two grey stone lions standing on either side of the steps leading up to the house kept any visitor under close watch. The house appeared to have a balcony facing in every direction. It wasn't especially stylish, but it was massive and set apart from the surrounding homes. Part of the reason for its seeming isolation must have been the size and shape of the rectangular plot, on both sides of which grew thick walls of spruce trees. Upon approaching from the street, visitors could not see the sea behind the house.

The front gates were locked, as were the doors of the double garage. At the front gate there was what looked like a buzzer; above it there was a speaker behind a grille, and a black, convex lens, beneath which a security camera was surely hidden. The imposing entrance was crowned with a sticker from a security company. It seemed the residents of Kaskisaari were more than prepared to deal with unwanted guests, though this was a place nobody ever visited. I was about to press the steel button on the buzzer when my phone vibrated in my pocket. I stepped back from the gates and moved round the corner.

Lab technician Susanna Salmela started talking before I'd even said my name. Sulphate, sodium, mercury, lead, zinc, manganese, lye. All thousands of times over the recommended maximum. The water was life threatening. Salmela asked where the sample had come from, and said that if it had come from the well at my family's farm then either we lived right next to a leaking nuclear reactor or I wasn't telling the whole truth.

I admitted I'd left out a few details. Salmela fell silent for a moment then asked for my email address so she could send the full written report.

The minute I ended the call, my phone beeped as a new email arrived. I rang the buzzer, clicked open the email and soon heard a familiar voice asking me what business I had there.

'Sulphates: forty-two milligrams per litre. Sodium: twenty milligrams per litre. Mercury, lead, zinc, manganese…'

'Who are you?'

'Janne Vuori, *Helsinki Today*.'

A short pause.

'What do you want?'

'To tell you what I know.'

The intercom crackled, indicating that the connection had been cut off. I took a few steps back. I looked up at the house but couldn't see anyone in the windows. The door at the top of the steps remained shut. Again I rang the buzzer. Nobody answered. I tried the gate; it was locked. Snow and silence surrounded the island, the house, and me. I was wondering what to do when the intercom gave another crackle, this time as the connection was opened again.

'Hello. Are you still there?'

I rushed back to the speaker and said, yes, I was still here.

'There was a small matter I needed to confirm. Please, come on in.'

Matti Mali's smile was friendly and open, and seemed to light his face both inside and out. The contrast with the rest of his appearance was striking. Mali's left eye was edged in shades of black and violet. A long, swollen wound ran the length of his forehead from the corner of his left eye to his hairline. His left arm was in a sling, its bandages lifting the collar of his shirt up almost to his ear.

Mali was a heavy-set, stocky man; his legs were spread apart and his slippers placed firmly on the floor. If it weren't for the injuries, he would look more like a pensioner from the bingo hall than the former CEO of a prominent mining company. The brown velvet trousers, the dark-blue cardigan with sagging pockets and the curly, silvery grey hair only served to heighten the impression. For a few seconds I realised I was questioning myself and my conclusions. Perhaps Matti Mali noticed it too.

'I recognised your name at once. I've read your articles. Let's go into the living room and talk.'

I left my coat and shoes in the hallway and followed my host, who, despite his injuries, moved naturally and fearlessly. Just as I had imagined him.

From the entrance hall we went down two steps into the spacious living room. The windows gave a panorama out to sea, which gleamed white from one side of the windows to the other.

We sat down in armchairs situated on either side of a coffee table. In relation to the other furniture in the room, the chairs were positioned at a slight angle. I understood why. From Mali's chair he could see both the sea and the television, which was behind me on my right. My chair offered a view out across the sea and the patio door, which was behind Mali, on his left. On the table were two coffee cups with saucers and a pot.

'Coffee?'

'Thank you.'

Mali poured coffee into the cups and slid one of them across the table towards me. I recognised the cup and saucer: the Singapore range by the Arabia ceramics company. I pulled the papers from my satchel. Mali looked at me. He said nothing as I placed them on the table and checked for the thousandth time that nothing was missing.

'Milk? Sugar?'

'No, thank you.'

'I take my coffee black, too. That's how it should be drunk, I say.'

I looked at Mali for a moment. 'I have here a number of documents that appear to reveal that—'

'Do you have a family?'

Sitting in the armchair across from me was an old man whose light-blue eyes were curious and friendly.

'Yes,' I said. 'Well, no.'

Mali smirked at my answer, and again his expression seemed more a look of sorrow than pleasure.

'I have a daughter,' I clarified.

'I don't have any children. I once had a wife, but now I'm alone. The housekeeper visits in the morning. This is a secret.'

'What is a secret?'

'This,' Mali nodded in front of him. 'Rather, it's been a secret for some time now: the fact that I no longer take part in the running of the company.'

'I realised that today.'

Mali didn't seem interested in what I had or hadn't realised. He looked out at the sea, crossed his right leg over his left and picked up his coffee cup. He blew on it, and steam cut across the edge of the cup. I took one piece of paper from the pile and pushed it to his side of the table. He glanced at it, sipped his coffee before putting the cup down, took a set of reading glasses from his pocket and picked up the paper. He read.

To: Matti Mali <matti.mali@finnmining.fi>
From: Hannu Valtonen <hannu.valtonen@finnmining.fi>
CC: Giorgi Sebrinski <giorgi.sebrinski@finnmining.fi>, Kimmo Karmio <kimmo.karmio@finnmining.fi>, Alan Stilson <alan.stilson@finnmining.fi>
Subject: Your offer

Dear Matti,
We had a meeting today to discuss your offer. We have decided to decline. We will not accept your offer, not now or in the future.

Yours sincerely,
Hannu Valtonen
Director of Research and Development
Tel: +35 8 46 8739 223
hannu.valtonen@finnmining.fi
Finn Mining Ltd – Commitment and Excellence in the Arctic

Mali placed the sheet of paper on the table, took off his glasses and replaced them in his shirt pocket. He looked out across the sea.

'The beginning of the end. For all concerned.'

His tone was neutral, as though he were talking about something that didn't affect him at all. He turned to look at me.

'It's a good job my father isn't here to witness this. The mining company was even more important to him than it is to me. But I've done what I imagined he would have done. Everything: though I wasn't very happy about some of it. Do you know what that piece of paper means?'

'Yes,' I said and pulled out another handful of papers. 'I believe I do. I have more documents that tell the whole story. Before that, I have to say that—'

'You have to say what?'

I looked at Mali's black eye, the wound across his forehead, his arm resting in its bandages.

'That fall of yours was quite convenient,' I said.

Mali looked at me, expressionless.

'When I'd read these papers and finally understood what I'd read, I made a single phone call and received a single answer. Nobody saw the attack. All the police have is your statement. The timing is a bit too perfect.'

Mali was silent for a moment. Then he smiled, and when his smile had disappeared he turned to face me fully.

'As you will have seen,' he began pensively. 'The steps out front are treacherous. I'm a practical man. You have to use any opportunities that present themselves. I needed a little time.'

'Time for what? You have no more time – that's precisely what I've come to tell you…'

Mali raised his right hand. I stopped mid-sentence.

'Would you like some chocolates before we get down to business? I think I'll have one. There's Belgian and Swiss, if you like.'

'Thank you, but—'

'I assure you, they're both excellent,' he said. 'If I remember, the Belgian chocolates have truffles in them. The Swiss stuff is dark. Wait a moment.'

Mali stood up from his armchair, walked through the open room, disappeared behind a wall and remained there for a moment. I heard a cupboard door closing, the clink of glasses. Mali returned carrying two crystal bowls, settled himself in his chair once again, took one of both chocolates and began noisily unwrapping them.

'Do you mind if I correct you as and when you make any mistakes?' he asked as he pushed a chocolate into his mouth.

This wasn't going as I had expected. I'd imagined I would at least have to try and threaten him – blackmail him with what I knew. I looked at him. He looked back and sucked his chocolate. I could see him clearly in the light of the reading lamp and the winter's day outside. Then it struck me. Alzheimer's. Dementia. Something like that.

'If you think for one moment...' Matti Mali began, '... that you've met a demented old man who hasn't the faintest idea who and what you are, and who might be suffering from some kind of memory loss, you can forget it.'

'Very well.'

'How old are you?'

'Thirty.'

'Not a boy any longer. You're old enough to regret one thing or the other.'

'Yes.'

'Good. We should all have things we regret. It will be our salvation. Sometimes it seems as if it's all we have, all that motivates us. Chocolate?'

I shook my head. Mali took another chocolate and stared out of the window. I stared outside, too. Snow was once again fluttering through the air. The blue sky had disappeared.

'Your father is probably very proud of you,' said Mali, and again turned to face me.

'He is. He says he is.'

Mali sucked ponderously on his chocolate. Then he took a deep breath.

'Please, begin.'

I placed the pile of papers directly in front of me, picked up the bunch on top of the pile – fourteen printed documents from the Register of Companies, plus employee records and financial statements – and laid it in front of Mali. He didn't look at the papers but kept his eyes fixed on me.

'Sebrinski, Karmio, Stilson and Valtonen together owned an investment company named North Venture Finland. A few years ago, when Finn Mining faced difficulty with meeting the costs of opening the mine at Suomalahti, North Venture came to the rescue. Finn Mining – that is, you – had to accept the terms of the deal. North Venture took over control of the operation, though it never became a majority partner. This confused me at first, as did the fact that North Venture's investment was split between four separate investment companies, whose funds are held in various limited partnerships whose owners, hidden away at the beginning of the chain, are – or were – Sebrinski, Karmio, Stilson and Valtonen.'

I paused, laid another sheaf of papers in front of Mali. He glanced at it, took his coffee cup from its saucer and sipped, all the while staring out of the window. The snow was beginning to thicken.

'North Venture began calling the shots at Finn Mining, though all the while you remained as the public face of the company.'

Mali glanced at me. Not angrily or showing that he was offended, but with a sense of determination. I took the hint.

'Well, for as long as they decided to keep you there, that is. I have a recording of a board meeting at which you are not present. The recording reveals that this group of four men was making decisions that directly affected operations at Suomalahti. They made one decision in particular whose ramifications we will be able to enjoy for decades to come. I'll come back to that point in due course.'

'So far everything you've said has been first class,' said Mali. He looked at me, his eyes keen and alert. 'Do you know what I see?'

'No, I don't.'

'I see happiness,' said Mali. 'There you are, surrounded by such happiness. You have everything you need. I imagine you don't really appreciate it. I imagine you simply can't appreciate it at all. It doesn't matter, you're certainly not alone in that respect. You probably worry about the future of your job; perhaps you have problems at home. You think other people are doing better than you. Let me promise you one thing. One day, when you look back on this, you'll think it was the best time of your life. And then your only wish – a futile one by that point – will be that you had realised you were as happy as it is possible for a man to be.'

I looked at Mali and revisited the possibility that he might be demented. His smile was warm and his voice soft as the snow constantly swirling behind the windowpane.

'You don't believe me,' he said. 'You will later. At the end of their lives, everybody does. Everybody believes in God, too. There isn't an atheist in the world who at the moment of death, at that final second, would dare to think that this truly is the end of the road. Anyone who says anything else is spouting hot air.'

'To go back to Suomalahti...'

'Do you believe in God?'

'No.'

'You believe that as a human you are the greatest, most potent force in the universe; that you are behind the universe, its original force?'

'I don't think that.'

'It certainly seems that way.'

'Do you believe in God, Mr Mali?'

'Don't be sycophantic.'

'Do you believe in God?'

'Of course. Every rational person believes in God.'

I looked at him. He picked up another chocolate, twisted it open, popped it into his mouth and dropped the wrapper on the table.

'Good,' I said, and picked up another bunch of papers and placed it in front of him. 'I've drawn up a timeline. This shows the main events.'

I ran my finger across the paper as I spoke.

'North Venture takes over Finn Mining. Then North Venture – that is, the four members of the board – realise there is no way of making the mine at Suomalahti profitable. No legal way, I should say. And so they make a decision to lighten up on some of the miserable mine's expenses. In other words, they decide to dump any unwanted shit straight into the surrounding environment. Once this has been going on for some time, Kimmo Karmio dies. Then Stilson. And so on. The only person left standing in this jigsaw puzzle is you, Mr Mali.'

'Your point being?' he said and raised his eyebrows.

'You want your company back.'

'Really?'

'Really.'

'And what if I don't want it back?'

I glanced outside. The light snow flurried diagonally across the window, like feathers falling from a pillow the breadth of the sky.

'The evidence is on the table. On my phone I have the lab results of the samples I took at Suomalahti. Everything points towards—'

'Did you always want to be a journalist? Have you always known it was the job for you; a calling, if you will?'

I adjusted my position in the chair.

'I must have been eighteen or nineteen, the first time I read an article and realised that whoever wrote it must have put in a lot of work that I couldn't see. I started thinking about what that work might be, how I could get my hands on information. I'd visit places, meet people, read, put things together. Write. That's what's most important. Something happened. I realised this was my profession.'

'Precisely. A calling. You're privileged. I'm sure you appreciate that.'

'What has this got to do with what's been going on at Suomalahti and Finn Mining?'

Matti Mali smiled again.

'You're impatient. It's all right. You can train yourself out of it. You'll see, impatience and youth disappear all at once.'

Mali lowered his hands and placed them on the armrests. He leaned his back more firmly against the chair and rested his head against the neck support. It looked as though he was waiting for a plane to take off, but without the trembling and shuddering. The house was utterly still and pleasantly warm. The snow outside hid us from the world like a feather duvet.

'I don't want anything to go back to the way it was,' said Mali. 'It's not possible. I'm not sure I'd want it even if it were possible. I want to correct my mistakes. There's a difference. I'm talking about the company; the company founded by my grandfather Harald Malin. I'm talking about the company I've run for over thirty years, a job I managed very badly.'

Mali looked at me more intensely than at any time during our meeting.

'I want to make amends,' he said. 'Do you know what that means?'

'I think so.'

'Good. That's a good start.'

I waited for him to continue.

'I wanted to be an architect,' said Mali. 'An excellent hobby, my father called it. He said I could stare at houses and admire buildings to my heart's content – as long as I did it on my own time, once we'd taken care of our work. By work, he meant the mine. The mines, plural, actually. And that's what I did. I accepted my lot. Don't get me wrong, it wasn't a bad lot, not in the least. My father had done the same. I never truly learned what he wanted from life. I don't know whether he had a specific calling. He died without answering all the important questions I had for him. I've since learned this is rather normal. People talk about this, that and the other for seventy years, but when they die these things still remain a mystery.'

Matti Mali looked at me.

'So now you know rather better why you are sitting there and why I'm telling you this.'

'Yes,' I said.

'So instead of being an architect, I studied and graduated as a geo-logical engineer. I was about as interested in the field as I was in last winter's snow. I became CEO of the company when my father sug-gested it. His suggestions weren't suggestions in the traditional sense of the word. For a long time everything went just as it should. Then things started to happen. Mining became the business of the future. That ought to have woken me up. But at that point … More coffee?'

'No, thank you.'

Mali poured some for himself. Steam rose from his cup as he leaned back in his chair again.

'The business of the future. A beacon for the mining industry worldwide. Things like that. I'd been in the business for decades, staring at our profit margins and the ore-depleted Finnish soil all my life, so I wondered quite what they were talking about. Before anyone paid this fact the slightest attention, suddenly a sixth of the country's surface area had been reserved for exploration. In 2013 the precise figure was 53,000 square kilometres of land, the majority of which was sold to foreign investors for next to nothing. It was entirely senseless. But that didn't matter. Politicians wanted to reinvent the wheel and declared that the mines would generate employment in Finland for decades to come and, in doing so, create affluence on an unprecedented scale. Nobody dared say out loud that one mine can operate very well on a staff of ten men; that mines are almost always unprofitable and that opening even one new mine would require tens, if not hundreds, of millions' worth of investments from the state; or that once they are decommissioned mines leave behind such a mess that the only way to clean it up is by using taxpayers' money. But you know all this, yes?'

'Yes.'

'Excellent,' said Mali. Again he managed to muster something resembling a smile, only for it to disappear in the blink of an eye. 'So now we arrive at the question of why I'm telling you this. When operations in Suomalahti were commenced, I simply couldn't see the whole picture. There was too much uncritical support for the project. That, if anything, tells you the business model can't last. If there's unanimous consensus that an idea is good, it more than likely isn't. The problems started almost immediately. I wasn't alert enough when they bussed in the first consultants. That's another sign of a burgeoning catastrophe – the appearance of consultants in increasing numbers. The consultants cost a fortune, but their fees were nothing compared to what it costs to keep the mine running. For that you need capital. Valtonen turned up with Stilson and the rest of them. Decisions were taken quickly because the situation required decisive action. When you work quickly, you have to trust what's going on.

Once you trust, then you have to find the right people. But that didn't happen.'

The last sentence seemed to make Mali's voice quiver. He coughed into his fist and looked out of the window. Snowflakes were gently tapping against the glass. I said nothing. Mali turned his head. His eyes were those of an old man.

'I lost control of my company; the company my father and his father before him had entrusted to me. The investment company represented by Valtonen, Karmio, Stilson and Sebrinski took over. They made the mine profitable, just as they had promised. But they achieved this by destroying Finn Mining. When it came to my attention that the industrial sewage was being pumped untreated straight into the local environment, I made one final attempt to put things right. Using my old contacts, I found a buyer and approached the four members of the investment company. I thought that if I could regain control of the company, I would be able to use all our remaining resources to correct the damage and decommission the mine with a semblance of honour. They declined my offer. Our family company, in operation since 1922, was heading for the most ignominious end imaginable, and before that it was going to turn these four criminals into millionaires. I simply couldn't allow it.'

The house was so quiet, I heard the almost inaudible hiss from the thermos of coffee as it gradually let out warm air. Mali looked at me.

'I made a mistake,' he said. 'And I intend to make up for it.'

At the beginning of our meeting Matti Mali had seemed like a friendly, relaxed host; now he looked like a man who regretted the course of his life, like an immeasurably fatigued old man.

'Did you record that?' he asked quietly.

'No.'

Mali nodded.

'Perhaps that's for the best.'

'You must be held to account for it though.'

'I didn't mean that.'

The pleasant warmth of the room had disappeared. I felt the

cool floor beneath my feet. The lights in the room – the floor lamp behind me, the two yellow-tinted lamps on the windowsill – were now only strong enough to illuminate contours, to sketch shapes in the dusk. Mali seemed to be sitting further away from me than he had a moment ago. My all-time biggest scoop, the story I'd come here to write, was no longer the story I'd been imagining on the journey to Kaskisaari.

I leaned towards the table to gather up my papers.

'If it helps you,' said Mali, nodding towards the papers, 'I'll corroborate what you said, what you showed me.'

I gathered the papers into a neat pile, and was about to stand up when Mali's gaze glided behind my back. He was startled at what he saw. I turned instinctively. All I could see was the wall clock. I turned back. Still he appeared to be looking at the clock. I waited a moment and stood up. Mali gave a start, then he too rose to his feet.

'Thank you for coming,' he said.

We walked into the hallway. I pulled on my outdoor clothes as Mali stood watching me at the edge of the dimly lit space. He moved as soon as I made my way to the door. Once at the door I turned and we shook hands. His voice was hushed as he spoke to me.

'Best of luck with everything. Make sure your mistakes are smaller than mine.'

Slowly he let go of my hand. I glanced back towards the living room. An exceptionally thick gust of snow passed the window, after which the snow on the window ledge crackled like a packet of sweets scattered on the floor.

I went down the steps and started walking. I wanted to get away from Kaskisaari.

10

He was skiing home. The snowfall made it slow and hard going, but he doggedly made his way forward. It didn't matter. Each time he pushed down on the poles, each time he raised a ski, he left the past behind. He had done what he'd promised, what he'd agreed. He would never do it again. That was his faith, his confession: *I was once a man like that, but I am not that man any longer.* It sounded simplistic, but who could really say something like that? He could.

The snow was white and pristine. Out at sea the wind pressed it into the ground and seemed to tear snow from the sky, ravenous and insatiable. From time to time a gust of snow blinded him and wet his cheeks. It felt cold, cleansing.

The love that had once separated them now unified them again.

He skied onwards.

Homewards. Finally.

11

BLOG
Janne Vuori *HT*
janne.vuori@helsinkitoday.fi
Twitter: @vuorijanneht

THE MINE THAT BURIED EVERYTHING

The Suomalahti mine is polluting its local environment in dangerous and ultimately irrevocable ways. All those responsible are dead. Nobody has won – not even the author of this exposé.

I freely admit that when I first heard the rumours about the nickel mine at Suomalahti operated by Finn Mining Ltd, I thought I was on to a scoop. Every reporter is on the hunt for a good scoop. A scoop is a story that goes viral, that is on everybody's lips. Many factors indicated that this was such a story. Now, as I look back at what happened and what this story is actually about, I realise that I was only partly right and that I acted wrongly with regard to virtually everything of any relevance. I will begin by explaining what I have learned about the company and a little of what I have learned about myself.

The nickel mine at Suomalahti was inaugurated in 2007. However, that is not where the story begins. Mauri Ylijoki's book *More Precious than Gold – The Story of the Finnish Mining Corporation* (Mineral Publications, 1994) explains where everything began and looks back almost one hundred years to 1922, when one Harald Malin, a thirty-two-year-old engineering student and heir to a family of pharmacists, founded the Finnish Mining Corporation, a company later rebranded as Finn Mining Ltd.

In many ways overseeing the operations of the Finnish Mining Corporation was a bold leap for Malin, a man more accustomed to working at a desk, and he duly enlisted both his own mother and a number of his friends to become supporters and patrons of the company. The principal objective in founding the corporation was, naturally, to make money. Thus the goldmine at Salla, the corporation's first venture, was an excellent start, both in terms of expectations and profile.

Things soon became far more complicated than Malin had first imagined. The north of Finland is cold and there is lots of snow throughout the year, with the exception of the short summer months, which end with the incessant rains of autumn. Malin, who until this point had lived and worked solely in Helsinki and the southernmost parts of Finland, wrote in letters and briefings about the great challenges the snow and rain presented for mining operations in the north. He described how the mining complex was at times entirely under water, how there was often so much snow that it stood several metres thick on the ground, and cursed that the unforgiving winter froze everything.

Malin also wrote extensively about the impact on local rivers and lakes, or rather he wrote about what angry ramblers, fishermen and residents told him was happening. The fish were disappearing, the water stank and had turned a shade of green. Either that, or the water was grey and the fish were green. It is to Malin's credit that the Finnish Mining Corporation not only understood the gravity of the situation, but also took action to rectify it.

It stopped draining water from the mining complex directly into local tributaries and began storing industrial sewage and treating it at the mine. Naturally this didn't come free, a fact of which Malin was only too aware. Thus the goldmine, which had only ever made a small profit, was now focussed solely on balancing the books. The company was not making a profit and was not losing money. This cycle continued for years. As technology developed, Malin eventually came to make a success of the goldmine at Salla and the Finnish Mining Corporation. Turning the company's fortunes around took almost fifteen years. In that time Malin shortened his name to Mali, in response to the wave of Finnish nationalist sentiment in the 1930s.

As mentioned, the Finnish Mining Corporation was eventually rebranded as Finn Mining Ltd, and the company used its English name from that point onwards. (From today's perspective it is hard to remember, and harder still to understand, that during the 1980s and 1990s the names of Finnish companies were routinely renamed with dynamic English titles or names in cod-Latin, meaning that the company's field and scope remained a mystery to all concerned.) Despite its new name, some things remained unchanged at Finn Mining Ltd. The CEO was still a member of the Mali family. After Harald Malin, the company was run first by his son Gerhard Mali, then by his grandson Matti Mali. The company was proud of its values and took care to nurture its public image – until that too came to an end. This is a period not covered in Ylijoki's book.

At the dawn of the new millennium Matti Mali rose to the top of the company. By now it was a company of which people expected great things. Either it had to be expanded or it would have to be wound down. Mali chose to expand. The choice seemed to reflect the values of the age. Innovators in Finland were frantically looking for new growth industries; more specifically they were looking for something that might just be the next money-spinner for the Finnish exchequer.

Matti Mali realised that his opportunity had come. He acquired mining rights for the area around Suomalahti for the sum of two euros and began an initial exploratory dig. It was easy to sell politicians promises of the positive impact the mine would have on local employment and the economy, because those same politicians seemed uninterested in how realistic the project was; and in particular weren't curious about anything that would last into the next and subsequent electoral cycles. Meanwhile it was easy to sell investors the financial side of the project; especially in a world where there is far too much money, and loans (and debt) can be acquired by any company or individual with a mind to do so; a world in which the need to build and the need for nickel would never end. Everybody involved in the project and all those lobbying in its favour were convinced that Finland was set to become the new innovative bellwether of the mining and mineral industry – this, despite the fact that our soil is notoriously ore-depleted, and that we in Finland don't have the kind of experience in either field that could be considered in any way exceptional in the global arena. Dissenting voices were immediately branded either eco-warriors or hardened communists.

The mine began operating in May 2007, and it was a disaster from the very outset.

If those involved in starting the project had taken the time to acquaint themselves with the history of the company and the difficulties experienced by Harald Malin, we would all have been saved a lot of trouble. The mine at Suomalahti employed a technique known as bioleaching, a process that had never before been used in a real-life situation. One can only wonder why the engineers at the mine decided to test-run this technique in the most demanding conditions imaginable. It quickly became apparent that the process was far too complicated, far too expensive and staggeringly ineffective; it also produced untold quantities of wastewater – as, indeed, the name already suggests. Plenty of rain and snow fell from the northern skies in Harald Malin's day, and this fact has not changed. There has never been any shortage of snow in northern Finland. Crucially, the owners of the Suomalahti mine only woke up to this fact once it was too late.

Retaining wastewater is an expensive business. Finn Mining Ltd was woefully unprofitable long before the winters of 2010–2012, which saw record snowfall. The financial crash of 2008 made sure there was no excess cash hanging around the company for the proverbial rainy day. In the spring of 2012, Matti Mali was forced to make a decision that would change the face of the company forever. The company's need for more capital had reached breaking point, and Mali acted fast. Finn Mining Ltd's new partner was an investment company named North Venture Finland, which itself comprised four separate investment companies linked in a limited partnership agreement. By following the money of the limited partnerships we discover the true identities of those behind North Venture Finland. They are the same men as those on the board of Finn Mining Ltd: Hannu Valtonen (Director of Research & Development), Giorgi Sebrinksi (Sales Director), Kimmo Karmio (Financial & Investment Advisor) and Alan Stilson (Head of Human Resources). As the balance of power shifted, North Venture Finland secured a voting majority within Finn Mining Ltd, and the four men duly became the new board of directors. Matti Mali remained a figurehead for the company, but beyond that he, like the Suomalahti mine, was left out in the cold.

The new board of directors decided to turn the company's fortunes around. No stone would be left unturned, both figuratively and literally. Staff were made redundant, the organisation was overhauled and operations streamlined. Still it wasn't enough. The problem was the same as it had been for Harald Malin: the volume of waste produced by the mining procedures and the high costs of treating that waste. Eventually the board decided to do away with these costs altogether. (A taped conversation between the four members of the board is available *here*. In conversation are Valtonen, Sebrinski, Karmio and Stilson.) A decision was taken to allow unprocessed wastewater to be drained directly into the local groundwater. Along the eastern edge of the mining complex, a series of ditches was excavated, a metre wide and a metre deep, from which vats of industrial sewage were emptied directly into local waters.

Precisely how much wastewater has been channelled into surrounding lakes and rivers is as yet unknown. But the samples, the collection of which ultimately cost biologist Tero Manninen his life, demonstrate that the damage is extensive and to some degree irreversible. (The full report on the state of the water in Kuusijoki can be found *here*. For instance, sulphate and mercury levels are tens of thousands of times higher than the legal limit.) It is hard to estimate the levels of wastewater dumped into the environment from the Suomalahti mine. Producing such estimates is challenging, and it will only be when spring and summer arrive that we will be able to assess what the future holds for the local rivers and lakes. What is abundantly clear, however, is that this is damage on a massive scale.

Furthermore, nobody will be held accountable.

All four members of the board (Valtonen, Sebrinski, Karmio and Stilson) are dead. The Helsinki police are currently looking into their deaths. Finn Mining Ltd is essentially bankrupt, and it is only a matter of days before the decommissioning of the mine will be officially announced. The task of cleaning up the area around the mine is left to the Finnish taxpayer. Having remained in operation since 1922, the Finnish Mining Corporation is set to disappear, as is the Mali dynasty. Matti Mali, who led the organisation for a long time, as had his father and grandfather before him, died at his home last night of a sudden illness. He had no heirs.

As attentive readers will note, the events outlined above contain at least three news items that could be considered scoops. If I were still the reporter who eagerly began work on this case, I would have saved each revelation for a separate article. The reason I did not do this is, paradoxically, that investigating this story has cost me too much and the benefit I receive from it is minimal. At least, that's what it feels like today.

The biologist Tero Manninen was murdered, as was Kari Lehtinen, a journalist who has investigated the company in the past. (One of Lehtinen's most memorable articles, 'A Bitter Pill – The Story of the Finnish Anti-Vaccination Movement' can be found *here*.) The men responsible for both murders are now dead. The repercussions of events at Suomalahti will last years and will cost millions.

Despite the longevity and severity of these events, people will talk about the story for a few days, perhaps a few weeks, then the story will be forgotten altogether. When the next mining project gets under way and starts jostling for political backing, nobody will recall or remember what happened at Suomalahti.

Or will they?

12

'Thank you,' said Emil and sipped his already tepid coffee. A moment ago he had been sitting by himself, waiting for the doorbell to ring and watching the morning brighten on the other side of the window. Minute by minute the sunlight had glowed warmer. The library too had come to life, people coming in and out.

He felt old but free. It wasn't a bad sensation.

'For what?' asked Janne and looked at him. A young man with glasses, his hair slightly ruffled and one side of his shirt collar stuck beneath the neck of his woollen jumper. His son had no idea that he was the first person in years whom Emil had invited to the flat, allowed into his home.

'I read your text. Twice. Your phone has probably been ringing off the hook.'

Janne glanced outside, stirred the long spoon through his coffee. Janne had asked for a coffee with milk and Emil had made him one.

'More than ever.'

'What are you going to do?'

Janne shrugged his shoulders. 'Not what I would have done before.'

Emil imagined he knew what his son meant.

'I'm sure you understand,' Janne continued. 'This hasn't been easy for me.'

'I've already said, I'd give my life…'

Janne shook his head. 'I don't want to hear that again. And I haven't said everything yet.'

'Very well.'

They sat in silence. Janne drank his coffee and wiped his upper lip.

'There are times when I wish I didn't know what I know.'

Emil said nothing.

'Then there are other moments…'

Janne looked as though he hadn't slept at all, or as though he'd caught at most a few hours' sleep on the sofa at his office. The crumpled clothes, the straggly hair and the bags beneath his eyes certainly suggested it.

'It seems you can't have everything,' he said.

'That's true enough.'

'Someone else can write the story. My boss is livid with me. I'll probably be able to keep my job, but I'll spend a long time writing pieces about twerking and things like that.'

'Twerking? What…?'

Janne looked at him.

'It doesn't matter. What matters is that Pauliina and I sort out our differences. She sent me a message, said she'd read the story and understood what I'd done, of course. We're meeting this evening.'

'I hope…'

'But that doesn't change the fact that something has to be done about this … matter. About the things you told me.'

Emil turned the coffee cup in his hands. The day would soon reach its lightest point.

'When we met for the first time – the first time in a long while, that is – you told me that writing means everything to you,' said Emil. 'That it's a way of working through your thoughts.'

'You read what I wrote this morning. I can't…'

Emil nodded and continued. 'Let's think about this from another angle. It doesn't need to be printed in the newspaper.'

Janne looked at him and leaned back on his chair. His appearance was still slightly dishevelled, but now he was alert, more alert than he had been only seconds before.

'Talk to me,' said Janne.

'What do you want me to tell you?'

'Talk about what happened in 1985.'

'Certainly.'

The more Emil spoke to his son, the lighter he felt. The adage was true: secrets were the heaviest burden of all.

'What next?' asked Janne.

'You can write about it.'

'And after that?'

'You've forbidden me from talking about it,' said Emil. 'I trust you'll do what you think is for the best.'

Janne looked at him. Light streamed through the window. Emil was about to say something when the doorbell rang. He hadn't invited anyone.

'I did what I thought was for the best,' said Janne.

Emil felt the decades gusting through him, felt everything he had learned and experienced pulling at him, the urge to stand up and prepare himself, position himself. He remained seated, though every cell in his body screamed for him to run, to retaliate. He allowed Janne to stand up and go to the door. Everything happened as though in a dream. The thought reminded him of the previous night, the first he could remember without nightmares. He'd woken up that morning feeling rested. It felt incredible.

Janne was at the door.

Emil still had a chance. His instincts were shouting, howling for action. His eyes made careful calculations of their own volition: the drawers in the kitchen, the knives, any loose objects, the toaster, the kettle, the heavy chopping board, even the chair where Janne had been sitting only a few seconds earlier. Everything could be used. He sat there, allowed his thoughts to ebb and flow, imagined himself using those objects. He was good at that. He had once been good at that. That was the difference that he stressed to himself once again. He heard footsteps.

He stood up, didn't lunge for anything; just stood there and decided to succumb to everything that was about to happen.

'Am I interrupting?' asked Leena. 'Have you had a chance to talk?'

Emil looked at her.

'After a fashion,' he heard Janne say.

Leena smiled.

'Hello, Emil.'

'Hello, Leena.'

'I should have guessed.'

'Guessed what?'

'Where you lived.'

They looked at each other.

'I think I'll get going…' said Janne.

Emil looked at him.

'No.'

Both Leena and Janne looked at him. Emil realised that he was no longer guarded. Everything that happened from now on was what was destined to happen.

'I mean … another coffee,' he said, then turned to Leena. 'Black, yes?'

He watched Leena take off her coat, watched as Janne took it from his mother's shoulders and put it on a hanger; watched mother and son sit at the table and admired them as the light from outside framed them like a painting. He heard their voices but was unable to speak.

At moments like this it was best to act. He made more coffee, concentrated on the movement of his hands. When the coffee was ready, he poured it into cups and sat down at the table.

Acknowledgements

Thank you to friends in Stockholm; the Salomonsson Agency: it is an absolute pleasure to work with you. Special thanks to Federico Ambrosini, whose support has been unwavering and invaluable. I'm grateful and happy to be able to call him my agent.

Thank you to friends in London: Karen Sullivan and so many others. Karen, you are amazing.

Thank you to friends in Helsinki: so many and so dear. I couldn't do this alone.

Thank you, Anu. I love you.

And, finally, thank you, Dad. This book is dedicated to you.

COMING SOON FROM ORENDA BOOKS

'A classic crime story seen through a uniquely Icelandic
lens ... first rate and highly recommended'
LEE CHILD

RAGNAR JÓNASSON

RUPTURE

'Jónasson's books have breathed new life into Nordic noir'
PRESS

COMING SOON FROM ORENDA BOOKS

THOMAS
ENGER

Which secret
would
you kill
to protect?

CURSED

A **HENNING JUUL** NOVEL **BOOK 4**

COMING SOON FROM ORENDA BOOKS

'Terse, tense and vivid writing. Matt Johnson is
a brilliant new name in the world of thrillers'
PETER JAMES

DEADLY
GAME

MATT JOHNSON

COMING SOON FROM ORENDA BOOKS

'A relentless page-turner with twists
and turns that left me breathless' **J.S. Law**

DEEP DOWN DEAD

STEPH BROADRIBB

COMING SOON FROM ORENDA BOOKS

SIX STORIES

MATT WESOLOWSKI

ORENDA CRIME

www.orendabooks.co.uk

@OrendaBooks